SATURDAY NIGHT MURDER

Maya marched up the gravel walkway to the front door of Diego's house. She was about to knock when she noticed the door was ajar slightly. Gently pushing it open, she poked her head inside.

"Diego?"

No answer.

She leaned in some more. "Diego, it's Maya Kendrick. Are you here?"

Still no answer.

Maya immediately felt a sense of dread.

She slowly pushed the door all the way open and entered the house.

A Prince song, "Little Red Corvette," was playing on Diego's Alexa home assistant, which she could see from the hallway was set up on the kitchen counter. She cautiously made her way down the hall until she was in the brightly lit kitchen.

Her eyes were instantly drawn to the floor where Diego Sanchez was lying facedown, an open cake tin next to him and crumbled cookies scattered all around.

Maya gasped, ran to him, leaned down and picked up his wrist, feeling for a pulse.

There was none . . .

D1198163

Books by Lee Hollis

Hayley Powell Mysteries
DEATH OF A KITCHEN DIVA
DEATH OF A COUNTRY FRIED REDNECK
DEATH OF A COUPON CLIPPER
DEATH OF A CHOCOHOLIC
DEATH OF A CHRISTMAS CATERER
DEATH OF A CUPCAKE QUEEN
DEATH OF A BACON HEIRESS
DEATH OF A PUMPKIN CARVER
DEATH OF A LOBSTER LOVER
DEATH OF A COOKBOOK AUTHOR
DEATH OF A WEDDING CAKE BAKER
DEATH OF A BLUEBERRY TART
DEATH OF A WICKED WITCH
DEATH OF AN ITALIAN CHEF

Collections
EGGNOG MURDER
(with Leslie Meier and Barbara Ross)
YULE LOG MURDER
(with Leslie Meier and Barbara Ross)
HAUNTED HOUSE MURDER
(with Leslie Meier and Barbara Ross)
CHRISTMAS CARD MURDER
(with Leslie Meier and Peggy Ehrhart)
HALLOWEEN PARTY MURDER
(with Leslie Meier and Barbara Ross)

Poppy Harmon Mysteries
POPPY HARMON INVESTIGATES
POPPY HARMON AND THE HUNG JURY
POPPY HARMON AND THE PILLOW TALK KILLER

Maya & Sandra Mysteries
MURDER AT THE PTA
MURDER AT THE BAKE SALE

Published by Kensington Publishing Corp.

Murder at the Bake Sale

LEE HOLLIS

KENSINGTON BOOKS
KENSINGTON PUBLISHING CORP.
www.kensingtonbooks.com

KENSINGTON BOOKS are published by

Kensington Publishing Corp.
119 West 40th Street
New York, NY 10018

Copyright © 2020 by Rick Copp

This book is a work of fiction. Names, characters, businesses, organizations, places, events, and incidents either are the product of the author's imagination or are used fictitiously. Any resemblance to actual persons, living or dead, events, or locales is entirely coincidental.

All rights reserved. No part of this book may be reproduced in any form or by any means without the prior written consent of the Publisher, excepting brief quotes used in reviews.

To the extent that the image or images on the cover of this book depict a person or persons, such person or persons are merely models, and are not intended to portray any character or characters featured in the book.

If you purchased this book without a cover you should be aware that this book is stolen property. It was reported as "unsold and destroyed" to the Publisher and neither the Author nor the Publisher has received any payment for this "stripped book."

All Kensington titles, imprints, and distributed lines are available at special quantity discounts for bulk purchases for sales promotion, premiums, fund-raising, educational, or institutional use.

Special book excerpts or customized printings can also be created to fit specific needs. For details, write or phone the office of the Kensington Sales Manager: Attn.: Sales Department. Kensington Publishing Corp., 119 West 40th Street, New York, NY 10018. Phone: 1-800-221-2647.

Kensington and the K logo Reg. U.S. Pat. & TM Off.

First Printing: December 2020
ISBN-13: 978-1-4967-3197-5
ISBN-13: 978-1-4967-3092-3 (eBook)

10 9 8 7 6 5 4 3 2

Printed in the United States of America

Chapter One

Sandra Wallage sat quietly in the passenger seat of the Chevy Bolt, debating whether or not she should bring up what was on her mind again. She had tried to broach the topic earlier in the day, but her partner, Maya Kendrick, had quickly shut her down. Maya's excuse had been legitimate, that they needed to focus on the case at hand, but now that they were parked outside a dingy bar in the middle of the afternoon, with nothing to do but nosh on the seasoned curly fries Maya had picked up from the drive-thru window at Jack in the Box, Sandra decided to give it one more try.

"I was thinking maybe a classy stenciled design. Jack is great with graphics, I'm sure he'd do a wonderful job—"

Maya sighed. "Sandra, we've been over this. Now is not the time—"

"But I've been a full-fledged partner for almost a year now," Sandra protested.

"Okay, first, you're not a full-fledged partner, only in your mind, and second, it has nothing to do with how long you've been helping me out at the agency. We can't afford it."

"But I'd be happy to take care of any additional expense—"

Maya quickly cut her off. "No. I told you, it's not because I don't think you're ready. I just don't want you writing personal checks for any of our expenses. That's not how I want to do business."

"I understand that. But this is something *I* want to do for the agency."

"First it's new signage for the door, then we have to get new business cards, and pretty soon you'll be shelling out money for an advertising budget so we can attract more clients . . ."

Sandra shot up in her seat. "That's actually not a bad idea!"

"No, Sandra, the last thing I want is for you to bankroll the whole business just because you can afford it."

Sandra slumped back down, defeated. She knew Maya was going to be intractable on this one. "Well, at least just think about it."

Maya popped a curly fry into her mouth. "I already have, so can we please table this discussion for now?"

Sandra stared out the window. "The new sign for the office door would practically be free of charge because Jack could design the logo as a school project for extra credit, and all I would have to buy are the art supplies—"

"Sandra!"

"You're right. I'm sorry. We can talk about it later."

Maya's phone buzzed and she checked the screen.

"Who is it?" Sandra asked.

"Our client. Just texting for an update."

Maya typed a quick reply and then put the phone back down in the cup holder.

Sandra glanced down at the phone curiously. "What did you tell him?"

"I told him we're very close to having some results."

Sandra stared back out the car window toward the bar entrance. "She's been in there since before noon."

Their client, Mark Langford, was the owner of a local car dealership in Portland, Maine, who, at the moment, was embroiled in a heated child custody battle with his soon-to-be-ex-wife, Deena. He had hired Maya and Sandra's private detective agency to gather evidence proving Deena was an unfit mother. Sandra initially was hesitant about taking on the case because she feared Mark was just using them to unjustly smear his wife. Maya, on the other hand, didn't spend too much time wallowing in the moral implications of accepting the case. She was just happy Mark Langford was willing to pay their fee with the promise of a generous bonus if they uncovered dirt that led to him winning full custody of their two preteen children.

Despite Sandra's early misgivings about the nature of the case, once they had begun digging into Deena Langford's personal life, it quickly became apparent that their client was right about his estranged wife's wildly erratic behavior. Quite frankly, the woman was an unapologetic mess.

And now, on a weekday afternoon, she was inside a bar getting drunk on her cocktail of choice, a gin and tonic, while her kids were at school. Around two thirty, after waiting outside the bar for almost three hours, Maya and Sandra finally spotted Deena Langford stumbling out of the bar, bleary-eyed and swaying from side to side as she fished through her pocketbook for her car keys.

"Her kids should be getting out of school soon! She

may be planning to go pick them up! We can't let her do that in her condition!" Sandra cried.

Maya flung open the driver's side door and hopped out, racing across the parking lot toward Deena, who was standing in front of her BMW, fumbling with the remote, trying to unlock her vehicle.

Sandra followed quickly behind Maya, catching up to her just in time to hear Maya say gently, "Mrs. Langford, I don't think it's a good idea for you to get behind the wheel of a car right now."

Deena looked up and glared at Maya with her bloodshot, watery eyes and spat out, "Says *who*?"

"Let's just say I'm a concerned citizen," Maya calmly explained.

"Well, let's just say I don't care *who* you are! You're not the boss of me!" Deena slurred belligerently as she finally managed to press the right button on her remote and a chirp indicated her car had just unlocked.

As Deena opened the door to get in, Maya physically attempted to stop her. Deena violently swung up her purse, clocking Maya in the head. She reeled backward, almost losing her balance.

"Get away from me!" Deena growled.

Before Maya had the chance to regain her senses and grab Deena, she was in the driver's seat of her BMW, doors locked, revving the engine.

Sandra instinctively sprinted forward and threw herself in front of the hood of the car to prevent her from leaving, but all it took was one determined, enraged look from Deena Langford for Sandra to realize the woman didn't care one bit about her blocking her escape, and was more than ready to run her over. As Deena cranked the gear of her BMW into the Drive position, Sandra dove out of the way just in time as the car roared away, tires squealing, kicking up so much dust and gravel in the parking lot that both Maya and Sandra were choking on it.

Before turning onto the highway, Deena sideswiped the back of Maya's Chevy Bolt, but Maya was too concerned about Sandra, who was splayed flat on the ground after a nasty fall, to care much at that point.

Maya darted over to her. "Are you okay?"

Sandra managed to sit upright, gingerly attending to a scraped knee. "I'm fine. Maya, you have to stop her before she kills somebody!"

Maya ran back to her now-damaged car and reached in to grab her cell phone. Within seconds she was on the phone with the police department, talking to one of her pals and reciting Deena Langford's license plate from memory.

As Sandra slowly climbed to her feet and hobbled over to Maya, who was still on the line with the cops, she sighed with relief when she heard Maya confirm, "They just pulled her over? Good, thank you so much." Maya hung up and turned to Sandra. "They're arresting her and charging her with operating under the influence."

"I feel bad for her, to be honest; she's going to lose her kids," Sandra said solemnly. "I can't imagine that."

"Well, until she gets the help she obviously needs, it's definitely for the best," Maya remarked. "I should call our client and bring him up to speed."

"It's just very sad all around," Sandra remarked.

"Except the part about our satisfied client, Mark Langford, sending us a nice, big, fat check for services rendered," Maya practically sang with a bright smile. Off Sandra's admonishing look, Maya quickly added, "But you're right. It's very sad."

Maya noticed Sandra's bloodied knee from her fall. "Come on, we need to clean that up. I think I have some antiseptic cream in the glove box."

"It's not so bad. And it doesn't really hurt much," Sandra said, limping back toward the car.

Maya shook her head. "Why on earth would you wear a white dress to a stakeout? I've told you dozens of times to always wear long pants so you're protected if something like this happens."

"I didn't have much of a choice. Jack's college interview is today and . . ." Sandra froze. "Oh God, what time is it?"

"Almost three," Maya said, checking her phone.

"I totally lost track of time. The interview is at five o'clock all the way down in Boston. Jack's probably at home going crazy I'm not there. . . . If we're superlate, it's going to look bad!"

"Well, come on, get in! I'll take you home! If you get on the road by three thirty, you could still make it on time, but it'll be close," Maya shouted as they jumped into her Chevy Bolt with the brand-new, big dent in the back, and squealed out of the parking lot and onto the highway back toward downtown Portland.

Chapter Two

Sandra's black Mercedes shot down the 95 southbound freeway as she gripped the wheel and pressed down her foot, almost as far as it would go on the accelerator. The speedometer teetered around 77 mph even though they had just zipped past a sign reminding drivers the speed limit was 65.

Next to her in the passenger seat, her oldest son, Jack, in a suit and tie, usually the calm, laid-back one, unlike her much more dramatic, high-strung younger son, Ryan, shifted in his seat nervously. "We're not going to make it, Mom."

Sandra glanced at the dashboard clock.

It was already 4:47 pm.

They had less than fifteen minutes to reach the Boston Tech campus, park and find the admissions building in time for the interview. It was looking impossible at this point, but Sandra was not going to let any of that affect her single-minded determination to get her son there on time for his interview.

"We'll make it," she said confidently.

"But we're sure to hit traffic once we reach Boston,

which will just slow us down even more." Jack sighed as Sandra flipped on the turn signal to pass a slow-moving pickup truck with a ratty old couch tied in the flatbed in front of them. "It won't look good if we're late."

"Stay positive," Sandra said, keeping her eyes fixed on the road. "Just concentrate on what you want to say in the interview."

"I'm leaning toward just getting down on my knees and begging them to take me," Jack groaned.

Sandra cranked the wheel, and the Mercedes zipped back into the right lane, now in front of the pickup truck. "It's going to be fine. Your grades are stellar and you wrote a fantastic essay."

"Yeah, maybe, but my SAT scores were nowhere near where they should have been. I'm surprised they're even letting me come in for an interview."

"Your SAT scores were just fine," Sandra argued. "*Above* average."

"Exactly. They should've been great. I'm so screwed. It's not like I can coast with a football scholarship, especially after the season we had last year."

Sandra pressed her foot down a little harder on the accelerator and kept her eyes fixed on the road. "You know what, Jack? If you don't get in, then it's their loss. But don't give up before you've had a chance to make your case."

They sat in silence for a few minutes, the lush fall terrain of New Hampshire zipping past them.

Sandra wanted to give her son the opportunity to collect his thoughts and figure out the best approach for the interview. She wasn't about to coach him, or offer suggestions. This was all about him, and she knew in her heart he would nail it.

If she managed to actually get him there in time.

Jack stared out the window for a few minutes and then turned his head back toward his mother, his eyes dropping down to her leg. "Your knee is still bleeding."

"What?"

Sandra glanced quickly down to see a trail of blood trickling down from the gauze she had quickly taped over her wound after she had gotten home from her stakeout with Maya. "Do me a favor. Look in the glove compartment to see if there is a box of Band-Aids."

"Why won't you tell me what happened?" Jack asked.

"I told you, I fell."

She didn't think it would be helpful to explain to her son that she had basically thrown herself in front of a drunk driver and had to dive out of the way in order to avoid winding up on top of the hood.

Jack fished around the glove compartment and found some Band-Aids. He opened one up and handed it to his mother. She ripped off the gauze with one hand as she held on to the steering wheel with the other. Then she slapped it over the wound, keeping her eyes squarely on the road the whole time.

"Did you know your dress is ripped?"

"Yes, I know, just a little, but I didn't have time to change. We were so late leaving already. I'm sure the admissions person won't notice."

"And there's a dirt stain."

"What?"

She wanted to look but knew she had to keep focused on her driving.

"How big is it?"

"Pretty big. The admissions officer is definitely going to notice."

"Well, luckily this meeting is not about me. It's about you. And you look very dashing and handsome and once you start talking, they'll see how smart you are too . . ."

"Mom . . ."

"Oh, come on, can't a mother compliment her son?"

"No . . . it's not that . . . look in your rearview mirror."

Sandra glanced up to see blue flashing lights behind them. Her heart sank. "Oh no . . ."

"We're never going to make it now," Jack repeated, resigned.

Sandra pulled over the car into the emergency lane of the freeway and slowly rolled to a stop. She dropped her head and closed her eyes, trying to come up with what to say. Finally, she opened her eyes and glanced up at the mirror to see a young state trooper get out of his cruiser and walk toward the Mercedes, moving up alongside the driver's window.

Sandra quickly turned to Jack. "I'm about to do something I swore I never would; it's wrong, and I never want you to ever try anything remotely like this, but we are in a code red situation, so I have no choice. Promise me you will never follow this bad example I'm about to set."

Jack stared at his mother, dumbfounded, but nodded. "Uh, okay."

Sandra pressed the button to roll down the window just as the state trooper appeared, a grim look on his face. She smiled brightly. "Good afternoon, Officer."

"Afternoon," he said glumly.

"I wasn't watching the speedometer, but I assume I was driving a little over the speed limit?"

"Not a little, ma'am. Twenty-two miles over the limit."

"Oh my, I had no idea. I'm driving my son to a college

interview in Boston and we're running late, and so I guess I just panicked a bit and lost all sense of how fast I was going."

"License and registration, please," he said, not cracking a smile.

"Jack, could you—?" Sandra asked.

Jack was already rummaging through the glove compartment for the registration as Sandra turned and reached for her purse in the back seat for her license. Jack retrieved the registration card first and reached over and handed it to the trooper. Sandra quickly followed with her license.

"It's an awful picture so I apologize in advance," Sandra joked.

The state trooper didn't find it funny. He just studied the name on the license, stone-faced.

Sandra hesitated, knowing she was about to do something completely inappropriate, but as it was 4:58 she steeled herself and just went for it. "It's pronounced Wallage."

The state trooper looked up at her.

"In case you didn't know how to pronounce it."

"Thank you, ma'am. I'll be right back."

Before he had a chance to head back to the cruiser, Sandra quickly said, "As in Stephen Wallage. *Senator* Stephen Wallage."

He nodded. "Okay."

"That's my husband."

The state trooper paused, studied the license again, then looked back up at Sandra, who smiled at him expectantly.

"I didn't vote for him."

And then the unimpressed trooper marched away.

Sandra dropped her head again, humiliated.

Jack chuckled. "I promise I'll never try anything like that, Mom."

"Thank you," Sandra muttered.

"Because it didn't work!"

Chapter Three

After the short, bespectacled admissions officer, Mr. Hanes, who in Sandra's opinion was rather doddering for a man in his forties, escorted Jack into his office for his interview, Sandra quickly retreated down the hall to the ladies' room to dampen some paper towels so she could scrub off the obvious dirt and grime that soiled her ripped white dress. She hoped Mr. Hanes hadn't noticed her disheveled appearance too much during their brief introduction.

What a day.

After managing to wipe most of the dirt from the fabric, she stood erect in front of the giant wall mirror above the sink to check herself out. Her hair was mussed, so she scooped a comb from her purse to try to bring it back down to earth a little bit. Then there was the small smudge on her left cheek, barely noticeable from her fall, that she hastily brushed away. Sandra sighed. This was about as good as it was going to get without doing a Yelp search for a hair salon and a nearby Macy's where she could pick up a new outfit.

Sandra wandered back out to the hallway and was

about to sit down on a bench to wait for Jack's interview
to wrap up when she spotted someone she knew at the far
end of the hall, huddled in a corner with a young girl
around seventeen or eighteen. The woman was Senator
Elisabeth Dooley, her husband's counterpart, the senior
US senator from the great state of Maine. Elisabeth had
first been elected in 2008, several years before Stephen,
and had been reelected in 2014. With her second term now
winding down, she had decided to try for a third, and was
currently in the midst of a robust campaign squaring off
against a conservative firebrand, who, surprisingly, was
not that far behind her in the polls.

Sandra had met Elisabeth on numerous occasions and,
to be honest, wasn't a huge fan. In front of the microphone, Senator Dooley was a dynamo, full of passion and
grit, but away from the cameras, she was far more reserved and, in Sandra's opinion, could come off as somewhat cold and remote.

Maybe they just didn't have much in common.

Stephen seemed to like her enough, but Sandra always
wondered if his fondness for her was out of political ne-
cessity rather than a genuine attraction to her personality.

In any event, Sandra decided it would be rude not to
say hello, so she marched down the hallway, heels clicking
on the marble floor, toward Senator Dooley, whose back
was now to her. When Sandra was close enough she
stopped suddenly, as she was now within earshot of
Senator Dooley's conversation with, it turned out, her
daughter, Kendra, if Sandra's memory was correct.

"You slouched in your chair the whole time. It was embarrassing," Senator Dooley spit out at the young woman.

"I said I was sorry," Kendra whined.

"How do you expect to get anywhere if you can't even

be bothered to present good posture? You mumbled your way through, I could barely hear what you were saying, and you gave so many one-word answers to Mr. Hanes's questions, the poor man finally gave up and ended the interview early."

"It wasn't *that* bad." She sighed.

"Yes, Kendra, it was *that* bad," Senator Dooley snipped.

"Parents aren't even supposed to be in there for the interview. He just didn't dare say no to you when you said you wanted to sit in," Kendra muttered.

"If I hadn't jumped in to help, he'd never even know about all your charity work or political involvement. You didn't even try to impress him. It's not like we have the luxury of leaning on your GPA or SAT scores."

Sandra wanted to do a one-eighty and spin off in the opposite direction, but at this point she was just too close to them. Any slight movement she made would be noticed instantly.

Senator Dooley had leaned slightly to the left, so Sandra now had a clear view of her wagging an admonishing finger in front of her daughter's reddened yet defiant face.

"I will be shocked if they let you in after that lackluster performance!" Senator Dooley hissed.

The girl shrugged. "What's the big deal? You're just going to strong-arm them into admitting me anyway because you're like this hugely important senator."

Senator Dooley reared back, raising a hand, almost as if she was about to slap her daughter across the cheek but thought better of it, slowly closed her hand and returned it to her side. "I do not appreciate you talking to me like that."

Suddenly the girl's eyes flicked toward Sandra, who

stood awkwardly in the middle of the hall, just a few feet away.

Her mother noticed Kendra distracted by someone and swung around, almost gasping at the sight of Sandra, who was forcing a smile, pretending she hadn't heard a word of the tense conversation between mother and daughter.

The anger in Senator Dooley's face swiftly melted away, and she was now all smiles and sweetness. "Sandra!"

"Elisabeth!" Sandra chirped. "I thought that was you."

Senator Dooley gripped her daughter's arm tightly, pushing her forward. "Kendra, you remember Mrs. Wallage, Stephen's wife."

"Hi," the girl said listlessly.

Senator Dooley released her grip and Kendra immediately shrunk back as her mother rushed forward to give Sandra the practiced warm and friendly hug she had probably used on voters countless times. "We must be here for the same reason."

"Yes, my oldest son, Jack, is in his interview right now, so I'm just pacing up and down the hall, trying to ignore how nervous I am," Sandra said.

"Jack's a really smart, awesome guy. Any college would be lucky to have him. I'm sure he'll get in," Kendra said, more to infuriate her mother than to alleviate Sandra's frayed nerves.

Sandra could see the fire in Senator Dooley's eyes as she shifted her attention toward her daughter and glared at her. But the senator kept that sugarcoated smile planted on her face the whole time, hoping Sandra wouldn't notice. Finally, after an awkward few seconds, Senator Dooley whirled back toward Sandra. "Kendra is a big fan of your son, so she tells me."

"I'm sure the feeling is mutual," Sandra said.

"How's Stephen? We haven't been able to see much of each other since I started campaigning," Senator Dooley said.

Sandra was certain the senator was aware that they had been separated for months now. But maybe she was just desperate to switch topics. "He's fine, thank you."

That was all she was going to say on the subject.

And because the scene Sandra had just witnessed had only managed to bolster her negative opinion of the senator, she wanted to be quite clear on the fact that the state of her marriage was absolutely none of this woman's business.

They heard a door open down the hall and Sandra turned to see Mr. Hanes escorting Jack out of his office. They shook hands and exchanged a few pleasantries.

Sandra turned toward the senator. "Excuse me, Elisabeth."

"Of course. Go," Senator Dooley said, still with that fake smile only a veteran politician could maintain.

Before rushing off, Sandra touched Kendra's arm lightly. "Good luck."

"Thanks," Kendra said sluggishly.

As Sandra clicked away back down the hall toward her son and the admissions officer, she could hear Senator Dooley berating her daughter again. "Stand up straight."

Mr. Hanes was just about to head back into his office when Sandra hustled up to them and put an arm around her son. "How'd it go? Were you the superstar I knew you would be?"

"*Mom*," Jack whined under his breath.

"Your son is a very remarkable young man," Mr. Hanes said, not ready or willing to give up anything more than that.

Sandra knew she should just say goodbye and leave, but she felt the urgent need to explain herself.

"Mr. Hanes, again allow me to apologize for us being so late for the interview today. I got tied up with work and we were unavoidably delayed, and then there was that speeding ticket—" Sandra realized her mistake the moment the words came tumbling out of her mouth. "Let me clarify. I was the one driving, *not* Jack."

Jack rolled his eyes, embarrassed.

Stop talking, Sandra thought to herself. *Just stop talking.*

But whenever she heard that voice, much to her own peril, she usually ignored it.

"It was the first time I have ever been caught speed-ing . . . *caught* might not be the right word. I don't make it a habit of ignoring the speed limit . . . or breaking any law for that matter. . . ."

"Mom, why don't you quit while you're behind?" Jack suggested through gritted teeth.

Mr. Hanes chuckled and said reassuringly, "I under-stand these things happen. It was a pleasure meeting you, Jack," Mr. Hanes said, shaking his hand one more time before returning inside his office and shutting the door behind him.

Jack turned to Sandra. "Way to go, Mom. You nailed it."

Chapter Four

"She's adorable!" Maya cooed, swiping through the photos on a phone of a cherubic, sparkling-eyed, happy baby. "She looks just like you."

Coach Vinnie Cooper, stout and with a buzz cut, his hands resting on his big belly as he sat behind his desk in his cramped office adjacent to the gymnasium at South Portland High School, grinned proudly. "You mean the chubby cheeks? Yeah, I suppose she gets those from me."

Maya's heart swelled as she swiped from one picture to the next. "She's gotten so big!"

She stopped at one photo of Vinnie standing in front of a Christmas tree holding the baby, looking precious in a reindeer jumper. She studied it for a moment, her bright smile cracking slightly as she said almost to herself, "She has her mother's eyes."

There was a painful silence.

Maya suddenly looked up, wanting to kick herself. "That just came out, I'm sorry. . . ."

Vinnie shrugged and said with sad eyes, "Don't be sorry. It is what it is."

Amelia's mother, Vinnie's partner of many years, was unfortunately out of the picture. Maya knew it was a difficult topic for the coach, so she wisely chose to steer clear.

She handed the phone back to Vinnie. "So I've heard a rumor."

Vinnie raised an eyebrow. "Oh? About me?"

Maya nodded. "I hear you're thinking of resigning."

"It's not true."

"Good, because I hate the idea of you leaving."

"I'm not thinking about it. I've already done it."

"Vinnie!"

"I know. I should've told you sooner. But it all happened really fast. I applied for a teaching job in Chicago, flew there for the interview last weekend, had an offer by Monday."

Maya nodded glumly, saddened, but she had suspected this news was coming.

"It's an amazing opportunity for me. I know the challenges ahead—single dad, demanding job—but my parents are moving with us and they're going to be a strong support system for me and Amelia. I think it's the right decision."

Maya wanted to argue with him—she could be a strong support system for him right here—but she knew on some level that he was right. It was probably a smart move and she couldn't allow her own feelings about Vinnie, and how much she was going to miss him, to get in the way of his decision.

"I'm going to miss you," Maya said, starting to get teary-eyed but trying her best not to show it.

Vinnie nodded sadly. "I know. Same here."

He reached over and grabbed Maya's hand with his own. They sat there silently, holding hands across the desk, smiling at each other. Finally, Maya couldn't hold it in any longer, and tears began streaming down her cheeks.

Vinnie, though visibly touched, pretended to be annoyed. "Oh come on, Maya, it's not like we're moving to Botswana. Chicago is like a two-hour flight from here."

Maya let go of his hand and wiped the tears from her face. "I know. Sorry to be so dramatic. You just caught me by surprise."

"We'll come back for Thanksgiving and Christmas. And you and Vanessa can come see us in the summer."

Maya nodded. He was making perfect sense. But she was still despondent over him leaving. She had always been proud of the fact that she was never overly sentimental, but there were a handful of people in her life—her daughter, Vanessa, of course, her ex-husband, Max, even her new partner Sandra, who she was still getting to know—who had wormed their way into her heart. And Vinnie Cooper was one of those people.

Vinnie stood up from his desk and circled around it, opening his office door. "Now get out of here. I have a football team on a big losing streak I need to whip back into shape."

Maya popped up and gave him a hug.

He wrapped his arms around her waist and held her tight, neither anxious to let go first.

"Hope I'm not interrupting," a man said from behind them.

Maya pulled away from Vinnie and spun around.

She was slightly taken aback by the clean-cut, athletic, handsome man standing in the doorway wearing a team jacket and a baseball cap.

"Maya, this is Josh Kirby," Vinnie said. "He's taking over for me."

Josh flashed a megawatt smile that nearly blinded Maya. She shook his outstretched hand. "Nice to meet you, Josh."

"The pleasure is all mine," he said, winking.

Was he flirting with her?

She couldn't be sure.

She was terrible at picking up those kinds of signals.

So her usual modus operandi was just to ignore them.

"Josh moved up from Worcester a few months ago to be my assistant coach never expecting to get promoted so soon to full-fledged athletic director," Vinnie said.

"I'll never forgive Vinnie here for dragging me all the way up here to work for him and then abandoning me," Josh said, playfully poking Vinnie in the belly.

"You'll be fine," Vinnie said. "The students love him, especially the girls."

Maya could see why, but she wisely chose to keep her mouth shut and not comment.

"Do you have a son or daughter here at the school?" Josh asked Maya.

"Yes, my daughter Vanessa."

"Kendrick." Josh nodded. "She's in my second-period gym glass. Nice kid."

"Thank you," Maya said. "I'd better go." Maya turned to Vinnie. "Don't you dare blow town without at least coming over for dinner."

"I'll email you later and we can pick a night next week," Vinnie said.

"I'm holding you to that," Maya said before smiling at Josh. "I'm sure the football team is being left in good hands."

"I'll do my best," Josh said, winking again.

Maya turned and was halfway down the hall when she heard Josh say to Vinnie in a low voice, "Please tell me she's a single mom."

She couldn't hear Vinnie's response.

In fact, she didn't want to because Vinnie loved playing matchmaker. And she wasn't looking for a boyfriend, least of all someone practically a decade younger.

Still, she couldn't overlook the fact that the new SoPo High head coach was unquestionably easy on the eyes.

Chapter Five

Sandra watched a video on her computer of a woman, looking stunning in a beaded blossom dress, her long, auburn hair styled in a mermaid shag, her pointy-toed pumps obviously Christian Louboutin. Sandra had an innate talent for identifying designers. Sandra's husband, Stephen, in a perfectly tailored, sharp Videl navy plaid suit, hovered next to her. Sandra didn't recognize the suit. It was probably a new addition. She had his entire wardrobe memorized. He looked good. Well-rested. Content. Sandra had to wonder if the woman next to him had anything to do with that. Sandra noticed Stephen's priggish, slimy aide, Preston Lambert, trying to show off in a skinny tuxedo jacket in green, geo-patterned sequins over an open black dress shirt, on his boss's heels, ready to elbow away anyone Stephen decided he didn't want to engage with at this high-priced political fundraiser.

Sandra was watching a video recorded at a Distinguished Citizen's Award Gala the night before in Washington, DC. The recipients included a former US secretary of state and the founder and CEO of a nonprofit organization whose mission was to disrupt poverty and empower inclusion for low-income youth. Both incredibly worthy objectives, in Sandra's mind.

Her eyes couldn't help but flick back to the woman with Stephen. Sandra had met her once in Stephen's office. Her name was Deborah Crowley. She was a lobbyist with the Commonwealth Fund. Stephen's attraction to the vibrant, articulate woman, in her thirties, was an easy call. But what she really wanted to know was if the two of them were actually dating. This video certainly was strong evidence suggesting they were an item, but Sandra couldn't be sure. They were, after all, also professional colleagues. They may not even have come to this event together, but had simply run into each other. Still, they appeared awfully chummy in the video, whispering in each other's ears, chuckling over a private joke, acting as if they were the Prince Harry and Meghan Markle of the DC social scene.

"Here's your Vanilla Sweet Cream Cold Brew," Maya said as she barreled into the office, just back from a Starbucks run. She handed the plastic grande cup to Sandra while taking a sip of her own Skinny Cinnamon Dolce Latte.

"Thanks," Sandra said, her eyes still glued to the video.

She and Maya had been bogged down with paperwork all afternoon, closing out the last few cases, and they both had needed a caffeine boost to get them through the rest of the day.

Maya slid in behind Sandra, who was sitting at her desk, and leaned down over her shoulder slightly. "She's pretty. Who is she?"

"A friend of Stephen's," Sandra said.

"*Just* a friend?"

"I can't tell. Although judging from their body language

and how happy they seem together, I'm guessing it might be more than just a platonic relationship."

Maya studied the video for a few seconds, just until Stephen rested his hand on the small of the woman's back, before she came to her own conclusion. "Yup. They're definitely sleeping together."

Sandra winced, just slightly but enough for Maya to notice.

"Does that bother you?"

"No," Sandra said, although not sounding too convincing.

"You two have been separated almost a year now, right?" Maya asked.

"Ten months."

"Don't you think it's time you stopped worrying about what he's up to and started focusing on what you should be doing?"

Sandra clicked out of the video and followed Maya with her eyes as she crossed over to her own desk and sat down. "And what is it you think I should be doing?"

"Maybe you should think about dating," Maya said matter-of-factly.

Sandra nearly spat out her Cold Brew. "*Dating?* Really, Maya, I don't think so."

"Why not?"

"Because it's *way* too soon . . ."

"It's been a year."

"Ten months," Sandra reiterated.

"Okay, *almost* a year."

"I think I should at least wait until Stephen and I make a decision about whether or not we're going to officially file for divorce," Sandra scoffed.

"Stephen's obviously not waiting."

Sandra couldn't argue with that point.

But she was still uncomfortable with this whole topic and was desperate to put an end to the discussion. "Besides, I'm too busy working here, taking care of the boys . . ."

"Stop making excuses. Jack's off to college next fall and Ryan's pretty much self-sufficient at this point and doesn't need or want you doting on him . . . and it's not like we're drowning in work here. . . . You need to take some time for yourself, see what's out there."

"I know what's out there and I'm *not* interested," Sandra groused.

"Just promise me you'll keep an open mind in case someone just happens to come along who turns out to be your type."

"No! I'm not promising anything. What about *you*?"

"I'm married."

"Your husband's in prison."

"He's still my husband."

"I thought you two had already divorced."

Maya paused, not anxious to reveal too much about her own private life, but then said quietly, "I never got around to filing the papers."

"What?" Sandra asked, surprised.

"Whenever I'd visit Max in prison with Vanessa, he'd always ask if I filed yet, and the hurt puppy dog look on his face would always just break my heart. It was so clear he didn't want to go through with it. But I thought it was the smart thing to do, make the break now so when he's finally paroled, we could both have a clean slate. But I kept dragging my heels, and finally I put the papers in a drawer and forgot all about them."

"When do you plan on filing?"

Maya shrugged. "I don't know."

"Do you still love him?"

Maya thought about it and shrugged. "I don't know . . ." She decided to turn the tables on Sandra and leaned forward, clasping her hands on her desk, asking pointedly, "Do *you* still love Stephen?"

Sandra gave her a wry smile. "I don't know . . ."

Maya cracked a smile. "What a wishy-washy pair we make."

Chapter Six

When Sandra pulled into the driveway of the nineteenth-century New England–style colonial house that she and Stephen had just finished refurbishing before they decided to separate, she felt bone-tired. When she had strong-armed Maya into allowing her to join her detective agency, she hadn't seriously considered the huge amount of hours that would be required to investigate a wide array of cases. Granted, she found the work exhilarating and challenging and rewarding in so many ways, but her former life as a US senator's wife, hosting luncheons and serving on the boards of a few nonprofit organizations, had been a breeze in comparison. Every night seemed to be the same over the last year. Home late, a rush to make dinner for her boys, reviewing a few case files before bed, and that was basically her life outside the office. She would not have traded it for anything, but she was looking forward to a break in the near future, maybe a spa weekend, quick but rejuvenating.

Sandra climbed out of her Mercedes and dragged herself toward the house, ticking off in her mind what she remembered was in the refrigerator that she could use to whip up some kind of nutritional meal for Jack and Ryan.

In the foyer she shook off her jacket and hung it on a rack by the door. She heard voices coming from the living room, one unmistakably her son Ryan's, but the other one she didn't recognize.

She wandered in, stopping at the sight of Ryan sitting on the couch next to a handsome boy—young man really—about Ryan's age with a handsome face, a lanky build and a buzz cut. They didn't notice her at first because they were too engrossed in their own private conversation.

"You can't say a word, Ryan; she made me promise not to tell *anyone*," the boy said urgently, in some kind of thick Eastern European accent.

"Dude, relax, you can trust me," Ryan assured him.

"I mean, we'll both be in a lot of trouble if this somehow gets out—" The boy stopped abruptly as he noticed Sandra standing across the living room in front of the fireplace.

"What's the big secret? I'm dying to know," Sandra said.

"N-nothing!" Ryan sputtered, startled to see his mother. "What are you doing here?"

"I live here," she said flatly.

"I know, but you usually work late and don't get home until close to seven," Ryan argued.

Sandra checked her watch. "Well, what do you know, it's five to seven." She crossed the room and extended a hand to her son's friend. "I'm Ryan's mother, Sandra."

"Hello," the boy said coldly, reluctantly reaching out to shake her hand. He appeared extremely nervous.

Ryan took a deep breath. "This is Anton. He's a buddy of mine from school."

"I see," Sandra said, studying them both, curious to know why they were both so jumpy about her walking in on their supersecret discussion. "I hear an accent, Anton. Where is your family from?"

"Russia," Anton muttered.

"Anton's an exchange student."

"Where in Russia?"

It pained him to make eye contact with Sandra, but Anton knew he couldn't be rude to a woman in her own house, so he looked at her and said quickly, "Kargopol."

"I've been there," Sandra said.

Anton's mouth dropped open in surprise. "You have been to Kargopol?"

"Years ago, just after college. I was in Moscow, sightseeing with friends, and we decided to tour a few of the surrounding areas. Kargopol was beautiful." She turned to Ryan. "It adjoins Kenozersky National Park, where we did some hiking and—"

"That's great, Mom," Ryan interrupted. "I'm sure Anton appreciates hearing your trip down memory lane, but we're doing homework."

Anton gave Ryan a puzzled look, which Sandra immediately picked up on.

"Oh, is that what you two were doing when I came in?" Sandra asked skeptically. "Discussing your homework?"

"Yes," Ryan persisted, sticking to his story no matter what.

Anton suddenly popped up from the couch. "I better go. See you tomorrow, Ryan."

Ryan nodded. "Okay. Call me if you want to go over those problems again later."

"Sure." Anton turned to Sandra. "It was nice to meet you, Mrs. Wallage."

"Nice to meet you, Anton," she said, watching him dash out of the living room before hearing the front door slamming shut. She slowly turned back to Ryan. "He seems like a nice boy."

Ryan nodded again, then reached out and picked up a script sitting next to his laptop on the coffee table. He flipped it open and began perusing it.

"More homework?" Sandra asked, suspicious.

Ryan shook his head. "No, just studying my lines for the fall play." He held up the cover for her to see. "*Noises Off.*"

"Funny show," Sandra remarked, not taking her eyes off her son. "So, what's the big secret you two were buzzing about?"

Ryan sighed. "Mom, I can't talk about it! I promised!"

"Is it something I need to worry about?"

"It has nothing to do with me! I swear! But I promised Anton I wouldn't betray his trust."

Sandra debated whether or not she should press further, but if Ryan was telling the truth, and the secret didn't involve him and wouldn't get him into any trouble, she was willing to let it go.

"Fine. I'm going to make dinner," Sandra said, turning on her heel and heading into the kitchen.

After a quick inventory of the fridge, Sandra decided her easiest option would be spaghetti and meatballs for dinner. She had all the necessary ingredients. There were also enough veggies in the crisper for a salad and two garlic cloves and half a stick of butter for some hot bread.

As she got to work preparing the meal, Jack ambled in, chewing a peanut butter protein bar.

"Hey," he said with his mouth full.

"Don't ruin your appetite before dinner," Sandra warned before cracking an egg over a bowl full of ground beef and bread crumbs.

"I won't." Jack sighed, taking another bite. "By the way, it's about a girl."

Sandra stopped what she was doing. "What?"

"The big secret. I was in the kitchen eavesdropping earlier. Anton's obsessing over some girl. But for whatever reason, he wants to keep it on the down low. The girl apparently is really freaking out that people at school are going to find out, which is ridiculous, because if a guy as cute as Anton was into me, I'd be Instagramming it like crazy!"

"You don't need a boyfriend right now. You need to focus on keeping your grades up until you get that acceptance letter from Boston Tech."

"I can multitask," Jack argued.

Sandra's son Jack was gay. Ryan was straight. And quite frankly, she would have preferred that neither of them had a boyfriend or girlfriend until college. But unfortunately, she had no control over that. Her boys were going to do what they were going to do. And she would just have to deal with it.

"Speaking of an acceptance letter, Dad called. He wants to call the president of the college and put in a good word because they're old friends." Jack sighed again.

Sandra grabbed a towel to wipe the grease from her hands and turned to her son. "How do you feel about that?"

"I told him no. I don't want him pulling strings. I want to get in on my own."

"I'm proud of you," Sandra said, smiling.

"That said, I told him we were really late for the interview and that might hurt, if not downright torpedo, my chances, so I still want the option of bringing him in to do damage control if I get a flat-out rejection."

"Did you tell him I got a ticket for speeding?"

Jack didn't answer. He just grinned at his mother.

"I'll take that as a yes." Sandra sighed.

"He thought it was really funny," Jack said, busting up. "He said you've always been a speed demon."

"I wasn't going *that* fast."

"It was like seventy-six in a sixty-five zone, Mom!" Jack howled.

Sandra tossed down the towel on the counter. "Okay, enough." And then she reached over and snatched the protein bar from Jack's hand just as he went to take another bite. "Not before dinner."

Chapter Seven

Maya pulled her Chevy Bolt to the curb outside SoPo High School and turned to her daughter, Vanessa, in the passenger seat. "Be outside right at three. We can't be late or we won't have time to get processed in time to see your dad."

Vanessa grabbed her backpack from the floor of the car. "I'll be here. Hey, I've been thinking . . ."

"That always worries me," Maya joked.

Vanessa rolled her eyes and ignored her mother's comment. "Next time we visit Dad, I'd like to bring Ryan along."

That stopped Maya cold. "Ryan?"

"Yeah. Dad wants to meet him."

"He told you that?"

"Yup."

"Are you and Ryan that serious?"

Vanessa thought about it for a minute and then tentatively nodded. "I think so."

Maya took a deep breath. "Then don't let him meet your father."

"Why not?"

"Because your father will try to scare him off. He doesn't like the idea of you dating. His sole mission is to get Ryan in front of him and intimidate him, make him nervous. He's already got the tattoo and orange jumpsuit going for him, not to mention the whole prison setting."

Vanessa chuckled. "I suppose you're right. But Ryan can handle himself. I believe he's up for the challenge."

"Let me talk to Sandra to see what she thinks," Maya said.

"You and Sandra need to accept the fact that Ryan and I are together."

"I hear you. Just let me talk to her to see where her head is at about all this. Not every mother is going to be cool with us dragging her son to the state penitentiary."

Vanessa sighed. "Fine. Whatever." She pushed open the door of the Bolt and hopped out, then slammed it shut behind her. She circled the car and gave her mother a quick wave.

Maya pressed a button to roll down the driver's side window, then shouted to her daughter, "Remember, this exact spot! Three o'clock sharp!"

"Yes, Mom, I know! Stop nagging!" Vanessa cried.

Before Maya could drive off, two high school girls eagerly approached Vanessa. One was a bit taller than Vanessa, with auburn hair, a pretty face, a shapely figure, and yet it was obvious this girl was not part of the in crowd but rather a bit awkward and out of step despite her natural beauty. With her was a much shorter, stout girl, with dark hair, plain features and a big, bulky sweater that did its best to hide her extra padding. Their arms were locked together and there was an easy familiarity between them. For a moment, Maya thought there might be something romantic going on with them.

The taller girl turned toward Maya and waved at her. "Hold on, Mrs. Kendrick! Don't go just yet!"

The shorter girl focused on Vanessa. "Have you talked to your mother yet about the bake sale?"

"No," Vanessa said. "She's not really the baking type."

Maya was totally caught off guard and leaned her head out of the window of the car. "What bake sale?"

The taller girl stepped over and smiled at Maya. "Hi, Mrs. Kendrick. I'm Cammie Lipton and this is my best friend, Daisy Wynn."

Daisy curtsied as a joke. At least Maya thought it was a joke. Maybe she just liked to curtsy.

Cammie bent down so close to Maya's face, she instinctively pulled her head back inside the car. "Our Spanish class is raising money for a trip to Barcelona next spring, so we are having a bake sale this Saturday. Can we count on you to donate some homemade sweets?"

"I'm afraid my daughter is right," Maya said apologetically. "I'm not going to be competing on *Cupcake Wars* anytime soon. But I do have a sweet tooth, so you can bet I'll be there to show my support and buy something."

Daisy gave Vanessa a troubled look. "We're a little worried not enough parents are going to contribute and the whole bake sale will be a bust. We can't raise money if there are no desserts to buy!"

"I've been dreaming of visiting Spain my whole life," Cammie wailed. "I'll just die if we can't go!"

Maya felt terrible. She wished she was the kind of mother who was a whiz in the kitchen. But the fact was, she was a disastrous cook. When she was married to Max, he would prepare most of the meals using the skills he'd learned from his Italian grandmother on his mother's side. Since his incarceration, Vanessa had mostly picked up the slack, or they ordered takeout. Maya had been meaning to ask Sandra for a few cooking tips but hadn't gotten around to it yet.

Cammie was in the midst of a meltdown, working herself up into a lather over the possibility that her eagerly anticipated trip to Spain might be canceled.

"Your class has plenty of time to raise money," Maya reassured her. "I'm sure you'll be just fine."

"You're just saying that to make me feel better!" Cammie snapped.

Yes, the kid was right. That was exactly what she was doing. Maya couldn't help but notice how odd these two girls were.

Daisy grabbed Vanessa's hands, startling her, and squeezed them tight. "We have to come up with more ideas on how to raise the money! We just *have* to!"

Vanessa just nodded, not sure what to say.

Suddenly Daisy was distracted by something and instantly released Vanessa's hands. Vanessa rubbed them together, trying to get her circulation going again.

"Hi, Mr. Sanchez!" Daisy practically sang.

"Hello, Daisy," a man said in a robust Spanish accent.

Maya turned her attention toward a drop-dead gorgeous man in his early-to-midthirties, Latino, with a muscular build and blinding white teeth revealed when he smiled. First the handsome new coach, Josh Kirby, and now this stunner. Was SoPo High recruiting their new teachers from a male modeling agency?

"Shouldn't you three be getting to class?" he asked.

"The final bell hasn't rung yet," Cammie said defensively. "We still have some time before first period."

Vanessa noticed him surreptitiously glancing over at

Maya in her Chevy Bolt, obviously curious to know who she was. "Mr. Sanchez, this is my mom."

He turned and smiled at Maya, extending his hand. "Diego Sanchez."

"Maya Kendrick."

He shook her hand. She felt a little jolt from his touch, which was both soft and commanding at the same time. His deep brown eyes were kind and inviting.

"I hope Cammie and Daisy aren't pressuring you about the bake sale. I keep telling them not to worry, we'll make our goal, but they're in full panic mode and won't calm down until we raise at least a thousand bucks on Saturday."

"Well, as I told the girls, if you want the bake sale to be successful, whatever you do, don't rely on me to make anything. The goal is to raise money, not make people sick."

Diego laughed and then gave Maya a flirtatious wink. "I'm guessing you might surprise people, maybe even yourself."

"Trust me, I may be good at a few things, but baking is definitely not one of them."

"Well, I'd be interested to learn about the things you *are* good at," Diego said.

He stopped, as if he couldn't believe what had just come spilling out of his mouth. There was a long, awkward silence. Maya smiled up at him, not sure what to say. Then she glanced over at Cammie and Daisy, whose mouths were dropped open in shock. They exchanged irritated looks. They were clearly jealous over the fact that their beloved Spanish teacher was fawning over Vanessa Kendrick's harried, unskilled-in-the-kitchen mother.

Finally, Diego cleared his throat and offered her a rueful smile. "Forgive me. That came out wrong."

Vanessa folded her arms, unconvinced. "Did it?"

"I just hope you'll consider at least attempting to make something for the bake sale. We'd all really appreciate it," Diego said, clapping his hands together, struggling to regain a little sense of professionalism.

Maya shrugged. "It's your funeral."

Diego smiled. "So, that's a yes?"

"I can't promise it'll be edible, but I'll do my best and take a whack at it," Maya said, wondering what she had just gotten herself in to, returning his wink.

Wait, Maya thought, *did I just wink back at him?*

"Thank you!" Diego said, reaching in and touching her shoulder before quickly withdrawing his hand, looking worried he had just crossed another line. He turned to Cammie and Daisy, who glared at Maya as if she was some kind of romantic rival. "Come on, girls. I'll walk you to class."

At that unexpected suggestion, Cammie and Daisy's angry expressions quickly melted away, replaced by elation that Mr. Sanchez was going to personally escort them inside the school. They both fell in beside him and practically skipped along as they all walked to the main entrance.

Vanessa slid the handle of her multicolored JanSport backpack across her shoulder and turned to her mother. "Well, that was supremely embarrassing."

"What?" Maya asked, perplexed.

"My Spanish teacher was flirting with you!"

"He was not!"

"Oh, come on!"

"I'm sure he talks to all the mothers like that!"

"Uh, no, he doesn't. And you didn't have to flirt back!"

"I was *not* flirting!"

Vanessa did her best impression of her mother. "*I can't promise it will be edible, but I'll do my best and take a whack at it*! Followed by a cute wink!"

Maya was stymied by how to respond. Mostly because deep down, she knew Vanessa was right. All she could think of to say was, "Three o'clock sharp!"

And then she shifted the gear of her Chevy Bolt into Drive and sped away.

Chapter Eight

"You still seeing that rich senator's kid?" Max asked Vanessa as they sat around a small, scratched Formica table in the main visiting room of the prison amid the other family and friends of inmates.

"His name is Ryan," Vanessa said. "And yes, we're still dating. If you play your cards right, I'll bring him here to meet you."

"I'd like that," Max sneered.

"Stop licking your chops like a hungry wolf about to feast on some poor, unsuspecting rabbit." Maya sighed.

Max cracked a smile. "What? I'll go easy on the kid."

Maya rolled her eyes. "Liar." Then she turned to Vanessa. "Don't say I didn't warn you."

Vanessa reached over and playfully swatted her father's arm. "He's really nice, so you better behave!"

Max shrugged. "I'm sure he can take it. If he's dating my strong-willed daughter, I'm guessing he's not a snow-flake."

Maya shook her head. "No, definitely not. He takes after his mother."

"How is that new partnership working out?" Max asked.

"Surprisingly well. What Sandra lacks in experience she makes up for with drive and ambition. And it helps that she has access to a world I don't know a lot about."

"Her fellow one-percenters?" Max asked.

Maya folded her arms and sat back in her chair. "Yes, but she doesn't come across the way you would expect. She's down to earth, compassionate. I respect her."

"I'm glad it's working out," Max said, casually reaching over and gently placing his hand over Maya's, which was resting on the table.

Maya didn't react on the outside, but inside, she felt an electrical charge at her husband's—or soon-to-be *ex*-husband's, touch. After his arrest and conviction for corruption in his role as a police captain several years ago, she had basically been prepared to write him off as the worst mistake of her life. Especially given how he had kept her in the dark about his illegal activities. She would never forget the day when a dozen FBI agents stormed the precinct where she worked as a cop and arrested her husband right in front of her eyes, the sense of betrayal that had swept through her, the sudden realization that her entire marriage had been an avalanche of lies. But there was one reason Maya had not immediately walked away and abandoned him at the time when he needed her most.

Vanessa.

That girl worshipped her father more than anything in the whole world.

And although the humiliation of her father's arrest had been crushing for a sensitive teenager, she withstood the whispers and stares from adults and the verbal and online taunts from some of her more mean-spirited peers, refusing to reject her father. She had told Maya in no uncertain terms that she wanted to maintain a relationship with her dad, and Maya made it her mission to take her daughter to the prison for as many visits as possible for the duration of Max's sentence.

Max, for his part, had proved to be the model prisoner. Teaching fellow inmates classes in English, history, even law enforcement, given his specialized background. He was determined to be granted parole the first time he was eligible. He had also kept in tip-top physical shape, working out at the gym, in the yard, even dropping the fact that he had taken up yoga.

It was an undeniable fact that Maya still found her husband irresistibly attractive. He always had been. His good looks had been her Achilles' heel. But it was his change in personality that now struck her the most. He had once been so arrogant, so overconfident, but now, after a few years in prison, he was far more vulnerable and introspective and, in some ways, kinder. Max had been steadfast in his goal to regain his daughter's trust, and also her mother's, for that matter.

And so far it was working.

Which might explain why Maya had never signed the divorce papers she'd had a lawyer draw up soon after Max's incarceration.

When Maya snapped out of her wandering thoughts and rejoined the conversation at the table, Vanessa was talking about her spring Spanish class trip to Barcelona. Max was listening intently but had a somber look on his face, which disturbed Maya.

Vanessa hadn't noticed because she was too busy prattling on about her new teacher. "Mr. Sanchez has been going all-out with the fundraising. Car washes, charity softball games, student art shows; we even have a bake sale coming up this weekend. . . ." Vanessa finally picked up on Max's sudden melancholy mood. "Is something wrong, Dad?"

"No," Max said too quickly. "It's all good. So this Mr. Sanchez—I haven't heard his name before. Is he new this year?"

"He started last spring, and he's *so* hot!" Vanessa gushed.

Max cocked an eyebrow. "Really?"

"Uh-huh, and he is totally in to Mom!" Vanessa laughed.

Max suddenly sat up, curious. "Oh?"

"He is not," Maya said unconvincingly. "Stop saying that."

"It was so embarrassing, the way you two were flirting this morning!"

Maya sighed and turned to Max. "I wasn't flirting."

"Oh, please." Vanessa laughed. "You promised to try to make something for the bake sale, and we all know what a terrible cook you are!"

Max had a tight smile on his face, but it was obvious he wasn't pleased to learn any of this.

"She's exaggerating. We had one exchange when I dropped her off at school. It was completely innocent," Maya insisted.

"You don't have to explain," Max said.

But he too was unconvincing.

They heard a buzzing sound.

Vanessa reached into her pocket to check something.

"Is that your phone?"

"No," Vanessa said, obviously lying.

"You were supposed to hand that over to the security officer when we checked in," Maya scolded.

"I know, but I was expecting a text from Ryan," she said, quickly reading what was on her phone screen.

"You get caught with that, they may toss you in here with me," Max chided.

Vanessa was unfazed. "I need to call him back."

"Well, take it outside," Maya huffed.

Vanessa stood up, flashed her mother a sarcastic smile and headed for the door guarded by one of the security officers. She turned on the charm, making sure he couldn't see the phone by stuffing it inside her jacket pocket. He opened the door and allowed her out into the hallway.

Maya turned back to Max. "You seem sad."

"Wouldn't you be if you were stuck in here for the foreseeable future?"

"No, it's something else. What was bothering you when Vanessa was telling you about her Barcelona trip?"

"I want to help, but in here I'm pretty much useless," Max said quietly.

"Help how?"

"I'd love nothing more than to be able to write a big, fat check for her class so they wouldn't have to worry about car washes or bake sales, but thanks to my colossal screwups over the past few years, I'm pretty much wiped out."

"Um, I'm acutely aware of your dicey financial situation, Max," Maya said. "We're still married, remember?"

There was a long moment of silence.

"We probably should sign those divorce papers," Max said quietly.

Maya was thunderstruck. "What?"

"You heard me."

"I . . . I thought . . . you didn't want . . ." Maya stammered, shocked that he was finally ready to proceed with finalizing their divorce.

"We've been putting it off for far too long, and you shouldn't stop living your life just because I'm stuck in here."

Maya leaned forward. "I'm not sure where this is coming from."

"Maybe you should think about dating this Spanish teacher Vanessa was going on about."

"So that's what this is about? Diego?"

"Diego? Sexy name."

"I mean Mr. Sanchez!" Maya cried, then looked around to see if anyone in the room had been distracted from their visits by her yelling. Mercifully, no one was paying any attention to her.

Max squeezed her hand. "I'm just saying, I don't expect you to wait around for me. If this guy is as cool and interested as Vanessa seems to think he is, maybe you should give him a chance."

Maya couldn't believe what she was hearing.

Max had always been the jealous type. If another man had looked at her sideways, he felt threatened. This was an entirely new side of him. And she wasn't sure how to handle it.

"I'm really not comfortable talking about this," Maya said. "First of all, I'm way too busy to think about dating anyone, least of all one of Vanessa's teachers!"

She had heard words to this effect before. Out of Sandra's mouth, when Maya had suggested that maybe it was time she started dating. And now her husband was giving her the same lecture? It was too weird to be believed.

"I'm not pushing you into anything; I just want you to know that if it's something you're open to, don't let me stop you. You have a green light."

Maya sank back in her chair, floored. "Who are you and what have you done to my husband?"

Max chuckled and gave her a wink.

Chapter Nine

The sudden, urgent, repeated beeps startled Maya, who was sitting at the dining room table in her modest, single-level home, typing a reply to a potential client setting up an initial meeting at the office with her and Sandra for the next day. It took her a moment to identify the piercing sound as the smoke alarm. Almost as quickly, she sniffed the air, which smelled of heavy smoke. Maya shot to her feet and raced into the kitchen, where she saw black smoke seeping out of the corners of the oven door.

She raced over, grabbed a pair of pot holder mitts and threw open the oven much too fast, because now the smoke billowed out, hitting her in the face, causing her to inhale enough that she began coughing and gagging. She tried waving away the smoke with her thick, cushiony mitts to no avail. Her eyes watering, still coughing, she turned away from the oven, took as deep a breath as she could, then turned back around and extended her arms inside the belly of the oven to grab either side of a cookie tray and yank it out. She hurled the little mounds, pitch-black and burned to a crisp, into the sink before flipping on the faucet to douse them in cold water. Still waving away smoke with her mitts, she let the water run for a while, until the black crisps broke apart from the force of the water and slid down into the garbage disposal.

She heard the front door slam open and pounding feet racing to the kitchen. Vanessa stopped in the doorway, a shocked look on her face, with her boyfriend, Ryan, hovering over her right shoulder, his mouth dropped open at the sight of Maya frantically waving her arms around like she was being attacked by a swarm of bees.

"Mom, what happened?" Vanessa cried, running over to the oven and switching on the cooling fan, which slowly began to disperse all the smoke.

"Nothing. I was just baking cookies," Maya said defensively.

"You nearly burned down the house!" Vanessa said.

Maya pulled off the mitts and tossed them on the counter. "Oh, don't be so dramatic. I just got distracted with some work I was doing and lost track of time."

"Why didn't you set the oven timer?" Vanessa asked.

Maya stared at her blankly.

"Is it because you didn't know the oven even had a timer?" Vanessa asked pointedly, crossing her arms.

Maya ignored the question, mostly because she didn't want to answer it. "Look, I never said I was an expert in the kitchen."

Ryan wandered over to the sink and peered at the remnants of the burned cookies. "What kind were they supposed to be?"

"Chocolate chip," Maya said quietly.

"Yummy," Ryan said, suppressing a grin.

"Mom, really, you don't have to do this. Ryan and I will go out and buy some cookies at the supermarket and you can arrange them on a plate with some plastic wrap and no one will ever know the difference."

"I'm not going to let you sell packaged cookies at a bake sale. If people are going to pay for baked goods, they should be homemade," Maya insisted.

"We'll go to the bakery then," Vanessa suggested. "That way they're homemade and no one has to know you didn't bake them yourself."

Maya stubbornly shook her head. "No. I'm going to do this."

Vanessa sighed. "I don't get it. Who are you trying to impress? Mr. Sanchez?"

Ryan could not suppress his grin any longer.

"Watch it," Maya warned. "You're still not too old for me to ground you."

"Uh, yes, I am." Vanessa laughed.

"You want to test me?" Maya asked.

Vanessa took note of the serious look on her mother's face and decided not to push it.

Maya spun around and went to the counter and started to pour more chocolate chips into a bowl from the bag.

"I think it's great you're trying to help out Vanessa with the Spanish class bake sale," Ryan said.

"Thank you, Ryan," Maya muttered.

"But . . ."

Maya stood up straight and slowly turned back around to glare at Ryan, bracing herself for what was about to come next.

Ryan instantly regretted opening his mouth. But it was too late now, so he had no choice but to blindly plow ahead. "My mother is a total pro in the kitchen. If you want a few tips, you should give her a call. I know she'd be more than happy to help you out."

Instead of her initial instinct to attack, Maya was actually impressed. Ryan's suggestion wasn't half bad. If anyone could help her whip up a tin of edible cookies, it was Sandra. She was like the Rachael Ray of the greater Portland area.

Maya crossed to the kitchen table where her brown leather bag was, fished through it for some cash, and then pressed two twenty-dollar bills in the palm of her daughter's hand. "I'm not going to have time to pick up some dinner, so why don't you two go out for pizza?"

Vanessa stuffed the money into the front pocket of her tight jeans and, with a knowing smile, said, "Now there is the mother I know and love!"

"Don't be smart," Maya warned. "Just be home by nine."

"Good luck, Mrs. Kendrick," Ryan said.

She waved them away and they headed back out the front door. Maya then scrubbed the burned cookie tray and let it soak in some soap and water before grabbing her phone and calling Sandra.

"Hi, what's up?" Sandra chirped.

"I'm baking cookies—"

"Oh my, that was the last thing I was expecting to hear from you—"

"Can I finish, please?"

"Sorry, go ahead."

"My first batch came out a little well done, so I was hoping I could put you on speaker and you could stay on the phone and kind of talk me through the whole process so I don't screw it up again."

"Can I ask why you're baking cookies? You're admittedly a lousy cook."

"I just want to be a typical mother, just this one time,

and make some cookies for my kid's bake sale so she can go to Barcelona."

"And this sudden desire to be Carol Brady has nothing to do with the handsome new Spanish teacher you were recently seen flirting with?"

This floored Maya.

It took her a few seconds to regain her composure.

"No," Maya barked, dismissing the notion. "And for the record, I was *not* flirting!"

"I'm just repeating what I heard."

"Who told you?"

"Look, I'd be happy to monitor you while you try baking a batch of cookies—"

"Who was it? Did Vanessa tell Ryan, and then he told you?"

"No, Ryan didn't say anything."

"Then who could you have heard it from?"

"Jack."

"Jack? How on earth did Jack find out?"

"His locker is next to a girl named Cammie's, and he overheard her talking about it to her friend Tulip or Petunia—"

"Daisy!"

"That's it. Daisy. Apparently, they both witnessed the whole thing."

"It was nothing! My God, where is this going to pop up next, TMZ? Why is everyone talking about this?"

There was a pause before Sandra spoke again. "You know, Maya, a good friend of mine recently suggested I think about dating again."

Maya felt her cheeks getting hot. "That's different!"

"Is it? You've been separated longer than I have, it's not like we're drowning in work right now, what's wrong with keeping an open mind if someone comes along you're attracted to?"

"Don't turn this around on me, Sandra," Maya warned.

"I'm simply saying you should think about following your own advice."

Maya knew in her gut that Sandra was right.

But she was nowhere near ready to admit it.

Instead, she snapped up her recipe book from the counter and perused the ingredients she was going to need for her new batch of chocolate chip cookies. "Okay, hold on while I get two eggs and two and one-fourth cups of unsifted flour."

"I'll be right here," Sandra said, chuckling.

Chapter Ten

Diego Sanchez wisely chose to hold the bake sale in the school gym on the same day as a home game happening just outside on the football field. Saturday games always packed the stands, so he was confident those football fans would eventually find their way inside for some delicious homemade treats during halftime, thus ensuring a banner fundraising day.

Sandra had told Jack, who was a starting running back, that she would pop outside to see as much of the game as she could, but she also wanted to help out the Spanish class and might spend a good part of the game inside at the bake sale. Jack, who had pretty much checked out of high school and was now solely focused on college, could not have cared less, but Sandra, trying to be the perfect mother, still felt the urge to explain it all to her uninterested older son.

Sandra perused the wide array of selections that filled all the long tables, including the staple gooey Rice Krispies treats, healthy peanut butter balls, banana crunch muffins and a vegan chocolate cake. Tucked in the far corner of the gym was a smaller table with some items that were expected not to be as popular as the more creative contributions. That was where Sandra found Maya glowering as she stood behind three paper plates stacked with her homemade chocolate chip cookies.

"I'm totally humiliated," Maya groused.

"Why?"

"You didn't tell me all the parents and students would bring their baked goods all gussied up in pretty bags and packages. I just piled mine on ordinary paper plates and covered them in plastic wrap!"

"Presentation only counts if the food tastes good," Sandra reminded her.

"Did you see the crazy mother outside protesting? What does she have against an innocent bake sale?" Maya asked.

"She's against us selling sugary and fatty foods to kids because of the obesity epidemic. She's very committed. Last year when I was PTA president she helped get the soda machines banned from the school."

"So what does she expect us to sell? It's not like the Spanish class will raise enough money offering celery sticks and nutrition bars!"

"Luckily, the football fans are pretty much ignoring her. Word on the ground is, if we keep going at this rate, we may hit a new sales record in school fundraisers."

"Well, we're certainly not getting any foot traffic over in this corner. I feel as if I've been banished to the Island of Misfit Cookies."

Sandra eyed Maya's plates of cookies. "They look delicious."

"Please don't patronize me," Maya snapped.

"Okay, maybe they look a little flat and lumpy because

you probably didn't listen to me when I said to use plenty of baking soda, but I'm sure they taste good."

"They don't."

"How do you know?"

"I tried one."

"You're always too hard on yourself. In fact, I'm going to buy a plate," Sandra said, reaching in her purse for some cash.

"You really don't have to do this, Sandra."

"No, I feel like I helped by staying on the phone with you while you baked them, so I want to see how they came out."

Maya sighed. "Ten bucks."

Sandra handed her the bill and picked up one of the paper plates of cookies. She unwrapped the plastic enough to slip one cookie out of the pile and took a bite. It was rock hard, and for a moment she was afraid she had broken a tooth. She tried not to react in any way, but Maya could see she was making a herculean effort to remain nonchalant.

"They're terrible, aren't they?"

Sandra shook her head.

"Don't lie to me."

Sandra crunched the cookie as much as she could before swallowing. "I'll admit, they're a little dry . . . and chalky. Did you use too much flour?"

"I don't know. Measuring isn't my strong suit."

"And did you put the cookies in an airtight container overnight to keep them soft?"

Maya stared at her blankly.

Sandra finally gave up. "Look on the bright side. You just made ten dollars for the Spanish class."

"I just want to get out of here," Maya whined, looking around. "Where is Vanessa? She is supposed to take over for me at halftime."

"I saw her outside watching the game with Ryan before I came in," Sandra said. "Don't worry. She'll be here."

"I should just dump these plates in the garbage right now and cut my losses," Maya said.

"Forget the cookies. I still haven't met the hot new Spanish teacher. Point him out to me."

"You're not going to embarrass me, are you?"

"I just want to see what he looks like."

Maya scanned the room and pointed in the direction of a table near the entrance, surrounded by people buying up boxes of eclairs, cupcakes and pies. It was clearly the most popular table in the room. Sandra instantly spotted the handsome Mr. Sanchez, hunched over, hands in his pockets, head bowed as a woman whose back was to Sandra appeared to be bawling him out over something while wagging her finger in his face. After an agonizing full minute of the woman cornering and badgering him, the woman finished dressing him down and then whipped around to walk away from him. It was Senator Elisabeth Dooley, visibly upset and irate. As she stalked off, she nearly mowed down the father of a boy selling cinnamon rolls, bumping into him and causing him to lose his balance, forcing his hand down on the table and smashing three of his son's product.

Mr. Sanchez smiled weakly at the gaggle of parents who were looking at him askance, wondering what the conflict had been all about, and then he excused himself and made his way across the gym, as if to escape all the gawkers. He spied Maya standing alone behind her table and made a beeline over to her. When he was close enough, he slapped on a pleasant smile. "Maya, I've been trying to find you."

"Oh, I've been right here . . . in Siberia," Maya joked.

Diego laughed heartily.

It was a strong, sexy laugh. And Diego was so strikingly handsome and appeared to have such a warm personality, at least from Sandra's first impression.

"This is my friend, Sandra Wallage," Maya said, gesturing toward her.

Diego turned, offering his hand. "Yes, I've heard a lot about you, Mrs. Wallage. It's a pleasure to finally meet you."

"Likewise," Sandra said. "I hear good things about you."

Diego smiled tentatively. "I appreciate that. I wish all the parents said that." He glanced over at Senator Dooley, who now had her daughter, Kendra, by the arm, and was dragging her alongside her toward some press photographers who were apparently following her around.

"It's hard pleasing everyone," Sandra said, a sympathetic look on her face.

Diego suddenly realized Sandra and Maya were both aware he was staring at Senator Dooley. "Oh, you mean Mrs. Dooley, I mean Senator Dooley. Yes, I seem to have gotten on her bad side."

"Nothing serious, I hope," Sandra said.

Diego paused, obviously not sure he should discuss another parent with a couple of relative strangers, but he kept staring and grinning at Maya, so clearly drawn to her, he finally decided to throw caution to the wind and trust them.

He leaned in and said in a soft voice, "It seems the senior senator from the great state of Maine doesn't appreciate my grading system."

"Ah, helicopter parents can be very challenging, especially when it's time for their kids to apply for college," Sandra remarked. "Every single grade counts."

"The thing is, Kendra is one of my best students. She scored the highest in the class for the first quarter," Diego said.

"But that doesn't make any sense. How can Senator Dooley be upset that her kid is number one in her class?" Maya asked.

"Because an A is not good enough," Diego cracked, shaking his head in disbelief. "Not when you expect your daughter to bring home an A *plus.*"

Maya and Sandra exchanged stunned looks.

"And I thought *we* were controlling parents," Maya said.

Sandra turned to see Senator Dooley, along with her daughter and husband, all smiles, arms wrapped around one another, in front of the scrum of photographers, projecting the meticulously cultivated image of the picture-perfect family.

As Sandra watched the senator's daughter holding up her pretty, pink box of yummy-looking lemon bars for all to see, smiling so wide the back of her neck probably hurt, a wave of sadness washed over Sandra as she pitied what that poor girl must go through on a daily basis.

Chapter Eleven

"This is the most amazing tart I've ever tasted!" Sandra crowed as she cut off another piece on her paper plate with a plastic fork and shoveled it into her mouth.

The exceptionally handsome Asian man standing next to her broke into a wide grin. "It's a cobnut pear and sticky toffee tart."

Sandra's eyes widened as she swallowed and pointed at what was left on her plate with her fork. "And you *made* this?"

"That's the official story," the man said before leaning in close and whispering in her ear, "I am lucky enough to have a couple of very talented bakers in my circle of friends."

"And one of them helped you make this?" Sandra asked, now curious.

The man nodded. "Paul John Hollywood."

"The judge from the *British Bake Off* show?"

He nodded again. "We met at Le Mans about five years ago, when we both competed in the Aston Martin Festival. And for the record, he didn't exactly assist me in making that tart. He actually made the tart for me. Is that cheating?"

Sandra laughed. "Uh, no. In fact, you should be touting the fact you had a world-class baker make these for our little fundraising bake sale. You could charge a whole lot more for them than three dollars apiece."

Henry Yang was a well-known tech millionaire whom Sandra had met when she was PTA president at the high school, before stepping down after deciding to join Maya's detective agency full-time. Sandra wasn't quite sure how Yang had made his money—the tech industry had always been somewhat of an enigma to her—but she did know he was wildly successful, personable and, again, disconcertingly good-looking. Yang's son Daniel was in Jack's class and the two of them were good friends.

Although Sandra had met Yang on several occasions at various school events, she didn't know very much about him other than what she read in the business pages of the *New York Times*, and in the tabloids five years ago, when he was going through a very public, very acrimonious divorce from his wife of nineteen years.

Sandra took another bite of the tart and moaned. "I may have to buy you out. How many tarts are left?"

"Just two, but you can have them on the house."

"The point is to raise money, not to do free giveaways."

"I'll make sure the Spanish class gets paid."

Sandra dropped the now-empty paper plate and plastic fork into a trash bin. "Well, I think it's very sweet of you to go to all this trouble, calling in a favor from a celebrity chef when you could have just written a check."

"My ex-wife went to a lot of trouble painting me as a distant, absent father when we were in the throes of our divorce a few years back, but I've always tried to be there for Daniel in any way I can. And I know this trip means a lot to him."

Sandra crossed to the table and pointed at the two remaining tarts. "How much for both?"

"Please . . ." Yang said, pushing the boxes toward Sandra and then extracting two hundred-dollar bills from his wallet and dropping them in the tin box where all the sales money had been collected.

"Thank you, Mr. Yang," Sandra said, picking up the boxes. "My sons are going to be very excited to discover who actually baked tonight's dessert at dinner."

Yang reached out across the table and gently touched her arm. "Sandra, before you go . . ."

Sandra stood in place expectantly.

"At the risk of coming across too forward, I've heard through the grapevine that you and your husband . . ." He paused, searching for the right word.

Sandra decided to help him out. "We're separated."

"Yes, and I don't mean for this to be awkward, but I've always been the kind of guy who just comes out with what he wants—it's served me well—so I was wondering . . . Would you like to have dinner with me sometime?"

Sandra was flabbergasted, and flattered to be sure, but this certainly was not what she was expecting. She hesitated long enough to make the moment a bit uncomfortable.

Yang decided to let her off the hook. "I understand if it's premature. I just didn't want to wait and let some other guy slip in under the radar. As you know, in my business and in my life, I like to be first."

Sandra chuckled. "Yes, I've read that about you."

"I realize now this is probably not an appropriate place to ask a woman out on a date."

"Would you mind if I think about it?" Sandra asked.

"Not at all. Take your time. Absolutely no pressure."

"Thank you."

"I'll call you tonight for your answer."

Sandra stared at him, dumbfounded.

"That was a joke. I'm not really going to call you. I'm going to be a gentleman and wait until you let me know your answer whenever you're ready."

"I'm embarrassed you had to explain that to me. I have to admit, I'm a little rusty at this kind of stuff."

"Believe me, so am I. Regardless of what you decide, it was very nice seeing you again, Sandra. I miss the days when you were PTA president."

"I sometimes miss it too," Sandra said. "I'll be in touch."

Yang flashed her a sexy smile, his eyes twinkling.

And then Sandra quickly turned around and beat a hasty retreat, still reeling. She spotted Ryan and Vanessa wandering inside after watching the game, holding hands and staring dreamily into each other's eyes.

Sandra marched over and blatantly interrupted the romantic moment. "Vanessa, your poor mother's been waiting for you to relieve her from selling her cookies."

"She's actually *sold* some?" Vanessa gasped, surprised.

"She's doing her best to support you," Sandra said, declining to directly answer her question. "And she needs a well-deserved break."

"Want me to come with you?" Ryan asked, trying to be a good boyfriend but clearly not wanting to be dragged into selling any baked goods.

"No, you should stay and help out your own mom," Vanessa said.

"She already sold out all her boxes," Ryan said before realizing how it sounded. He quickly turned to Sandra. "I mean, you lucked out and got a really sweet location with heavy traffic, right? No wonder you moved so much product—"

"You don't have to do this, Ryan. I already know *your* mother is actually a talented baker." She gave him a kiss on the cheek. "I'll meet up with you later."

Vanessa scampered off toward the back of the cafeteria, leaving Sandra and Ryan alone. Sandra looked over at her son, who was suddenly distracted by something that was causing him to crack a knowing smile. She followed his gaze over to his Russian friend Anton, who was huddled in a corner with a woman at least ten years older than him, very attractive, with flawless dark skin and a mass of full, curly black hair, wearing a billowy beige blouse and dark slacks.

"Who's that?" Sandra asked.

Ryan reacted, surprised his mother had zeroed in on the scene he was observing. "Oh, that's Anton; remember, you met him when he was over at the house?"

"I know Anton. I don't know the lady he is talking to," Sandra said directly to her son.

"That's the new art teacher, Miss Forsythe," Ryan said, seeming as detached and uninterested as possible.

"I heard they hired a new art teacher. How is she doing? Do the kids like her?"

Ryan shrugged. "I guess so. She seems nice enough."

Sandra watched as Anton rested a hand on the small of Miss Forsythe's back. She frowned, obviously distressed by the intimate gesture, and surreptitiously reached back and pulled away Anton's hand. She looked at him sternly, without saying a word, and he instantly retreated, quickly stepping away from her and dropping his hand back down to his side.

"Well, it certainly appears your friend likes Miss Forsythe," Sandra remarked.

Miss Forsythe instantly parted ways with Anton, fixing her eyes straight ahead and flagging down another teacher she wanted to talk to about something. Left alone, Anton glanced around, catching sight of Ryan. He ambled over, without noticing Sandra standing nearby, and with a wolfish smile said to his friend, "Emma wants to meet up with me later."

Ryan shook his head and pleaded with his eyes for Anton to stop talking, but it took the boy a few seconds too long to get the message.

"Emma? First-name basis, huh?" Sandra cracked.

Anton froze in place, working hard not to act surprised or nervous at the presence of Ryan's mother. He slowly turned around to face Sandra. "Hello, Mrs. Wallage."

"Nice to see you again, Anton," Sandra said.

Anton shifted uncomfortably. "A lot of teachers prefer we call them by their first names. They like to treat their students as friends."

"How progressive," Sandra said, folding her arms. "Well, it certainly looks like you two are quite friendly."

Anton's face reddened, but he never wavered from remaining stoic and unemotional, in his very typically Russian way. "I'm just being nice to her so I can get a good grade."

Sandra waited for him to continue, but he was done. Anton glared at her. "Do you have a problem with that?"

"No, not at all. I'm sorry; I didn't mean to make you feel uncomfortable."

Anton shrugged, still trying to come across as cool and laid back but not quite succeeding. "Doesn't matter to me.

I've got nothing to feel uncomfortable about. Like I said, it's all about getting a good grade. I'll see you later, Ryan."

And then Anton scooted away, completely discombobulated.

Sandra turned back to her son, who was not eager to continue this conversation in any way, shape or form. "I'm going to go find Vanessa."

Ryan hurried off, leaving his mother behind.

Sandra scanned the crowd, locating Emma Forsythe, who was now engaged in a deep conversation with a woman Sandra recognized as one of the English teachers. She had not intended to open such a can of worms with the moody Russian exchange student, but now that she had, she was resoundingly curious to find out exactly why Anton was so disturbed by her prying.

Chapter Twelve

"Mom, why don't we just call it a day? Nobody's going to buy these cookies." Vanessa groaned, her arms folded, as she stood behind the table and stared down at the near-empty cashbox.

"Give it a little while longer. You never know," Maya insisted before grabbing her bag from a chair and slinging it over her shoulder. "I have to get to the office. I just got a call from a potential client who wants to meet in an hour."

"On a Saturday?" Vanessa whined.

"Yes, having your own business is not a five-day, forty-hour-a-week job," Maya said, checking her watch. "And we both know I need clients. If you see Sandra, tell her I'll call later to give her an update."

A pair of cheerleaders with ponytails, fresh from their halftime routine, passed by the table and glanced at Maya's cookies. One of the cheerleaders, with her nose in the air, asked Vanessa, "Are they gluten-free?"

Vanessa sighed. "Sure. Why not?"

The cheerleader eyed her suspiciously, not sure whether or not she should believe her.

Maya quickly intervened. "No, I'm afraid they're not gluten-free." She then threw Vanessa an annoyed look and raced out of the gym.

Outside, Maya hurried to her Chevy Bolt, which she had parked in the far reaches of the lot, given the fact that she had arrived late in the morning and couldn't find any spots closer to the building. Next to her car, the trunk of a Tesla was popped open and a man, whose back was to her, was loading boxes of baked goods into the trunk from a large plastic milk crate.

"Someone's got a sweet tooth," Maya cracked.

The man stood upright and turned around. It was Josh Kirby, the new teacher taking over for Vinnie.

"Oh, hello," Maya said, smiling.

"Maya, right?" Josh asked.

Maya nodded.

Josh looked down at all the boxes still left in the crate. "I may have gone a little overboard."

"Well, it's for a good cause."

"Actually I have really high triglycerides, so my doctor tells me I should avoid sugar, but that's easier said than done. Besides, I want to show my support."

"You must have spent hundreds of dollars," Maya said as Josh finished loading the boxes into the trunk of his car. "That's a lot of support."

"To be honest, it's not easy replacing a legend like Coach Vinnie Cooper, so any way I can win a few hearts and minds at the school is a win for me."

"I totally get it." Maya laughed.

"I'll donate most of them to the First Baptist Church food pantry."

Josh slammed the trunk shut, and Maya noticed for the first time the pristine, deep-blue metallic, prohibitively expensive Tesla that Josh, a coach living on a teacher's salary, was driving.

"Nice wheels," Maya remarked.

"I'm a big Elon Musk fan. I not only want to drive his car, I want to be one of the first people on his commercial SpaceX flight," Josh said, giving her a wink before realizing Maya might require a little more information to explain such a pricey purchase, given his low-paying career choice. "My parents bought the Tesla for me. I told them to pay off my student loans instead, but they like to spoil me." He looked at Maya intensely, trying to gauge whether she believed him or not.

But Maya kept on her poker-face and just said, "Enjoy the rest of your weekend."

"You too," Josh said, hopping in his Tesla and backing out of his spot. Maya watched him peel away before turning and unlocking her far-more-affordable Bolt with her key fob. Across a few rows of parked cars, she spotted Diego Sanchez, Spanish teacher and all-around school sex symbol, at least in her opinion, holding a box of cookies while arguing with the pretty art teacher, Emma Forsythe, whom Maya had met at Vanessa's last parent-teacher conference. She was too far away to hear what they were squabbling about, but she could see Miss Forsythe's face flushed with anger as she sharply pointed a finger in Diego's face. Diego, for his part, was waving his arms around as only a hot-blooded Spaniard could. It all seemed to reach a head when Miss Forsythe abruptly spun around on her heel and stomped away from him. He yelled something at her, trying to get her to come back, but she refused. She stormed back inside the building.

Diego turned around suddenly to get into his car. Maya thought about ducking down out of sight so he wouldn't see her but didn't react in time. She was caught in his direct line of vision, and he spotted her instantly. He gave her a little wave and a smile. God, not only did he have a gorgeous face, he had the most perfect teeth too.

Maya casually returned his wave and opened the driver's side door of her Bolt, but before she could climb inside, Diego was bounding across the parking lot toward her. She stood frozen in place, knowing a fast getaway was now out of the question. On second thought, however, she wasn't all that anxious to get away.

"Hey, I'm glad I caught you," Diego said, soulful brown eyes twinkling in the sunlight.

"I wasn't trying to eavesdrop on your conversation with Miss Forsythe, I swear," Maya quickly explained. "I just happened to look up as I was walking to my car and saw you two talking. I promise I didn't hear a word of what either of you were saying."

"It was no big deal." Diego chuckled. "She's just mad at me because I won't let her piggyback onto my trip to Barcelona."

"How do you mean?"

"My kids have been working really hard to raise money. I've already told them I don't want their parents writing big checks to pay for all their travel expenses. I want them to earn their own way throughout the school year. It's still a big question mark whether we'll make the final goal, but it's challenging enough planning an international excursion with sixteen students, let alone adding sixteen more from Emma's art class."

"I can see how that would be a little overwhelming."

"She just doesn't get it. I'm going to be responsible for all those kids in a foreign country. As it stands, I'm going to need to recruit volunteers to be chaperones on the trip. Keep that in the back of your mind, by the way."

Maya was taken aback. She had never considered she might be asked to go along on the trip. Her initial thought was, *I could never take that much time off from work*. But then, thinking about it some more, she decided it might be fun exploring Barcelona with a stunning Spaniard who would already know the lay of the land. She decided to go for a quick, nonchalant reply. "Okay."

"Anyway, Emma just won't take no for an answer, so our exchange got a little heated."

"I'm sure it will all work out," Maya said, turning to go.

"Maya, wait. . . ."

She wheeled back around, an expectant look on her face.

"It's been a long day and I'm wound up and need to blow off some steam after catering to the needs of all my students *and* their parents. I was wondering if you would consider meeting me later for a drink. I mean, if you don't already have plans. I know it's last minute, and a Saturday."

Maya opened her mouth to politely decline. After all, as good-looking and charming as Mr. Sanchez was, he was Vanessa's teacher, and it would probably be highly inappropriate for her to date him.

Or would it?

Was there some written rule that said she had to say no?

She hesitated, not sure how to answer.

Her head was saying no. Every other part of her body was saying yes.

"I completely understand if you don't think it's appropriate," Diego said softly.

There was that word again.

Appropriate.

Maya despised that word because it usually meant not following your heart.

"Yes, I would love to," she heard herself saying.

Diego beamed, flashing those perfect teeth again. "Great. How about the North Port, eight o'clock?"

"Sounds good."

"Great. See you there," Diego said as he ambled off toward his Ford Fiesta, a far cry from the new coach's fancy Tesla. Maya found Diego's choice in automobile refreshing and, well, less suspicious.

Sandra suddenly appeared at Maya's side. "Vanessa told me you were heading to the office for a client meeting. Why didn't you tell me?"

"Because I can handle it by myself, and I didn't want to take you away from the bake sale."

"But I sold all my cookies."

Maya frowned. "Of course you did."

Sandra saw the Spanish teacher fumbling around for his car keys beside his Ford Fiesta. "Was that Diego I saw you talking to?"

"He asked me out."

"On a *date*?" Sandra gasped.

Maya watched Diego, now inside his car, try a few times to get his Fiesta started. It finally chugged to life, and he managed to drive off in it. "I think so . . . I'm not entirely sure yet. . . ."

Sandra shook her head. "Well, guess what? I got asked out too."

Maya turned to Sandra. "You did?"

"Yup. When did school bake sales become the new singles' bars?"

Chapter Thirteen

Maya stared at her reflection in the mirror, leaning in for a closer look at her face, making sure she hadn't applied too much makeup, and then stepping back for a full view. Her yellow floral print, long-sleeved blouse wasn't too dressy, especially with her Lucky Brand Sweet 'N Straight Leg jeans and brown leather ankle boots. She was going for casual chic, and if not entirely successful, she was at least in the ball park. Maybe a bracelet or simple neck chain might spruce up the whole look. She wasn't sure.

"Is that what you're wearing?"

Maya saw Vanessa through the mirror, leaning against the doorframe to the bathroom behind her, giving her mother the once-over.

"Why? What's wrong?"

"Nothing. You look good. The blouse might be a bit busy."

Maya studied herself in the mirror again. "I'm kind of in to it. You don't like the floral print?"

"I'm not a big fan of bright yellow, but don't listen to me. Mr. Sanchez loves loud colors. He's Spanish."

Maya grimaced and said sarcastically, "That's not stereotyping at all."

"I can get away with it because I'm half Mexican on my mother's side."

"I'm going to stick with it," Maya said, turning away from the mirror to face her daughter. "So, are you okay with this?"

Vanessa shrugged. "Yeah, why?"

"You don't think it's weird for me to be going out with a guy who's not your father?"

Vanessa thought about it for a few seconds. "I guess it's okay. What's weird is you going out with one of my teachers."

"If it bothers you—"

Vanessa raised a hand to stop her. "No, it's fine. I can deal with it. . . ." Her eyes fell to the tiled floor of the bathroom. "I've handled my dad going to prison, I can handle my mom dating my hot Spanish teacher."

Maya chuckled. "We're just having a drink. I'm certainly not ready to rush into anything."

Vanessa raised her eyes to meet her mother's, her expression serious. "Mom, I love Dad so much, and I miss him being around, and it's been really hard, and the last thing I would ever want is to see him get hurt because I know that he . . . and me. . . we've both been holding out hope that maybe someday you two might get back together . . . or not. . . ."

"I get it. I really do," Maya whispered.

"But . . . just because Dad and I want that doesn't mean you do . . . and I don't want to stand in the way of you being happy."

Maya shook her head. "How did I get so lucky and wind up with such a mature kid?"

Maya walked over and kissed Vanessa on the cheek. She scrunched her shoulders and made an *Oh God, Mother!* face.

"I won't be late," Maya said, squeezing her arm and passing by her out of the bathroom and down the hall toward the foyer. She could hear Vanessa following behind her as she grabbed her black leather jacket from the rack near the front door.

"Ryan's coming over," Vanessa tossed off, as if it was the most natural thing in the world to say.

Maya spun around as she dipped her arms into her jacket. "This is news to me."

"What? If you can have a date, why can't I?"

She couldn't necessarily argue with her, except maybe to try the I'm-the parent-you're-the-child, we-have-separate-rules defense. But she knew Ryan was a responsible kid, and Maya had worked hard to make him scared of her if he got out of line with her daughter, so she decided to let it go.

"Text me when you're on your way home," Vanessa said.

Maya rolled her eyes. "And give you an advance warning? Forget it. I'm never giving up the element of surprise."

"We're just going to hang out and watch a movie!" Vanessa wailed.

Maya headed out the door to her Chevy Bolt, ignoring the butterflies flapping around in her stomach as she thought about going on her first date in a very long time.

Maybe she was putting too much onus on the word "date." Diego had never officially called it that, just a drink. But she knew she was nitpicking. A drink more often than not meant a date. If it was just a parent-teacher meeting, it would not be at a bar at night, but rather at school during school hours.

As Maya gripped the wheel of her car and drove toward the bar located in the Old Port, she told herself over and over again to stop overthinking this. *Just have a drink with him and don't overanalyze.* Who knows? Maybe after five minutes with the guy, she'd be making up an excuse to leave. After all, she had only met him twice. She really didn't know that much about him. Except for the fact that he was good-looking.

Astoundingly good-looking.

Maya arrived at the North Port, a laid-back, unpretentious bar and restaurant, before Diego, so she had the hostess seat her at a corner table, where she ordered a dry martini to calm her nerves. She only took two sips after the waiter brought it to her because the last thing she wanted was to get tipsy before Diego even sat down.

She texted him a quick message. *I'm here. Corner table in the back.* Then she tossed her phone back in her bag and set it down next to her chair.

Twenty minutes passed, and Maya finally allowed herself to have another sip of her martini. After thirty, two more sips. She finally pushed the martini glass over to the opposite side of the table and checked her watch.

He was now thirty-five minutes late.

Not good form.

Not good form at all, in fact.

Maya sighed.

Of course he was a flake.

She was more annoyed that she had taken so much time picking out her casual, cool outfit and putting on makeup and the guy was a no-show.

Her phone buzzed in her bag.

Maybe it was him.

As she rummaged for it, she hoped his excuse was a flat tire or something unavoidable. If he was just running late because he couldn't get his act together, she was going to pay the check and go home.

The text wasn't from Diego.

It was from Vanessa.

Ryan and I are dying to know how it's going.

Maya typed back, **It's not. He stood me up.**

Within seconds, her phone was ringing. It was Vanessa calling.

Maya answered. "I'm coming home."

"No, Mom, Mr. Sanchez would never do anything like this. He's like the most considerate, responsible teacher I've ever had," Vanessa insisted. "Right, Ryan?"

Ryan was mumbling something in the background, but she couldn't hear what he was saying.

"Well, people can be terrific at teaching but not so great when it comes to their personal lives," Maya argued.

"Did you try calling him?" Vanessa asked.

"I texted him and never heard back."

"Something's wrong," Vanessa said ominously.

"You're damn right something's wrong. I never should have agreed to this. Make sure you make enough popcorn, because you and Ryan are about to get a third wheel for your movie night."

"Wait, hold on," Vanessa said.

Another text came through from Vanessa.

It was a local address, not too far from SoPo High.

"I just sent you his home address. It's listed on the

faculty contact sheet on the school website. You should go over there to check up on him and see if he's okay," Vanessa suggested.

"Are you out of your mind, Vanessa? I'm not going to show up on his doorstep after he ghosted me."

"*Please*, Mom. If you don't go, Ryan and I will."

Maya sighed. She knew her strong-willed daughter would have no compunction about driving over to her teacher's house on a Saturday night and banging on the front door.

She was going to have to do this.

"Fine. You two stay put. I'll swing by on my way home. But if he forgot, or is entertaining another woman, and I'm totally humiliated, there are a multitude of ways I can make your life miserable."

"Call me when you know something," Vanessa said, ignoring her mother's threat.

Maya stood up from the table, threw down some cash and headed for the exit, apologizing to the hostess on her way out. She didn't need Waze directing her to the address because she knew the neighborhood well. It was a short ten-minute drive, and when she pulled up next to the curb across the street and looked at the small, one-story house where Diego Sanchez lived, there were lights on inside. He was obviously home.

Her gut told her to just drive away.

Leave a disappointed message on his voice mail and call it a night.

But she had promised Vanessa she would at least make sure he hadn't had a heart attack or slipped in the shower and knocked himself out.

Maya sighed and got out of her Bolt. She started to

cross the street when suddenly she was blinded by a pair of headlights engulfing her. She twisted around to see a car speeding toward her, straddling the yellow line.

Maya threw herself out of the way, tumbling to the pavement and rolling until her back cracked against the curb on the opposite side.

The car kept going, not even slowing down, screeching around a corner before disappearing down another residential street.

Maya did manage to recognize the make and model.

It was a Nissan Sentra.

Dark blue.

But she only had time to get the last part of the license plate: 7UR.

She made a mental note of it because she had half a mind to call in a few favors at her old police precinct when she was a beat cop and track down this clown and get him or her written up for reckless driving.

Maya climbed to her feet and brushed herself off before marching up the gravel walkway to the front door of Diego's house. She was about to knock when she noticed the door was slightly ajar. Gently pushing it open, she poked her head inside.

"Diego?"

No answer.

She leaned in some more. "Diego, it's Maya Kendrick. Are you here?"

Still no answer.

Maya immediately felt a sense of dread.

She slowly pushed the door all the way open and entered the house.

A Prince song, "Little Red Corvette," was playing on

Diego's Alexa home assistant, which she could see from the hallway was set up on the kitchen counter. She cautiously made her way down the hall until she was in the brightly lit kitchen.

Her eyes were instantly drawn to the floor where Diego Sanchez was lying facedown, an open cake tin next to him and crumbled cookies scattered all around.

Maya gasped, ran to him, leaned down and picked up his wrist, feeling for a pulse.

There was none.

Beloved Spanish teacher Diego Sanchez was dead.

Muy muerto.

Chapter Fourteen

Maya had been wandering around in a heavy fog during the week following her accidentally stumbling across the dead body of Diego Sanchez. The events immediately following her grim discovery had been a big blur. The frantic 911 call. The grueling three-hour interview at the police station. The high school shutting down for the rest of the week to allow students to properly grieve. The heartbreaking memorial service at which students and fellow teachers paid tribute to the beloved Spanish teacher.

And then, with time, life began to slowly find its way back to normal. Even Maya, who had been so shaken and disturbed by her own role in the tragic events, was finally starting to emerge from the mist and regain a sense of normalcy.

But then, an explosion rocked the high school, indeed the whole city, when an intrepid reporter from the *Portland Press Herald* got her hands on a copy of Sanchez's autopsy report, which the police were initially trying to keep under wraps, and leaked a key detail to the public that traces of a fast-acting poison, ricin, were found in Mr. Sanchez's bloodstream.

And if that wasn't enough of a shock, the report also concluded, after forensics tested one of the half-eaten cookies found near his body, which he had bought at the bake sale, that it had contained the same toxin that was found in Sanchez's system. Which meant that someone at the bake sale had wanted Mr. Sanchez dead. And a poisoned cookie he had bought to support the class trip to Spain he was organizing had been used as the weapon to get the job done.

Maya was more than happy to allow the police to handle the case. She was too close to it anyway, given that she was a key witness. But as the Rolling Stones song will tell you, "You Can't Always Get What You Want." Because now she was sitting at her desk, surrounded by fifteen high school students crammed into the tiny office, some leaning against the walls, some sitting cross-legged on the floor like it was some kind of college protest, her daughter Vanessa perched on the edge of her mother's desk, legs swinging. Sandra stood in the middle of the room waving her arms to get the chattering kids to settle down.

"Is anyone hungry? Should I order some pizzas?" Sandra shouted.

A few of the kids nodded and excitedly yelled, "Yes!"

But most of them ignored her, not even listening.

Sandra shrugged, and called across the room to Maya, "I think that place around the corner delivers."

Maya had heard enough. She stood up and bellowed, "No pizza! Now everybody shut up!"

Vanessa tossed Maya an irritated look. She didn't appreciate her mother yelling at her classmates, but Maya's authoritative tone seemed to do the trick. The kids stopped jabbering, at least for the moment.

"Look, I know you're all upset about what happened

to Mr. Sanchez, but trust me, as a former cop, the police are doing everything they can to—"

"It's not enough!" screamed a short, stout, militant girl with heavy black mascara, wearing a red beret as if she was one of Patty Hearst's kidnappers. "Why should we sit around and wait for them to solve this? They never will, and then they'll just move on to something else, and Mr. Sanchez will be forgotten! We can't let that happen!"

The kids cheered in agreement.

"They were hiding the real cause of death!" The girl, who was now on a roll, galvanizing the crowd, charged, fist pumping.

"No, they chose not to make the public aware of the facts while they're still investigating. That's very different," Maya explained.

"Doesn't sound like it to me," the militant girl grumbled.

"Look, Mom, we're not here to argue the facts, we're here to hire you," Vanessa said, sighing.

There was a pause.

Sandra gave Vanessa a puzzled look. "*Hire* us?"

"Yes. We don't trust the police to do it, so we want you to find out who killed Mr. Sanchez," Vanessa said.

Another pause.

"Hiring us costs money," Maya said matter-of-factly.

"Maya—" Sandra interrupted.

Maya held up a hand for her to stop. "No, Sandra, you live in a big house and drive a Mercedes and don't need to worry about scholarships so your kids can go to college, but I live in the real world and I simply cannot afford to work for free."

"We're not asking you to." Vanessa sighed, embarrassed.

Daisy, who was huddling with her BFF Cammie near

the door to the office, waddled forward. "We can pay you with the money we raised from the bake sale."

Maya noticed all the kids staring at her with looks of fierce determination. They were dead serious. And they clearly had held a strategy meeting before showing up at the office like an unruly mob.

"But that money's for your trip to Spain. . . ." Sandra said.

"We're not going to Spain anymore," Ryan, who was one of the boys on the floor in the lotus position, piped up. "That dream died with Mr. Sanchez."

Sandra wasn't ready to let it go. "But I'm sure we can find another teacher who is willing to—"

"No, Mom," Ryan snapped. "We took a vote. None of us want to go to Barcelona without Mr. Sanchez."

Cammie crossed the room and planted her hands on top of Maya's desk. She leaned forward close to Maya's face, and with sad, desperate eyes, pleaded, "Please, Mrs. Kendrick, we need to know who killed our teacher. And Vanessa thinks you're the ones who can find out."

Maya flicked her eyes toward Vanessa, who smiled.

"I told them I have complete faith in you and Sandra," Vanessa said.

"Me too," Ryan added.

"That's so sweet," Sandra couldn't help but blurt out.

Everyone kept their eyes focused on Maya.

She felt as if she was stuck in the whole rock-and-a-hard-place cliché. She didn't want to take the case and get in the way of the police detectives currently investigating. But she also didn't want to profoundly disappoint the kids in Sanchez's class who were so desperate for answers. Maybe there was a way they could work in tandem. After all, despite Maya's abrupt departure and her husband's corruption conviction that had torn the department apart, she still had friends at her former precinct who might be willing to help her out.

Sandra eyed her partner. "Maya, I know how you feel about pro bono cases—"

"That's a lawyer term, not a private detective term," Maya groused.

"Okay, but in the spirit of pro bono, which is free work for the good of the people," Sandra said, gesturing to the fifteen kids crammed into the office, "I am sure we could juggle this alongside our other cases."

The kids were oblivious, but Maya knew Sandra was making a strong point for her ears only. They had no other cases. And until they did, there was no reason why they shouldn't do this for the Spanish class.

It was obvious to Maya that Sandra had absolutely no intention of accepting any money for their efforts whatsoever, operating costs be damned. Maya could also tell that Sandra was going to be unwavering in her demand that those kids were all on a plane to Barcelona come springtime.

Maya finally threw up her hands in surrender and sighed. "Fine. We'll look into it."

The kids erupted in more cheers.

Vanessa practically threw herself across the desk to hug her mother.

"No charge!" Sandra quickly added. "Save your money for Spain! Go as a tribute to Mr. Sanchez!"

Ryan jumped up to his feet. "So what do we do first?"

Maya cocked an eyebrow. "*We?*" She gestured to all the kids in the room. "*We* don't do anything. I want you all to go back to school and learn a few things like you're supposed to, while Sandra and I stay here and put together a game plan."

Daisy held up a hand.

Sandra pointed at her, like a prim algebra teacher in front of a chalkboard. "Yes, Daisy?"

"If you want to talk suspects, Cammie and I have a big one."

That got everyone's attention, and the room fell silent.

"Who?" Maya asked.

Daisy glanced furtively toward Cammie, who nodded encouragingly, and then Daisy announced, "Anton Volkov!"

Ryan spun around angrily, confronting Daisy. "What? Oh, come on, Daisy, that's crap and you know it!"

Daisy's face flushed, embarrassed, but shakily continued. "He's the only one in our entire Spanish class who refused to come here today! I find it highly suspicious that he is so against us getting to the truth!"

"Just because he didn't want to be a part of this doesn't mean he's a cold-blooded killer! You're just being stupid!" Ryan snapped.

"Ryan!" Sandra admonished.

"It's him! I know it!" Cammie shouted in a show of support for her best friend.

"You don't know anything!" Ryan barked.

Sandra quickly stepped between them, placing a hand on each of their shoulders. "Okay, okay, calm down. There's no need to fight over this." She turned to Daisy and Cammie. "Now, girls, it's a little premature to be pointing fingers, so give us a chance to gather the facts and see where we are, all right?"

Daisy and Cammie solemnly nodded in unison.

Ryan got a hold of himself and managed to cool off.

The rest of the kids began to file out of the office, thanking Maya and Sandra for their willingness to help them.

One athletic boy, dragging his heels, complained, "I thought we were getting pizza."

Daisy and Cammie were the last two kids to leave. The two of them were huddled together in a corner, whispering. Maya strained to hear what they were saying, but the words were unintelligible.

Sandra marched over to them, sensing Maya's eagerness to get rid of them. "Was there anything else, girls?"

"Just make sure you don't ignore Anton," Daisy warned. "He's hiding something for sure."

"I promise you, we will follow every lead," Sandra assured them.

This seemed to satisfy the girls and, after mumbling a half-hearted "thank you" to both Maya and Sandra, they pranced out of the room hand in hand.

Sandra turned to Maya, who rested her elbows on her desk and dropped her head into her hands.

"What have you gotten us into?" Maya moaned.

Chapter Fifteen

Sandra hovered outside the classroom of Melanie Tate, a creative writing teacher, as students filed out, chattering and laughing and heading off to their next class before the bell. Sandra waited patiently in the hallway until the last student had emerged, but Ryan's buddy, Anton Volkov, had stopped in front of the teacher's desk, holding up an iPad in front of Ms. Tate as he argued with her about something.

Sandra casually moved in front of the doorway, where she was close enough to pick up bits and pieces of their conversation.

"I don't understand why you failed me," Anton growled. "It's not fair. My essay was good."

"Your essay was plagiarized," Melanie Tate barked at him as she sat behind her desk, sucking on one of the temple tips of her reading glasses. She was an attractive woman, maybe with a little too much mascara and lipstick, well-endowed, a bit on the heavy side, with a cascading mass of curly red hair. Sandra's eyes were drawn to her long, perfectly manicured pink nails, which gave her a shot of glamour.

Anton's body stiffened at his teacher's accusation, and he stuttered, alas unconvincingly, "I did not copy someone else's essay."

Ms. Tate put on her glasses and glared at him as she snatched away his iPad from him and set it down in front of her. She scrolled down to read his work, stopping to focus on one passage as she lowered her glasses to the bridge of her nose. "This part right here, when you talk about your aunt from St. Petersburg, who was so cruel to you, and then died when you were eleven years old, you say, 'I didn't attend the funeral, but I sent a nice letter saying I approved of it,' that's very clever."

Anton smirked. "Thank you."

"I'm curious, though," Ms. Tate said. "How did you come up with that?"

Anton shrugged. "I guess it just popped into my head as I was writing."

"Is that so?" Ms. Tate asked, leaning back in her chair, closely studying her student's body language. "Popped in your head? Just like that?"

Anton nodded nervously.

Ms. Tate returned her attention to the iPad and read some more before looking up at him again, pointing out a specific passage on the screen with her index finger. "What about this part here, where you discuss your appendix rupturing at summer camp and being rushed to the hospital and it was touch-and-go for a while and you say, 'The report of my death was an exaggeration.' That phrase just popped into your head as you were writing too?"

Anton, stiffening again, nodded defiantly.

"You didn't lift those quotes from a book on Mark Twain? Because he was the one who originally said them."

"Maybe I read about that Twain guy somewhere online,

and those quotes were already in my head, but I didn't intentionally steal—"

"Mark Twain had another famous quote, Anton. 'If you tell the truth you don't have to remember anything.' Just because Mr. Twain died in the early 1900s doesn't mean his words died with him. You cheated, Anton." She then folded her hands and rested them on her desk. "You may expect to get an easy A in art class from Ms. Forsythe, but in my class, your failing grade stands."

Anton bristled at the mention of Ms. Forsythe. Then he grabbed his iPad away from her and stormed out of the classroom, ignoring Sandra as he whizzed past her.

As Melanie Tate watched him go, she suddenly noticed Sandra lingering. "Mrs. Wallage, so nice to see you again. Are you here about Ryan? He's one of my most talented students. Quite the wordsmith."

"He gets that from his father," Sandra said as she crept inside the office and quietly shut the door behind her.

The move surprised Melanie, who sat up in her chair, suddenly concerned by the urgent need for privacy.

"I'm actually here to talk about you," Sandra said, crossing over to the desk, her heels clicking on the shiny floor.

"*Me?*" Melanie asked with a searching look.

Sandra had dreaded this conversation, but after interviewing all the students in Diego Sanchez's Spanish class, including her own son and Maya's daughter, the name that kept popping up was the voluptuous, gregarious creative writing teacher, with her bright-green, affable but appraising eyes. According to all the students, it was an open secret that Mr. Sanchez and Ms. Tate had dated last spring for a period of time, but the romance apparently had soured during the summer months. No one had offered a clear reason why, though some assumed it had just petered out due to a lack of chemistry. Others believed that the stunning Mr. Sanchez had a roving eye and got bored very quickly with women, and had decided it was simply time to move on. In any event, what everyone seemed to agree on was that Ms. Tate, who lived by herself in a small studio apartment near the Old Port, did not take the breakup in stride. There were rampant rumors that Melanie was brokenhearted and bereft, eventually becoming hardened and bitter by the way she had been so unceremoniously dumped by the "playboy" Diego. One of the boys in the Spanish class, who happened to live on the same street as Mr. Sanchez, had spotted Ms. Tate driving by his house at least three times one day while the boy was out mowing his lawn. It was common knowledge that by the time Labor Day had rolled around poor Ms. Tate had become what Vanessa called "a little stalkerish."

And so Sandra knew she had to proceed with caution so as not to spook Melanie and cause her to shut down before Sandra even had time to assess just how obsessed she had become with the strapping Spanish teacher.

"I wanted to drop in to see how you're doing. I know you and Diego Sanchez were close," Sandra said soberly.

Melanie suddenly became weepy at the mention of his name. "I still can't believe he's gone," she sniffed. "It's devastated the entire school. He was such a vibrant presence here."

Sandra paused, then delicately slipped in, "I was so sorry to hear you two had broken up over the summer."

Melanie tensed. "How did you know we were even dating?"

"Oh, you know how word gets around in a high school."

"Well, you shouldn't pay too much attention to what a

bunch of gossipy students might blab to anyone within earshot."

"I actually spoke with Principal Williams, and she confirmed it."

Melanie's mouth dropped open. "I had no idea my personal life was such a subject of interest in the administration office."

When Sandra had asked Principal Williams about the relationship, she had expressed her discomfort over the idea that two of her teachers had been romantically involved. It was her utmost priority to run a tight ship, and she did not want even a whiff of impropriety among her staff. But because it had apparently ended over the summer, she had decided not to make an issue of it.

But now that Diego Sanchez was dead, poisoned by a cookie he had obtained on school grounds, she was revisiting his relationship history with renewed interest. As was everyone at SoPo High, students and teachers alike.

"I'm sure you can understand, given the tragic circumstances," Sandra tried explaining.

This did not seem to satisfy Melanie, who continued pouting. "I just didn't think everyone would be talking about me behind my back."

"I'm not going to lie, Melanie. People are curious about your relationship, especially now that—"

Melanie held up her hand for Sandra to stop. She couldn't bear hearing anymore. "Please, don't."

"I know this is hard, but I'm in the process of trying to get to the bottom of what happened."

"Why you? Isn't that what the police are for?"

"I've recently become a part-time private investigator," Sandra said.

Melanie stared at her for a few moments, bewildered

and speechless, then burst out laughing. "Senator Wallage's wife is one of *Charlie's Angels*? Oh, he must *love* that," Melanie said, cracking herself up.

Sandra noticed that Melanie Tate wasn't as genial as she had appeared upon her arrival.

Nor was she as visibly grief-stricken.

Perhaps the creative writing teacher was creative in other art forms as well, like acting.

Melanie finally stopped laughing. "Are you saying someone has hired you to find out who poisoned Diego?"

"Yes, his senior Spanish class," Sandra said.

Melanie's eyes widened. "You can't be serious."

"I'm dead serious."

"So you're working for a bunch of high school kids?"

"High school kids who want answers. They're pretty helpful too. And resourceful."

"How so?" Melanie asked, a skeptical look on her face.

"They were raised on social media. It's amazing how much they're on it. In fact, just this morning, before school, there were a bunch of kids at my house, practically the whole Spanish class, who spent about an hour pooling all their Instagram photos from the bake sale. Each posting dozens of photos from all angles of the gym."

"How does that help?" Melanie sneered.

"I was hoping you would ask that. You see, with all those photos from all different locations in the gym, all time-stamped, they were able to create a timeline that basically retraced Mr. Sanchez's steps for the entire morning: where he was, who he was in the vicinity of, who he interacted with and, most importantly, who he bought cookies from."

Melanie's face fell.

After an agonizing pause she cleared her throat. "I'm sure he bought cookies from a bunch of different people."

"No," Sandra said, shaking her head. "Just *you*."

Melanie opened her mouth to speak, but she did not appear to know what to say, so she simply shut it again.

"I have to compliment you on those adorable pink boxes you put your cookies in; you'll have to tell me where you found them."

"I didn't poison Diego," Melanie seethed. "And I resent you trying to point the finger at me."

"I'm sorry, that was not my intention."

"I made cookies for Diego when we dated—he loved my oatmeal raisin the best—and so when he told me he was having a bake sale to raise money to take his students to Barcelona, I wanted to help in any way I could, so I participated."

"That was very sweet of you, considering how things ended between you."

"I don't know what you heard, but we parted ways amicably, and anyone who tries telling you different doesn't know what they're talking about. We are . . . we were good friends."

"Were you around your boxes of cookies the whole time during the sale, or was there any point when someone could have slipped—"

"No! Stop insinuating it was one of the cookies from my box that killed him! It's hard enough knowing he's gone! Now you're implying that it's somehow *my* fault!"

"I never said—"

"Yes, you did!" Melanie cried. "I should sue you for defamation! I bet your big-time politician husband up for reelection next year wouldn't like that one bit!"

A threat? Really?

"Now, please go, Mrs. Wallage. I have another class starting in a few minutes," Melanie spat out, thrusting her hand toward the gaggle of students gathered outside the door, waiting to be let in.

"I won't keep you. Thank you for your time," Sandra said quietly, turning to leave.

Sandra had not expected her to unravel so quickly.

As Sandra marched to the door and opened it, a wave of students began pouring in, some gabbing, some rough-housing, most with their eyes fixed on their phones.

Sandra glanced back at Ms. Tate, who was tottering near her desk, seemingly lost in her thoughts, clearly not listening to the two students prattling on to her about some assignment that was, unfortunately, going to be late.

Sandra could not be 100 percent certain that the poisoned cookie that killed Diego Sanchez had come from the pretty pink box he bought from Melanie Tate. But she also could not be 100 percent sure it didn't. All she knew at this point was that the jittery and jumpy Ms. Tate was acting more guilty than innocent.

Chapter Sixteen

Sandra burst through a side door of the high school into the jammed parking lot. She searched the sea of cars while talking on her phone with Maya, who was back at the office. "I got her to confirm that she and Diego had dated last spring, broke up during the summer and that she was the one who sold him that box of cookies he took home with him."

"Which appears to be the murder weapon," Maya said.

"Who knew baked goods could be so dangerous?"

"Are you coming back to the office now?"

"No, I'm going to stick around here a while longer. School will be out in another forty minutes. I want to wait for Melanie to leave, then follow her to see where she goes. Maybe it will tell us something. . . ."

Sandra walked up and down the rows of parked vehicles. "There's always a crush of people in the lot after the last bell and I don't want to lose her in the crowd, so I'm looking for her car so I know when she leaves. Ryan told me she drives a Nissan Sentra. . . ."

"A Nissan Sentra?" Maya asked quickly.

"Yes," Sandra answered before spotting it at the end of a row, half-parked on a patch of grass. "Found it."

"Do me a favor," Maya said. "Take a look at the license plate and give me the last three letters or numbers."

Sandra circled around the car and bent down to get a good look at the plate. "7UR."

"She was there," Maya gasped.

"Where?"

"At Diego's house. On the night I found his body. She nearly ran me down in the middle of the street."

"Maybe she was just driving by, like all those times the neighbor boy saw her after the breakup," Sandra suggested.

"Or she was running away from the crime scene," Maya said solemnly.

"Should I go back inside and confront her with this?"

"No, we need someone a little more intimidating at this point to scare the truth out of her."

"What, you don't think I can be intimidating?"

"No, Mary Poppins, I don't."

Sandra couldn't suppress a smile. She knew how she came across. Sweet, perky, perfect. But she also knew she had a strong backbone, and that was all that mattered.

"So, who do you know that's a real badass?" Sandra asked.

"I have just the person."

Lieutenant Beth Hart was what people might call a ballbuster. She was a pint-size, five-foot-two-inches tall, but she made up for her small stature with her forceful personality. Tough, outspoken, and never one to take guff from anybody, least of all from her fellow male cops, some of whom were uncomfortable taking orders from a woman. Beth and Maya had graduated from the police academy just months apart, and had risen through the ranks together. When Maya's career was sidelined by her husband's corruption scandal, Beth had continued to flourish, and was now on her way to becoming the first African American female captain.

Despite Maya's persona non grata among some of the officers, who had felt betrayed by Max and blamed her by association, Beth had remained steadfast in her support of Maya, making the distinction that the sins of her husband did not translate to Maya being guilty in any way. Beth was one of the few cops at Maya's old precinct she felt comfortable calling when she had information or needed advice on a case. So, after Sandra had snapped a photo with her phone of Melanie Tate's car and texted it to her, Maya was instantly on the phone with her buddy.

Within an hour, Beth had dispatched a pair of officers to SoPo High. They approached Melanie at her car, with Sandra watching from a distance, and requested that she come down to the precinct for questioning.

Melanie had seemed utterly discombobulated and in a sheer panic at the possibility that she was even a person of interest in Diego's murder, but she'd cooperated and promised to follow the stern but polite officers, one male, one female, in her car to the police station.

Maya had nearly gotten pulled over by a traffic cop as she rolled past a stop sign, trying to get to the precinct as fast as she could to watch the interrogation from behind their two-way mirror, something she had done hundreds of times while working there as a cop.

When she arrived, Lieutenant Hart was already sitting in the interrogation room across from a visibly upset Melanie Tate, who jiggled her knee up and down nervously under the table.

"There's no need to be nervous. I just have a few questions," Beth said softly, almost motherly.

"It's just that I've never been in any kind of trouble before. . . ."

"You're not in trouble," Beth assured her, although Maya knew that was just a tactical line to make the suspect lower their guard.

Melanie's shoulders relaxed just a bit.

"I just want your help filling in a few key details."

"I don't know how I can help because I don't know anything, but I'll try . . ." Melanie offered apprehensively.

Beth peppered her with a few questions about her relationship with Diego. Melanie was more than happy to discuss that it was Diego who had pursued her, that she had turned him down several times in the early spring before finally agreeing to go out with him. That the romance had heated up in May and June, during graduation season, but had started to cool off around the Fourth of July, when they had planned to attend a fellow teacher's barbecue together and he stood her up. He had stopped calling after that, and her repeated attempts to get in touch with him had failed. He'd essentially ghosted her, and she thought that was rude and indicative of his character.

Beth leaned forward, her piercing brown eyes locked on Melanie. "I've talked to a few people who have a slightly different recollection."

Maya smirked. Beth hadn't talked to anyone. Maya and Sandra had been the ones doing all the legwork. This was coming directly from their clients, the high school kids who knew all about the ill-fated romance between their hot Spanish teacher and the curvaceous, emotionally volatile creative writing teacher.

Beth calmly confronted Melanie with her knowledge that Diego had pulled away because she was becoming too obsessive, too needy in the relationship.

"That's not true!" Melanie snapped, her face reddening.

Maya could tell by watching her from behind the two-way mirror that Melanie was stung by the accusation.

The truth sometimes hurts.

The more Beth pressed, the more Melanie dug in her heels, denying that she had behaved improperly at any time.

"So you didn't continue chasing after Mr. Sanchez after the two of you broke up?" Beth asked with a raised eyebrow.

"No, of course not!"

"What if I told you we have an eyewitness who saw you drive past Mr. Sanchez's house multiple times after you two ended the relationship?"

"I would say that person is lying." Melanie sniffed.

"What if I told you I have another eyewitness who saw you at Mr. Sanchez's residence on the night he was killed?"

"I would say—" She stopped. This one appeared to trip her up. Her bottom lip began to quiver slightly.

Beth sat back and crossed her arms, waiting for Melanie's answer.

"I . . . I mean . . ." she stuttered. "Who? Who saw me there?"

"A reliable witness," Beth said flatly.

Melanie's eyes darted back and forth. Maya knew she was desperately trying to come up with some kind of explanation that would put her in a good light, but failing that, Melanie finally gave up and sighed. "Yes, I went to his house that night."

"And what did you say to him?"

"Nothing. He wasn't home."

"Why did you go there?"

Melanie buried her face in her hands. "Why do you think? I wanted to try to get him back. You're right. I was having a little trouble . . . moving on . . . but I was *not* a stalker! I hate that word!"

Most stalkers did, in Maya's opinion.

"I was hoping that if we just sat down and talked, maybe he would reconsider and we could try again. I must have knocked on the door a dozen times. The door was open a little bit, and I debated with myself for almost twenty minutes about whether I should go in or not, but finally I decided against it and just went home. I had no idea he was inside . . . already dead."

The image appeared to make her shudder.

"Do you remember almost hitting someone with your car as you drove away?" Beth asked evenly.

Melanie bristled, shocked that the lieutenant knew this specific detail from that night. But there was no denying it. She slowly nodded and copped to it. "Yes. I was upset and crying when I left, and maybe I wasn't paying attention to my driving, and suddenly there was this woman right in the middle of the street, and I almost hit her. . . ."

"Why didn't you stop?"

"I didn't hit her. She was fine. But maybe I should have. Like I said, I was very upset."

Beth continued asking questions.

But Maya had heard enough. If Melanie was indeed telling the truth, and that was still a big if, how had that poisoned cookie gotten inside her box?

Who had put it there?

Who wanted Diego Sanchez dead?

Chapter Seventeen

When Sandra opened the front door of her house to find Henry Yang standing on the welcome mat dressed in an expensive, navy-blue sports coat, an open white shirt and gray slacks, looking so refreshed and handsome, her heart did a slight pitter-patter, which was a good sign.

Sandra had gone back and forth, wondering if it was a good idea to accept a date with the tech billionaire, but in the end she relented, figuring now was as good a time as any to at least open her mind to the possibility of finding someone new, especially if she and Stephen were officially going to go through with the divorce. She knew in her bones that she was not looking for anything serious right now because she was going to need a good deal of time on her own before jumping headfirst into something new. But what harm could come of just dipping her toe in the water to see what it felt like?

Henry got off to a strong start by complimenting Sandra's new, plum Iris & Ink Marne pleated crepe dress, which she had bought just for this occasion.

Their evening began at Sandra's favorite local watering hole, Top of the East, boasting panoramic views of Portland

and Casco Bay, where Henry ordered her cocktail of choice, a Bayside Basil, a yummy gin concoction, and the two of them talked about the challenges and stresses of the college application process they were both currently going through with their sons. From there, it was off to the Merrill Auditorium in downtown and a concert featuring the famed gospel troupe the Kingdom Choir, their stirring rendition of "Stand By Me" closing out the show.

They had perfect seats, and when Sandra had asked Henry how on earth he knew she was such a fan of the Kingdom Choir, having first seen them perform at the wedding of Prince Harry and Meghan Markle, he smiled warmly but remained tight-lipped, obviously attempting to remain a little mysterious.

Sandra's head was in the clouds as they left the auditorium. Henry escorted her to his Audi A6 in VIP parking, where they were able to zip away before the crush of traffic and head to the Old Port and Sandra's most cherished farm-to-table eatery, Fore Street.

It was now past ten and the restaurant was closed to other customers, but Henry had arranged for them to remain open to serve just the two of them a late-night, romantic dinner. Sandra could not imagine what that must have cost him. But she was having too good a time to question it.

Before she even had time to pick up a menu, Henry had ordered them a rare, age-worthy bottle of pinot noir, one of Sandra's favorite wines, a plate of roasted Maine mussels with garlic almond butter and selections from a chilled and smoked seafood platter. They shared a delectable hangar steak and a parade of artisan cheeses, chocolates and, finally, the meal was topped off with an unforgettable apple crumble dessert, another Sandra favorite, along with two spoons.

"I'm astounded by the precision planning that went into this evening," Sandra marveled, taking a sip of the cappuccino the waiter had just delivered to her.

"We tech guys can be very goal-oriented," Henry said with a sly smile.

"Kudos on your success."

"So you had a good time?"

"Good time? This was like a dream date. You certainly did your research. The only thing you didn't include from my possible wish list was a trip to Paris."

"How about next weekend?"

Sandra laughed, but he didn't seem to be joking. If anyone had a private jet at his disposal, it would be this guy.

"Seriously, the Kingdom Choir, Fore Street, how did you know how much I loved those things?"

"That Alexa device in your kitchen, the one you tell to play your favorite song or set a timer for the oven or dim the living room lights, it hears *everything*," he said.

Sandra's eyes widened in surprise as she sat back in her chair.

"I'm kidding," Henry said, chuckling.

She relaxed a little.

These tech guys knew so much about data collecting, how could she not believe him? Whenever she researched buying new shoes online, she would be inundated with ads for the exact shoe she had been considering. The internet was downright spooky these days.

"Actually, all I had to do was enlist the help of my son Daniel. I corralled him into pressing Jack and Ryan for information on a few of your favorite things, as the song goes, in order to help me prepare for tonight. The boys were a fountain of ideas."

"Well, I like a man who does his homework."

"So, I managed to impress you?" Henry asked hopefully.

Sandra grinned and nodded. "Yes, Henry, I would say you did."

Henry clapped his hands, triumphant. "Good. So does that mean I've earned a second date?"

Sandra remained composed, not wanting to appear too eager because she was still slightly reticent about the whole idea of dating again. But she had to admit she liked the handsome Henry Yang with his bright smile. And she was duly impressed by his herculean efforts to impress her.

"Paris, huh?"

Henry didn't even blink. "Let me make a few calls. Can you leave in the morning next Friday so we make our dinner reservation at Guy Savoy?"

"I was *joking*!" Sandra gasped.

Henry clearly wasn't. He was already on his phone, tapping the screen.

"Who are you texting?"

"The pilot of my jet to see if he's free next weekend to take us. Don't worry. I have another pilot on standby if he's unavailable."

Sandra reached across the table, grabbed the phone out of his hand and held it against her chest. "A simple dinner right here in Portland will do just fine, Henry, thank you. Like I said, you've already impressed me, so there is no reason to go overboard."

"As long as our second date has been given the green

light, I'll take you to McDonald's for a quarter pounder with cheese, if that's what you want."

Sandra chuckled. "As lovely as that sounds, I'm actually okay with a restaurant that has maybe one or two more stars than that."

Chapter Eighteen

There were seven yellow school buses lined up in front of South Portland High, indicating the end of the school day. Students poured out of the building, some filing onto the buses, others hanging out on the grass chatting, a few of the boys engaging in horseplay. It was a crisp, sunny, late fall day, still a few weeks away from the bone-chilling winter temperatures that would eventually grip the state for what would feel like endless months, so the kids were taking full advantage of the nice weather while it lasted.

Maya pulled up in her Chevy Bolt and parked it in the student lot. She emerged from her car and made her way toward the main building. A few of the boys stopped their rabble-rousing to whistle and catcall at her. She tried ignoring them at first, but they were relentless, so she finally made a sharp turn and marched back directly toward them. The boys suddenly realized they were in for a direct confrontation, and their heckling and hollering quickly died down.

"Do you really expect that kind of thing to work?"

Maya asked, eyes narrowed, glaring at the boys. "I thought your generation was supposed to be more enlightened."

The boys exchanged nervous glances, not sure how to respond.

One of them, the obvious ringleader, finally piped up. "You should be flattered we noticed."

Maya chuckled. "Seriously? I should be grateful that a gang of pathetic, pimply faced high school boys with racing hormones are yelling at me to cover up their own gross insecurities because they can't get a girl to like them?"

The ringleader's mouth dropped open and he shifted uncomfortably.

The others looked down at their Air Jordans.

"I'm somebody's mother, for crying out loud. Show a little respect. If a couple of you did, you might have a fighting chance of growing into decent men. But at this rate, I'm not holding my breath," Maya growled.

"Mother!"

Maya turned away from the boys to see Vanessa standing nearby, knapsack hanging off her shoulder, listening to her berate a few of her fellow students. Maya pivoted back to the boys. "I'm going to walk away now. If I hear one whistle, tongue-click, or hoot, I'll be back to knock some heads together."

One of the boys hiding behind the others managed to croak out a barely audible, "Sorry." The others remained chastened and silent.

Maya whipped around and walked over to Vanessa. "Before you say anything—"

"I have to go to school here! I can't have you chewing out half the football team!" Vanessa wailed.

"They deserved it."

"What if I liked one of them, I mean *really* liked one?"

"First of all, you don't like any of those boys because you like Ryan, and Ryan would never act like a Neanderthal construction worker from the 1980s."

"Mom, I'm just saying, please don't embarrass me anymore on school grounds."

"You can't expect me to hold my tongue when—"

"Yes, I *can*," Vanessa said sharply.

"Am I supposed to just ignore that kind of behavior?"

Vanessa didn't answer the question. She just folded her arms and stared icily at her mother.

Maya threw up her hands in the air. "Fine! I promise not to engage with anyone under eighteen."

"Thank you." Vanessa sighed. "Now, what are you doing here?"

"Following up on a lead," Maya answered, not wanting to be too specific.

"But I thought the case was closed," Vanessa said. "I heard the police arrested Ms. Tate."

"No, they just brought her in for questioning. I was there and heard most of the interview and—"

"Hi, Mrs. Kendrick!" a cheery voice interrupted.

Maya and Vanessa swiveled around to see Daisy and Cammie, both bright-eyed and grinning from ear to ear, traipsing toward them.

"We just wanted to thank you personally for solving the case," Cammie gushed.

"I still can't believe it was Ms. Tate who killed poor Mr. Sanchez!" Daisy gasped, shaking her head.

Maya slowly stepped toward them. "Girls, I was just telling Vanessa—"

"I suppose it makes sense." Cammie shrugged. "Given

how obsessed she was with him after he broke her heart into a million pieces."

"I could tell she was really sad about something when we came back for fall semester," Daisy commented. "It was like the light had gone out of her eyes."

"She was delusional if she thought a man like Mr. Sanchez was going to marry *her*. I mean, he could do so much better!" Cammie sneered.

"Well, I don't know about that, but as far as I'm concerned, the case against Ms. Tate is far from open and shut," Maya insisted.

This got the girls' attention and they stopped talking.

"She freely admitted to the police and to me that she sold Mr. Sanchez the box of cookies that he took home with him, but she adamantly denied poisoning him. And it's entirely possible someone else could have slipped a tainted cookie into that box when no one was paying attention."

"She is clearly lying!" Daisy argued.

"Maybe. But what gnaws at me is why she would be so obvious," Maya wondered, quieting the girls again. "If she really wanted to kill Mr. Sanchez, why be so open about it by directly selling him a box of poisoned cookies in front of half the school? It would be a pretty stupid move. She would have had to have known she immediately would be a suspect."

Neither Daisy nor Cammie had an answer for that.

And Vanessa was mulling it over in her mind as well.

"Well, I never liked her!" Daisy snapped. "She's always been nicer to the boys than the girls in her classes. I think it was her!"

"Me too!" Cammie agreed. "As far as I'm concerned, the case is closed!"

The girls sauntered off, hand in hand, excitedly whispering to each other, seemingly convinced that their creative writing teacher was a cold-blooded killer.

"So who are you here to see?" Vanessa asked her mother.

"I'll tell you what: If it turns out to be something interesting, I'll let you know."

"Technically, I'm the client, so it's your *duty* to keep me informed," Vanessa argued.

"You heard Daisy and Cammie. They believe the case is closed. I'm no longer working for your Spanish class; I'm on my own now, so I don't have to tell you anything."

Maya made a beeline for the building, leaving her exasperated daughter behind her.

Chapter Nineteen

Maya was surprised to find the door to Emma Forsythe's classroom locked already. Students were still milling about the hallways after the last bell, and it was standard procedure for teachers to remain behind until most of the kids had cleared out in case they had questions or needed to talk about a grade or a class assignment.

Maya peered through the window of the classroom door to make sure Miss Forsythe had truly vacated the premises. She was just about to walk away when she suddenly caught a flash of movement. An easel in the corner with a student's impressionist painting experiment on it moved slightly. Maya waited, and after a few seconds, she saw Miss Forsythe emerge from behind it, buttoning her red blouse before adjusting her hair. Maya cocked an eyebrow. What was the pretty art teacher doing back there? She didn't have to wait too long to find out. Following quickly behind her was one of her students, looking flushed and happy. Maya recognized him instantly. It was the Russian kid from Vanessa's Spanish class. Anton Volkov. While Miss Forsythe looked harried and nervous, Anton appeared practically euphoric and giddy.

Miss Forsythe fumbled as she unlocked the door and opened it, composing herself before turning back to Anton, "Get me some sketches by tomorrow so I can approve your project, but so far, I like your ideas, Anton."

"Thank you, Miss Forsythe," Anton drawled in his thick Russian accent as he acknowledged Maya with a curt nod and made a beeline for the hallway. Maya watched him go before turning back to the pretty art teacher.

Emma Forsythe shifted nervously. "He's really quite a talented artist."

"I'm sure he is," Maya muttered.

Miss Forsythe ignored the comment and babbled on. "When he was fifteen, he participated in the Art Vision competition at the Moscow International Festival Circle of Light and placed second."

"Impressive," Maya said.

"He's having trouble settling on a final project, so I was giving him a few suggestions."

Maya remained tight-lipped, which seemed to further ruffle Miss Forsythe.

Maya's eyes fell upon Miss Forsythe's exposed bra strap; she'd buttoned her blouse wrong. She quickly rectified her mistake and managed to button it properly, covering herself up.

"Excuse me," Miss Forsythe mumbled; then, attempting to shift the focus from her disheveled appearance, she said with a friendly smile, "You're Vanessa Kendrick's mother. She's not taking art this semester."

"I know," Maya said coolly. "I'm not here to talk about Vanessa."

"Oh . . ." Miss Forsythe's voice seemed to trail off

as her whole body stiffened. "What can I help you with today?"

"I came to ask you about Diego Sanchez," Maya said flatly, letting her words hang there.

Miss Forsythe tried projecting a mask of calm but ultimately failed. She raised a hand to pull some of her curly, cascading hair behind one ear. "What do you want to know, other than that the whole school is devastated over his passing? It's such a tragedy. We're all waiting for some answers as to exactly what happened."

"I'm not sure you're aware, but the police have ruled his death a homicide."

Miss Forsythe's bottom lip trembled as she nodded. "Yes, I did hear that. I can't imagine anyone wanting to harm poor Mr. Sanchez."

She obviously hadn't heard about the police questioning her coworker, Melanie Tate.

"Were you and Diego close friends?" Maya asked pointedly.

The question seemed to startle her. She thought about it for a few seconds before answering. "No, not really. We were more colleagues than friends. That doesn't mean I didn't like him. He was very spirited and fun, and his students adored him." It suddenly dawned on Miss Forsythe that it was odd that a parent was in her classroom giving her the third degree. "I'm sorry, why are you asking?"

"I'm not sure you're aware, but I'm a private investigator."

Miss Forsythe's eyes widened in surprise. "Well, how about that? No, I didn't know."

"And I've been hired to find out who killed Mr. Sanchez."

"Who hired you?"

"His senior Spanish class."

"The *students*?" Miss Forsythe gasped.

"Like you said, they adored him."

"I'm confused," Miss Forsythe said, nervously readjusting her hair behind her ear again after some of it fell back in front of her face. "What could I possibly be able to tell you?"

"The thing is, I saw the two of you arguing in the parking lot on the day he was poisoned."

Miss Forsythe stumbled back, floored. "Do–do you think I had something to do with—?" She stopped herself, too upset to continue.

"No, I'm just trying to retrace his steps on his last day alive, and the disagreement between the two of you I witnessed stuck out in my mind."

"I–I barely re–remember what . . ." Miss Forsythe stammered. "It was so inconsequential . . ."

Maya wasn't prepared to tell her that Diego had already offered her an explanation when she asked him about it at the time because she wanted to know if Emma Forsythe would corroborate his story.

"Miss Forsythe . . ."

"Please, call me Emma. When you say Miss Forsythe, I can't help but think of that board game Clue. It was Miss Forsythe in the drawing room with the candlestick. The whole idea of being some kind of suspect makes me very uncomfortable."

"That's not my intention. I'm just curious about what you two were at odds about."

"Fine. If I remember correctly, I had Saturday detention duty that day, and he had agreed to cover for me because I had a family commitment, but he bailed on me and I was ticked off at him for leaving me in the lurch."

Diego's story had been completely different.

He had claimed Emma had wanted to horn in on his Barcelona trip with her art class when it was challenging enough to raise the money for one class of sixteen kids to go to Spain.

One of them had to be lying.

Emma noticed Maya's puzzled look. "What?"

"That's just not what Diego told me."

The blood drained from Emma's face. "You talked to him about it?"

"Yes, right after it happened. We ran into each other in the parking lot. His explanation doesn't line up with yours at all," Maya said matter-of-factly.

"W—what did he tell you?"

"That you were upset about his refusal to include your art class in the spring trip to Barcelona."

There was enormous relief written all over Emma's face. "Yes, I remember now; that's what we argued about!"

"Why didn't you just tell me that?"

Emma stayed mum, obviously not wanting to say anything else that might incriminate her.

Maya studied her, then said, "Unless you both made up stories to cover up what you *really* discussed?"

Emma grabbed her bag out from underneath her desk and brushed past Maya.

"That's a lovely perfume you're wearing," Maya remarked.

"Thank you," Emma replied.

"I noticed your student, Anton Volkov, was wearing the same scent."

"I'm reasonably certain Anton doesn't wear women's perfume," Emma said in a clipped tone as she slowly continued toward the door to leave.

Maya shrugged. "I guess some of yours must have just rubbed off on him, then."

Emma froze in her tracks, her back to Maya. "I'm not sure what you are implying."

"I think you're pretty sure."

Emma spun back around. "Mrs. Kendrick, I'm offended if you think anything improper has transpired between me and one of my students."

"How far has it gone?"

Emma stood her ground, maintaining a steely gaze.

"Look, I saw you two behind the easel. There's no point in lying to me," Maya said.

Emma's body slumped, slightly defeated. "Please, it's not what you think. . . ."

Maya folded her arms, skeptical.

"Okay, yes, we have been having something of an inappropriate relationship, but it's been nothing more than a little . . ." Emma couldn't help but squirm as she faced what must have felt like an inquisition. ". . . kissing, some heavy petting, but nothing beyond that, I swear! I've been struggling with this ever since the whole thing started. It just happened. I wasn't looking for it. He came on so strong . . ."

"Does that even *matter*?"

Emma vigorously shook her head. "No. Of course not. I'm humiliated and ashamed about my behavior." Emma gave Maya a pleading look. "But Mrs. Kendrick, please, I'm begging you, don't say anything to anyone. I've worked so many years cultivating my teaching career. I don't want it to blow up because of one monumentally bad decision on my part."

Maya's eyes narrowed. "End it. Now."

"I promise, I promise," Emma panted, clasping her hands together.

Maya brushed past Emma and out of the classroom. She was halfway down the hall toward the exit when Vanessa fell in beside her.

"I was just outside the door. I didn't hear much, but I saw Anton come rushing out of Miss Forsythe's classroom. What was that about?"

"No comment."

"You know there's a rumor going around—"

Maya cut her off. "Don't you have a class to get to?"

"It's only study hall. Plus, I have a hall pass. So, is it true what people are saying about Miss Forsythe and Anton?"

Maya still refused to confirm or deny. Instead, she leaned in and gave Vanessa a light kiss on the cheek. "I'll see you at home later." And then she quickly made a break for the exit door.

Vanessa called after her, "You know it speaks volumes when you refuse to answer a question!"

Chapter Twenty

Maya knew she was adding too much salt to the big bowl of freshly popped popcorn, but she was feeling decadent. It had been a long day and she just wanted to curl up on the couch with her favorite snack and watch some mindless TV. She padded down the narrow hallway and rapped on her daughter's bedroom door.

"Hey, I'm going to watch a Hallmark Christmas movie. Care to join me?"

"Mom, it's only October!" Vanessa sighed from inside her room.

"Yeah, so? It's never too early for a schmaltzy Christmas movie. This one sounds good too. A cute bakery owner unlucky in love pours all her energy into her shop during the Christmas season, but then her ex-boyfriend unexpectedly opens a rival bakery across the street and the sparks fly."

"Let me guess. They fall back in love in the end." Vanessa moaned.

"It's not about the final destination, it's about the journey getting there," Maya argued.

No response from the bedroom.

"I take it that's a no?"

"I'm doing homework. But I can blow it off if you really don't want to watch a cheesy movie alone."

"No, keep at it. Sorry to bother you," Maya said, shoveling a handful of popcorn into her mouth and heading back toward the living room, where she plopped down on the couch in the lotus position, the bowl of popcorn resting in her lap, and punched the numbers for the Hallmark Channel on her black remote.

Maya excitedly settled in for the show. She knew how dumb and predictable these movies could be, but she had grown fond of watching them every holiday season when she worked as a cop. She was exposed to so much of society's ills, like rampant drug use, base indefensible human behavior, lies and corruption, that these inconsequential little stories touting love and the best of the human spirit were so comforting. They allowed her an escape from what she had to endure throughout most of the day.

Snow was falling on the picturesque tiny town, probably shot somewhere in Canada, and the opening credits were just beginning to roll when the doorbell rang.

Maya glanced up at the wall clock above her flat-screen TV. It was a few minutes past nine o'clock.

It struck her as odd that someone would drop by unannounced at this hour. She set down the popcorn bowl on the glass-top coffee table in front of her, jumped up and crossed to the front door. When she opened it, she couldn't hide her surprise.

It was Emma Forsythe.

She appeared to be in a distressed state, hair mussed, mascara running down her face from crying, her complexion a pale white.

"I hope you're satisfied!" Emma hissed.

"I'm sorry, Emma, I'm not sure I understand what—"

"I was called into an emergency meeting with the principal and the school board this evening. They knew everything about me and Anton. They said I was unfit to teach, and if I didn't resign immediately, they would hold a long, protracted disciplinary hearing about my violation of the school's moral clause that would surely end in my dismissal. So I quit, hoping it would all stay quiet and I could eventually find a job somewhere else. But somebody leaked what happened at the meeting. It's all over social media. I'm a pariah! You should see the terrible things people are saying about me!"

"I . . . I didn't know . . ." Maya said softly. "I haven't been on my computer much today—"

"Was it *you*? Did you rat me out to Principal Williams?"

"No, Emma. I swear, it wasn't me."

Emma studied Maya's face carefully, as if trying to assess whether she was being truthful or not.

"Believe me, I never said a word," Maya assured her.

"Well, *somebody* did," Emma whispered, her eyes welling up with more tears.

"Maybe Anton confided in one of his friends and word got around—"

"Anton would *never* do that!" Emma snapped, wiping her eyes, her head down. "Teaching meant everything to me. It's all I have ever wanted to do. And now my whole life is ruined because of one stupid little mistake. . . ."

Maya wanted to remind Emma that it wasn't a "little mistake"; no, it was a whopper of a mistake, and she was lucky she hadn't been arrested. But Emma was in such a fragile state that she resisted the impulse.

"What am I going to do?" Emma wailed. She reared

back, as if she wanted to lash out and hit something, dispel some of the rage and grief that was consuming her. Maya gingerly took a step back in case Emma decided to take a swing at her.

"Would you like to come in?" Maya asked tentatively.

Emma sniffed back the tears and shook her head. "No. I don't know why I even came here. You're the last person I should be around, given what else people are saying."

"What are they saying?"

"That I poisoned Diego Sanchez. You practically accused me of murder in my own classroom! What else would anyone think?" Emma glared at Maya with fury in her eyes. "Thank you, Mrs. Kendrick. Thank you for all you've *done*!"

And then she covered her mouth with her hand to stifle the heavy sobs, spun around, and dashed off into the night.

Maya closed the door. The house was eerily quiet, except for the bouncy dialogue from a meet-cute scene in the movie playing on the television.

"Wow, I guess that torpedoes my plan to take art as my elective with Miss Forsythe next semester."

Maya turned to find Vanessa hovering behind her in the foyer. "How much did you hear?"

Vanessa shrugged. "Um, pretty much all of it. It's hard to ignore a teacher from your high school having an emotional breakdown right at your front door."

"Have you been talking to your friends?"

"Mom, it wasn't me. But like I tried telling you at school today, people have been talking. It could have been anyone, even a teacher. Let's face it, Miss Forsythe and Anton haven't exactly been geniuses at keeping things on the down low."

Maya considered this.

Vanessa was right.

Word was spreading fast about this scandalous teacher-student affair.

But she was fairly certain now that one of the first people to discover what was going on between the attractive art teacher and the adoring Russian exchange student was Diego Sanchez.

And that knowledge may have cost him his life.

Chapter Twenty-One

"I want to help you in any way I can," Sandra offered as she walked alongside Emma Forsythe in Fort Williams Park in Cape Elizabeth, the Portland Head Lighthouse looming in the distance.

When Sandra had called Emma earlier, suggesting that getting some fresh air might do the beleaguered teacher a world of good, Emma had jumped at the idea. She had told Sandra she had been holed up in her house ever since her abrupt dismissal from SoPo High, avoiding social media, contemplating how to put her shattered life back together. Sandra knew Emma saw her as an ally, having been a big booster of her when she was PTA president.

Sandra wasn't sure if Emma was aware of her new job working with Maya, but she had decided when she arrived to pick up Emma at her rented apartment on a quiet residential street in Gorham that it would not be on the list of topics to be discussed during their hike.

Emma smiled gratefully at Sandra's kind offer. "Thank

you. I appreciate it. It all happened so fast, I didn't even have a chance to tell anyone my side of the story."

Sandra noticed a flicker of doubt on Emma's face, as if she was silently questioning whether or not Sandra had the influence or clout to really do anything to help.

And she was right. Sandra knew Emma's chances of getting her old job back were slim to none, and nothing she could do would help change that. The new principal struck her as a calm, reasonable, fair woman. But Principal Williams was too smart and political to entertain the possibility of bringing back Emma in any capacity and risk an onslaught of protests from a mob of angry parents. Despite Emma Forsythe's adamant claim that her inappropriate relationship with Anton had never progressed into a prosecutable crime, she was simply too toxic to have around. And quite frankly, Sandra agreed that Emma's reckless behavior had been completely inappropriate. What Sandra was hoping to do was help find Emma a new position, perhaps at a college or senior center where she could start fresh, because Emma's remorse struck her as genuine and she was a good teacher. Sandra was willing to give her the benefit of the doubt that although her behavior had reached the edge of no return, ultimately nothing illegal had transpired between her and Anton Volkov.

"The whole thing started because I was trying to counsel Anton. I knew he was dealing with a lot of problems. . . ."

"Problems?"

"There had been a few incidents reported at a previous school in Minnesota, where he first landed in the foreign exchange program."

"What kind of incidents are we talking about?"

"Some boys made fun of his thick accent, and he overreacted—"

"How?"

"There was a violent outburst. One of the boys ended up in the hospital with a broken jaw."

"Emma—" Sandra gasped.

"I know, it's bad, but back in Russia, Anton was raised in an abusive home situation. His father was a mean drunk—"

"That doesn't excuse violence of any kind."

"I know that," Emma snapped defensively. "I'm just saying, there were extenuating circumstances."

"You said a few?"

Emma pointedly ignored the question. "I was just helping him put his past indiscretions behind him and start fresh at SoPo High."

Beating up a kid was a little more than a past indiscretion, but Sandra chose not to keep pounding home her point.

"To be honest, what Anton needed most was a hug." Emma sighed.

Sandra resisted the urge to say, *And that's how it all started?*

But Emma could read the thought on her face and grimaced before attempting to make her case for rehabilitation. "Maybe once Principal Williams learns the nuances of what happened, how it wasn't as base and sordid as what people are saying on Facebook and Twitter and Instagram, she might just be willing to have me back next semester. . . ."

Sandra parsed her words very carefully. "I'm sure we'll find you the right situation."

Sandra felt awful for not being forthright with the truth, but she hated the idea of bursting Emma's bubble, which was filled with so much hope of reclaiming her old life. Sandra knew that was one wish that would probably never come true. But she also knew that Emma needed to come to that realization in her own time.

Emma babbled on breathlessly as they power walked down a park trail. "I understand that right now things at SoPo High are a little hot. It's like we've entered *The Twilight Zone*. People actually believe I was the one who killed Diego! I mean, it's completely crazy! Anyone who really knows me will tell you I am the least violent person in the world. Believe me, I'm the one who scoops up the spider in the kitchen with a napkin and sets him free outside."

"I know it's frustrating—"

"Yes, it is! Frustrating and unfair! I wish people would just mind their own business. That's what I told Diego. . . ." Emma suddenly stopped herself and began circling her arms around to loosen herself up.

"Exactly what did you tell Diego?" Sandra asked gently.

Emma had a sour look on her face. "Nothing. I didn't mean to say that. It just came out."

"Emma, please, I can be more effective in helping you if you level with me."

Emma sighed. "Okay. I trust you. . . ." But a furtive look from her suggested otherwise.

After a long pause as Emma had some kind of internal debate with herself, she finally continued. "On the day Diego died, we had an argument."

"About combining your classes for the trip to Spain?"

"No. That's apparently what Diego told people it was about to protect me. But it was actually about Anton."

"So, Diego knew what was going on between you?"

"He suspected. And he confronted me about it. I was so shocked to have him call me out like that, my defenses went up, I denied everything, and I told him to mind his own business!"

"Did he threaten to go to Principal Williams?"

Emma slowly shook her head. "No, he just warned me that if I didn't put a stop to it immediately, it would adversely affect my career. And boy, was that the understatement of the year," she said with a wry smile. She then turned and placed a hand on Sandra's arm, stopping her in the middle of the trail. "Diego was very sweet. He didn't want to destroy my life. He just wanted me to do the right thing."

"He sounds like a very kind, thoughtful man."

"He was. At the time I couldn't see it, though. We weren't close, and suddenly I felt like he was butting into my personal business. I was so angry at him, I refused to participate in his bake sale. I didn't contribute anything, so I couldn't have poisoned him."

Sandra studied her face.

She seemed sincere.

But then again, people could be good actors, good liars.

"Besides," Emma added, eager to put the spotlight on anyone else, "I heard Diego's ex-girlfriend, Melanie Tate, was arrested."

Sandra folded her arms and said solemnly, "The poisoned cookie came from a box she sold to Diego."

Emma clapped her hands together, almost triumphant. "Well, there you go. Case closed. I'm innocent."

"I just don't think Ms. Tate would be dumb enough to be so blatantly obvious as to hand the murder weapon to her victim publicly, in front of dozens of people, if she was actually the killer."

Emma shrugged. "You never know. People do dumb things sometimes." And then she trundled off down the trail, unable to suppress her joyful smile at the fact that there was another, far more likely suspect on law enforcement's radar.

Chapter Twenty-Two

Sandra hurriedly pulled into the driveway of her large, Colonial three-story house and hopped out of her Mercedes, phone clamped to her ear, listening to Maya's thoughts after filling her in on her walk in the park with Emma Forsythe.

"If Anton knew Diego was threatening to expose his affair with Emma to school officials, he could have poisoned him to keep him quiet," Maya suggested forthrightly.

"I just can't get my head around the possibility that one of my son's friends is the culprit." Sandra sighed.

"He's a strong suspect. He's got a history of violence we didn't know about," Maya reminded her. "Have you talked to Ryan?"

"I just got home. I'll speak to him, see what he has to say," Sandra promised, clicking up the cement walkway to the front porch and then throwing open the front door with a flourish and charging inside.

Her sons were in the living room, Jack sprawled out on the couch, Ryan in a leather chair near the crackling fireplace. Both boys had somber looks on their faces as their mother shook off her coat and stood in the entryway.

"Where have you been?" Jack asked.

"Working," Sandra answered vaguely, dropping her phone in her Tom Ford shoulder bag.

"On Mr. Sanchez's murder?" Ryan asked with a raised eyebrow.

"Yes, as a matter of fact. Why the long faces?" Sandra was curious to know.

The boys exchanged furtive glances.

Jack cleared his throat.

There was a long, drawn-out pause as Sandra waited for an answer.

"*Well?*"

Finally, Ryan spoke up. "He didn't do it, Mom."

"Who?"

"Anton. He didn't kill anybody."

"What makes you say that?"

"Because I know the guy. He's a buddy of mine. Yes, I'm aware he was in some trouble at his last school, but he's not like that anymore. He really wants to make his time at SoPo High productive and successful before he has to go back to Russia."

Sandra studied Ryan, who struck her as sincere. Then she glanced over at Jack, who maintained a poker-face. She swiveled back to Ryan. "Did you know about his affair with Miss Forsythe?"

Ryan scoffed. "I wouldn't call it an *affair*."

"Okay, how about a wildly inappropriate relationship? Does that work better for you?"

Ryan shrugged. "He was the one who chased her, not the other way around."

"It doesn't matter who started it. She should have known better."

Jack finally joined the conversation. "Anton was here earlier."

Sandra's mouth dropped open. "Here at the house?"

Jack nodded. "Ryan wasn't home yet. He was really upset that Miss Forsythe was fired because of him. Worse, she told him not to call her or email her or contact her in any way, and that's driving him crazy because he really has strong feelings for her."

"Well, if he honestly wants to be successful at SoPo High, he's going to need to get over those feelings," Sandra said bluntly. "I'm going to get dinner started."

Sandra made a move toward the kitchen when Jack stopped her cold by asking nonchalantly, "So, are you going to see Henry Yang again?"

Sandra slowly pivoted back around to face her sons. "I honestly don't know. . . ."

Ryan cracked a smile. "For the record, according to Daniel, his dad thinks you're really hot."

"I respectfully would rather not hear that news from my own son, thank you very much," Sandra replied flatly.

Ryan chuckled. "It's true."

Jack sat up on the plush couch, resting his feet on the floor. "Are we going to have to start calling him 'Dad'?"

"Of course not," Sandra said. "We've only had one date."

The boys stared at her, waiting to hear more.

"And . . . and I'm not even sure there's going to be a second. . . ."

"There is," Jack said. "He's already sent you a text, according to Daniel."

Sandra blinked at her sons skeptically, then fished

through her bag for her phone. Sure enough, there was a text from Henry suggesting dinner tomorrow night.

"How is it you two know more about my social life than I do?" Sandra asked.

"He's planning a nice surprise, from what I hear," Jack said. "Very romantic."

"Oh no. What?" Sandra asked with a sense of dread.

"Wouldn't be a surprise if I told you," Jack insisted.

Sandra marched into the living room and sat down on the couch next to him. "Tell me honestly. Is this awkward?"

"You dating our friend's father?" Ryan asked.

"No, me dating period," Sandra said.

Ryan nodded. "A little."

Jack piped in, "I think it's great. Why shouldn't you date? Dad—" Jack caught himself and stopped in mid-thought.

Ryan looked his way, curious. "Dad what?"

"Nothing."

"No, Dad *what*?" Ryan pressed.

Sandra was stunned.

Jack knew about Stephen's relationship with Deborah Crowley. Either Stephen had admitted it himself or Jack had discovered it on his own while he was visiting his father in DC last month. But clearly Ryan was still in the dark.

"Is Dad dating someone too?" Ryan demanded to know.

"I don't know," Jack said quietly.

Sandra always knew when her older son was fibbing. He always bounced his right leg up and down nervously.

Just like he was doing now.

Ryan was about to press the issue further, but Sandra interrupted him before he had a chance. "This thing with Henry Yang, whatever it is—I haven't quite figured it out yet, but it's in the very early stages and not at all serious. But if it does progress into something more substantial—and that's a big if—I will not move forward without consulting the two of you. Is that clear?"

Both boys nodded, satisfied.

Sandra was desperate to change the subject. "Now, I think I have enough ground beef in the fridge to make tacos. You interested?"

"Yes," Jack replied for the two of them.

Sandra offered them both a bright, motherly smile and then retreated to the kitchen to collect herself. She was not comfortable discussing dating anyone with Maya, let alone her own sons. As she peeled the plastic wrap from the pound of meat she had retrieved from the fridge, she could hear Jack and Ryan whispering to each other in the living room.

She knew in her gut that Jack was quietly relating the news about their father's possible new girlfriend to his brother.

And she couldn't help but be bothered by it.

No formal decision had been made between her and Stephen regarding either reconciling or divorcing. But in her mind, with both of them having now taken a deep dive into the dating pool, it was becoming increasingly clear this separation was heading in the direction of a permanent break.

Chapter Twenty-Three

The crash startled Maya, who was in the kitchen stirring a pot of vegetarian chili on the stove with a wooden spoon.

The loud noise had come from outside.

She was listening to some Frank Ocean on the Alexa device planted on the counter that Vanessa had insisted they buy for the house.

"Alexa, stop music," Maya instructed, setting down the wooden spoon on the kitchen counter.

Frank's melodious voice evaporated, and the only sound Maya heard was the hissing gas powering the blue flames heating up the chili on the burner. She cranked the knob on the burner, lowering the heat. Then she crossed over to the back door leading outside and opened it.

She heard a rummaging sound around the corner.

"Hello?"

No response.

Just more rummaging.

Maya cautiously stepped outside, looking around and spotting no one, before tiptoeing over and peering around the side of the house. That was when she spotted her trash bin tipped over on its side, a plastic garbage bag ripped open, and a hungry racoon foraging through the discarded leftovers from last night's dinner, feasting on some old, mushy spaghetti noodles covered in marinara sauce.

Maya took one step forward, alerting the racoon, who reared up on his haunches and hissed at her, irritated that his meal had been so rudely interrupted.

Maya clapped her hands together a few times, trying to scare him off, but he just stared at her defiantly for a few moments before finally deciding to waddle off and find someone else's trash to rifle through.

When the racoon was halfway down the driveway, Maya turned on her heel and walked back into the house, shutting the kitchen door behind her. She returned to the stove, picking up the wooden spoon and stirring the chili so it wouldn't burn in the pot. Then she opened the cupboards and took out two bowls, setting them down on the counter. She assumed Vanessa would be hungry when she got home from studying with friends at the school library. The last time Vanessa had claimed to be studying at the library, it had turned out, after a lengthy interrogation, that she had actually been hanging out at the mall with Ryan. But she had just spoken to Sandra a few minutes earlier, and she had confirmed that Ryan was home with her, so Maya was willing to give her daughter the benefit of the doubt this time.

She inspected the bowls to make sure they were clean because she had been having a problem with her dishwasher detergent leaving a white residue on her plates and cutlery. Satisfied, she set them back down and turned to get some cheddar cheese and onion to top the chili with when the sight of a knife-wielding intruder in front of the fridge caused her to scream and jump back, her lower back slamming into the edge of the counter.

She instantly recognized the invader.

It was Anton Volkov.

He was wild-eyed, maddened and gripped the knife like his life depended on it. It was a small pocketknife, nothing as intimidating as a sharp butcher's knife, but still dangerous enough to do serious bodily harm.

Maya knew she had to remain calm and steady.

She couldn't let on that she was actually scared out of her mind.

"What are you doing in my house?" Maya yelled.

Anton didn't answer her at first.

He just stood in front of Maya's refrigerator, his shoulders slumped, his eyes wet, his face flushed and vexed, as if he was trying to figure out for himself why he had come here and what he was planning to do.

Maya kept her eye focused on the sharp edge of the knife. He held it up in front of him, but he wasn't thrusting it toward her in a threatening manner.

"Anton, if you don't put down that knife, you're going to be in a whole world of trouble—"

He cut her off. "I loved her so much, we were so happy together, and then you had to go and ruin everything!"

Maya slowly, deliberately shook her head. "No, Anton. I'm not to blame. Your relationship with Miss Forsythe was doomed from the start. She never should have allowed it to progress—"

"Stop talking like she did something wrong! She's a lovely person. Kind, generous, caring. And now, thanks to you, everybody is talking about her like she's . . . some dirty . . ."

"I don't think that. I just believe she made an impulsive decision that—"

"Shut up! I'm tired of listening to people judging her and punishing her just because . . ."

The back door suddenly swung open and Vanessa bounded in. "Sorry, I missed your text about dinnertime—" She froze in her tracks at the sight of Anton Volkov standing near her mother in the kitchen brandishing a pocketknife.

Vanessa's sudden arrival distracted Anton, allowing Maya to grip the counter with the palms of her hands, lift herself up high enough so she could swing out her right leg. The heel of her boot smacked against Anton's wrist. He yelped in pain and dropped the knife, which clattered to the floor. Maya sprang into action, kicking the knife underneath the fridge and out of Anton's reach while simultaneously hurling herself at him, knocking him back off his feet. Maya spun him around, wrenched his right arm behind his back and shoved his whole body up against the refrigerator, his left cheek smashed against the stainless-steel door.

"Vanessa, call 911!" Maya ordered.

Vanessa reached for her phone in her backpack but hesitated before unlocking the screen.

"Do it now!" Maya cried.

Vanessa looked at her phone screen, then back up at her mother. "Mom . . ."

"I'm not kidding around. He broke into our house and threatened me with a knife."

"I know it looks bad, but I don't believe Anton would actually hurt anyone—"

"He's done it before. At his last school, for instance."

"If anybody bothered to ask, they'd find out there were extenuating circumstances. He was the target of bullying," she argued.

"Vanessa, I'm not going to have this discussion with you. Now unlock your phone and call 911. Do you hear me?"

Vanessa hesitated again. She focused on Anton, helpless in Maya's powerful grip. "Did you come here to hurt my mom?"

Anton shook his head and sniffed. "I just wanted to talk to her, find out why she had to break me and Emma up."

Anton's body wilted and he silently wept.

Maya loosened her grip a little, allowing him some breathing room.

"We loved each other so much. . . ." Anton choked out. "I wanted us to run away together, and now she won't even return my calls. . . ."

Maya took him by the arm and led him over to the kitchen table, pushing him down in a chair.

"Can I get you something to drink, Anton?" Vanessa asked.

Maya shot her a look. "He is not a guest in our home, Vanessa. We're not serving him milk and cookies!"

"I . . . I'm sorry, Mrs. Kendrick. It was wrong of me to come here. . . . I just . . . I just needed someone to blame. . . ."

"Did you blame Mr. Sanchez?" Maya asked pointedly.

Anton raised his eyes to meet hers. "What?"

"Mr. Sanchez. He knew about your relationship with Miss Forsythe. He warned her to end it immediately."

"I . . . I . . . did hear that . . ." Anton stammered.

"Did that make you angry?" Maya asked, eyes narrowing.

Anton slowly nodded.

"Angry enough to *kill* him?"

"No!" Anton shouted, suddenly panicked. "I didn't poison him! You have to believe me!"

"You just broke into my house, recklessly waving around a knife. Why on earth would I believe you're not capable of targeting Mr. Sanchez?"

"Because Emma never told me Mr. Sanchez found out about us! Not until after he was dead! I had no reason to kill him because I didn't know!" Anton cried, babbling some more in Russian without even realizing it.

Vanessa's eyes flicked toward her mother. She firmly believed her classmate. Maya wasn't so sure.

But if he was telling the truth, any kind of motive would be off the table. If he didn't know about the argument in the school parking lot between Emma and Diego, he would have had no reason to kill him, which would essentially put him in the clear.

Maya studied the kid's distraught face.

He was still chattering in Russian before he finally noticed the quizzical look on Vanessa's face and caught himself. Then he fell silent.

Maya dropped to her knees, slid her arm underneath the bottom of the fridge and retrieved the pocketknife. She held it up in her hand. "I'm keeping this."

Anton nodded solemnly.

"Now, come with me," Maya ordered, grabbing him by his jacket sleeve and dragging him toward the door.

"Are you taking me to the police station?" Anton asked, almost resigned.

"Mom!" Vanessa protested.

Maya shot her a look, which hushed Vanessa, then she looked back at Anton, who appeared so shrunken in size from the intimidating posture he had adopted when she first saw him hovering in her kitchen holding the pocketknife.

Maya sighed. "I'm giving him a ride home. There's chili on the stove. Eat before it gets cold."

And then she roughly escorted Anton out.

Chapter Twenty-Four

Sandra had always found New York City, with its soaring skyline, so mesmerizing and magical whenever she visited, but now, sitting next to Henry Yang in his company helicopter soaring down the East River past Roosevelt Island, staring up at the tall buildings that stretched all the way up into the clouds, she couldn't quite believe she had such a bird's-eye view of the city's beauty. This was the last place she had ever expected to be on what would have been a normal, uneventful Thursday night.

When she had accepted Henry's last-minute invitation to join him for dinner at one of his favorite haunts "a little ways out of town," she had expected a twenty-minute car ride to Freeport or Ogunquit, but she was picked up in a limo and delivered to the Portland Jetport, where Henry waited for her. From there, they boarded a private jet to LaGuardia Airport, where they were met by the seasoned, exceedingly polite pilot of Henry's personal chopper, and now they were en route to a helipad near Wall Street, where they would be having dinner.

After a smooth landing and a salute and a smile from their former military pilot, Henry led Sandra through the whipping wind caused by the helicopter's rotor blades to a private rooftop entrance, and then to an elevator bank that carried them down to street level. After a five-minute walk, they arrived at an out-of-the-way restaurant known, according to Henry, for their "thick-cut steaks and out-of-this-world wine list." Sandra made no arguments about his restaurant choice and eagerly followed as they were escorted to a table set off from the main dining room. Henry, of course, was treated like a returning, conquering king by the staff, and Sandra was reasonably sure he had called ahead to give them advance warning to make sure his date felt special.

After a stunningly beautiful waitress in a gender-bending black tuxedo complete with a bow tie poured two glasses of wine with one arm behind her back and the fussy host came back around to make sure everything was to Henry's satisfaction, including the room temperature, Henry caught Sandra's awed expression.

"Too much?" Henry asked.

"A little," Sandra answered with a laugh. "When you asked me to have dinner with you, I honestly didn't expect to leave the state."

"I promise to have you back in time for Stephen Colbert's opening monologue," Henry said with a wink. "I understand it's a school night."

"I expect my sons will be waiting up for me when I get home. I'm not sure exactly when our roles got reversed."

Henry chuckled. "My son's parting words as I left the house tonight were, 'Don't screw it up, Dad.'"

"Well, he need not have worried. You're doing just fine."

"Daniel says I haven't looked happy in a long time, so he was thrilled when he found out we had connected."

"I know. He reported the news to Jack and Ryan."

"Sorry about that. He worries about me spending too much time alone in my room. Who knew my son would grow up to be my mother?"

Sandra laughed and looked at Henry, whose eyes seemed to be sparkling in the dim light of the restaurant.

Henry picked up his wineglass. "To sons who are protective of their parents."

Sandra raised her glass, they clinked and she took a sip, moaning, "Oh, that's divine."

She was tempted to sneak a look at the wine list to see how much it cost, because she knew it had to be a small fortune, but she resisted the urge. *Just stay in the moment*, she thought, *and don't obsess over the details*.

After a delectable shellfish chateau appetizer, a crisp, clean Caesar salad topped with anchovies, and finally a twenty-eight-day, dry-aged porterhouse steak for two, Sandra let herself relax completely and enjoy the decadence. They talked a little bit more about their kids and their marriages, although Sandra did not divulge too much because she was still legally attached to Stephen. She stopped drinking wine after two glasses because she was not about to risk getting sloppy and spilling more information about her famous husband than she should.

She had just sampled the foie gras when the evening took an unexpected turn.

"Tell me about this private detective agency you've gotten mixed up with," Henry said casually.

Sandra's guard instantly went up.

It wasn't the words he said but the attitude with which he said them.

Almost dismissive.

And perhaps slightly bothered.

Sandra decided to plow ahead and ignore the couched judgment. "Last year I ran into a woman I went to high school with. Maya Kendrick. She was a police officer who was married to a captain, and he—"

"Yes, I know all about Maya Kendrick and her incarcerated husband."

Again, Sandra was disturbed by his tone.

And the evening had been going so well.

Sandra exhaled a breath and continued. "Anyway, as I'm sure you remember, there was a presumed suicide at the high school; the assistant principal supposedly hanged herself. It was all over the news. The woman's sister hired Maya to find evidence of foul play, and I, well, I just kind of inserted myself into her investigation. . . ."

"Because you're nosy?"

Sandra sat up in her chair, taking umbrage. "I prefer to say naturally curious."

Henry nodded, a thin smile on his face. He seemed to be trying very hard not to show his disapproval but was doing a terrible job of hiding it.

"After she wrapped up the case with my help, we decided to keep working together. I know it's an odd match, but I admire her so much. She's strong, stubborn, good at what she does and I've learned quite a lot from her."

"To what end?"

The question took her by surprise.

"Do you want to start your own private investigation firm? Be a full-time detective?"

Sandra thought about it, then shrugged. "For now I just like working with Maya. Where it ultimately leads, I have no idea."

Henry nodded again, then gulped down the rest of his wine and flagged the waitress with the bow tie and ordered another bottle.

Sandra wanted to let it go, but she couldn't. "You don't approve?"

Henry feigned innocence. "What? Me? No. Whatever floats your boat, I always say."

Sandra picked up her fork and steak knife and started to saw through a piece of the porterhouse. Henry went back to poking at the last remnants of his salad. They ate in silence for at least a minute. Sandra knew in her bones that Henry was not finished discussing this and waited for him to pick up the conversation again.

She only had to wait a few seconds.

"I just don't know how I'd deal with someone I was involved with rummaging through garbage for grocery receipts or following people around in the dark, snapping pictures of them cheating on their spouses."

Sandra had heard enough. She put down her fork and knife and picked up her ironed cloth napkin from her lap, delicately wiping the sides of her mouth. "So you're look-ing for a trophy wife?"

Henry's eyes widened. "What? No, that's not what I meant."

She looked him squarely in the eye, trying to assess his sincerity, then dropped her napkin and continued. "I have to admit, I made an excellent trophy wife for Stephen. Hosting rubber chicken luncheons, standing by his side through endless speeches, competing with the wives of his Republican campaign rivals in a stupid bake-off to see whose cookies tasted yummier. I smiled my way through years of that crap, standing by my man, as Tammy Wynette once said. I didn't know how much I resented it until I met Maya, and she introduced me to a whole new world."

"Of danger and excitement?"

Sandra thought this over. "No, of fulfillment."

The waitress returned with the fresh bottle of wine, popped the cork and poured a little for Henry to taste. After his nodding approval, she filled their glasses and took her leave.

Sandra and Henry finished the rest of the meal with mindless chitchat rather than discussing anything more substantive. After sharing a walnut fudge tart accompanied by a dessert wine and coffee, Henry paid the bill and they stood up to leave. He circled around to help Sandra on with her coat, and as they crossed through the main dining room to the door, Henry turned and whispered to her apologetically, "I didn't mean to belittle your latest endeavor in any way."

"I appreciate you saying that," Sandra chirped, although she suspected Henry was desperately trying to salvage the date more than restate his position. His initial reaction to her recent career change was loud and clear and nothing he could say now could possibly lessen the damage already done.

Or maybe she was being too sensitive. Too hard on him.

He was just being honest.

Stephen had been much harsher when he had found out about her new work arrangement with Maya. But his opinion was coming from a self-serving place. They were still married, his constituents continued to firmly believe that Sandra was the loyal and adoring wife of their senator, and he didn't need her running around pretending to be a grown-up Veronica Mars.

At least Henry had tried to quickly backtrack. Which was a clear sign he liked her.

And that had to count for something.

She promised herself to keep an open mind.

As Henry opened the door, allowing Sandra to exit ahead of him from the restaurant out onto the street, they were suddenly besieged by a crush of reporters and photographers, who had somehow been alerted that the famous tech billionaire was currently romancing the wife of a US senator who, by all accounts, was still married to her husband.

"How long have you two been dating?" one reporter yelled.

"Does Senator Wallage know where you are tonight, Sandra?" another crowed.

Sandra threw up an arm to cover her eyes from the dozens of cameras relentlessly flashing and blinding both her and Henry.

Sandra felt Henry's arm encircle her waist as he pushed her through the throng of paparazzi, leading her up the narrow side street toward the looming Freedom Tower and the building where they could escape to the roof and be spirited back to LaGuardia and the hour jet ride home to Maine.

Chapter Twenty-Five

Sandra wasn't happy reliving the events of the previous evening, walking into a press firestorm when leaving the Manhattan restaurant with Henry Yang. But here she was, standing in her kitchen, while her sons scarfed down omelets and hash browns at the table, staring at a news clip from the CNN app on her phone following every movement. Her deer-in-the-headlights gaze into the blinding camera flashes, Henry's arm protectively around her waist to rush her to safety, her hand up, trying to cover her face. She looked so guilty, as if she had been suddenly caught in some criminal act, and yet she had just had dinner with a man she wasn't even sure about. And now everyone was talking about it.

Jack had even shown her an article on his own phone criticizing her for getting on the helicopter that spirited them down to the southern tip of Manhattan, and its withering effect on the environment, not to mention the reporter's breathless speculation that she might be a climate change denier. It was all too much.

And then there was Ryan, the artist, her political activist, the community protester, who she knew had kept his opinion of Henry Yang to himself. He was decidedly not a fan. There were too many reports of unethical business practices, such as bribery connected to foreign expansion, privacy concerns and creative accounting. He had kept mum about what he really thought of his mom's new beau, but now that the budding relationship was trending on Twitter, he couldn't help but voice his opinion because everyone else on social media felt free to do so.

Ryan set down his glass of orange juice and stared at Sandra solemnly. "I didn't want to say anything before, Mom—"

"I know, Ryan, you don't approve of me seeing Henry Yang."

Ryan caught Jack rolling his eyes. "His company paid zero in taxes last year!"

"So what?" Jack scoffed. "Look at how many people he employs all over the world."

"Yeah, and I wonder how many of those people are slave labor putting together all his gadgets for like three cents an hour!"

Sandra raised her hand. "Please, let's not get into this. I realize now this was probably a huge mistake. I never should have allowed myself to get involved with Henry."

Jack shook his head vigorously. "Mom, don't let Ryan's ridiculous bleeding heart get in the way of something potentially good."

"Henry Yang is an unapologetic corporate menace!" Ryan yelled.

Jack sighed. "Here we go . . . the idealistic, artsy type who thinks anyone making over a hundred grand a year is a Bond villain. Mom, trust me, Daniel's one of my close friends, and I've spent some time around his dad and I think he's a decent guy."

Ryan angrily shoved a forkful of his veggie omelet into his mouth and glared at his older brother.

Jack noticed and shrugged it off.

Sandra's phone buzzed and she glanced at the screen.

It was Stephen, calling from Washington.

Sandra knew this could not be good.

He had probably been inundated with texts from his staff monitoring his wife's recent activities before his six a.m. morning alarm even went off playing yacht rock tunes.

Sandra gave the boys an exasperated sigh and walked out of the kitchen clutching the phone. She overheard Jack say to Ryan in a hushed tone, "Bet it's Dad."

Sandra went into the living room, answered the call and said in a low voice, "Good morning, Stephen."

"Well, you've certainly been busy," Stephen said, trying to strike a jocular tone but failing. She had known him too many years. He was clearly rattled.

Sandra said nothing.

Stephen was knocked a little more off-balance by her calm silence but seemed to decide to press on. "Listen, I don't have a lot of time to talk. I'm going into a meeting—"

"To discuss how to counteract the narrative that I'm head over heels in love with Henry Yang so you can tamp down all the social media hysteria?"

"No, actually, it's about paid leave legislation," Stephen snapped. "But now that we're on the subject . . ." He paused to collect himself and choose his words precisely. "How serious is this?"

"Is that any of your business, Stephen?"

"No, I suppose not. And if you'd rather not tell me, I'll respect your decision."

"I feel a 'but' coming."

"But doesn't it make sense for us to coordinate our

responses so it doesn't come off as if we're on opposing sides?"

Stephen was acutely aware that her approval rating among his constituents was twenty points higher than his own and he didn't need the headache of voters assuming they were fighting or on the verge of divorce. They had sent out what Sandra had considered a mild, rather bland statement a while back, announcing "a trial separation," and that had sparked a flurry of salacious, mostly false headlines in the tabloids. Stephen knew people liked to take sides, and if that happened, he would take a hit politically.

"My only response is that my private life is nobody else's business," she said.

A long pause.

She could almost hear Stephen's mind racing.

"I get that. I do, Sandra, and if that's what you want us to say, we'll put that out. But I have to know, as your husband—and I still am your husband, at least last time I checked—"

"We've had two dinners. I'm not sure where it's going to go; probably nowhere, but I'm also not going to dismiss the possibility of a relationship out of hand, not yet. I should at least get three dinners to decide."

Stephen chuckled and then exhaled, as if relieved she and Henry weren't already shopping for an expensive engagement ring, one he personally could never afford. She just wished she knew for sure whether he was relieved because of his political future or because he still loved her.

Sandra wanted to ask him about Deborah Crowley.

How serious was that relationship?

If there was one. She still honestly didn't know.

But didn't she have the right to ask before she had to endure the third degree from him?

But she didn't.

She refrained from saying anything.

Sandra didn't know if the boys had reported back to Stephen about their conversation regarding Dad's new girlfriend, and she didn't want to make an issue of that now. She didn't need this call blowing up into a silly skirmish over who started dating first.

"Stephen, the last thing I want to do is make things harder for you in Washington. You can tell your press contacts whatever you want. I never intended for any of this to become public—"

"A private jet, a romantic dinner at a five-star restaurant with Henry Yang of all people; how could you not expect—"

"As I just said, handle this however you deem appropriate. I have to go."

Sandra abruptly ended the call.

She felt a squeamishness in her stomach.

This was the last thing she wanted to deal with this morning. Especially when she and Maya had made so little progress on the Diego Sanchez poisoning. She needed to focus on that and find some answers fast.

But she was irked by Stephen's call.

There seemed to be a double standard on how they should comport themselves during their separation.

It bugged her, and she wanted to call him back and confront him about it, but she stopped herself. It was best to just try to let it go.

At least for now.

Chapter Twenty-Six

Sandra felt guilty.

Here she was at a swanky Old Port restaurant rocking an Elie Tahari bright-red, ruffle-sleeve sheath cocktail dress, sipping champagne. Donors had paid a thousand bucks to rub elbows with Senator Elisabeth Dooley, not to mention the junior senator from Maine, Stephen Wallage. Meanwhile, Sandra's detective partner Maya was immersed in meticulously compiling a list of every parent she remembered seeing at the bake sale to talk to all of them in the hope that perhaps one would remember seeing something unusual, something plainly out of the ordinary, involving Diego Sanchez on his last day alive.

But Sandra had committed to this fundraiser months ago, and Maya, being a good sport, had graciously given her blessing to Sandra bowing out of working the case with her this one time.

Stephen had made a big show of their arrival, sweeping into the party with his wife on his arm, daring the gaggle of reporters outside to inquire about the state of their marriage. Indeed, most of them shouted questions about Sandra and Henry Yang, and Sandra had felt Stephen's grip on her nervously tighten, but they had ignored the press and kept their eyes forward, refusing to make eye contact.

Stephen had pretty much abandoned Sandra once they were safely inside the restaurant to confab with a few high-priced donors whose support he needed to secure for his own upcoming reelection in two years' time. Sandra had wandered around the room exchanging pleasantries and small talk with a few people, trying to act interested and engaged with whatever gossip was on top of mind with the donors. After about fifteen minutes, Stephen dutifully returned to her side.

"Sorry about that. I had to touch base with that guy." Stephen sighed, pointing to a short, rubber-faced, balding man conversing with Senator Dooley in a corner. "Gordon Astrof. His grandfather started a shoe company in Millinocket way back in the 1940s. Now he's worth one point three billion. Deep, deep pockets."

Sandra nodded knowingly.

Stephen caught himself and paused, then reached down and squeezed Sandra's hand. "By the way, you look stunning tonight, in case I didn't say it before."

"You didn't," Sandra said, taking a sip of her champagne.

"Well, you do, and I appreciate you still coming tonight, now that we're . . ."

It seemed he couldn't say it.

Separated.

The word just got caught on his tongue.

They stood there awkwardly for a few moments.

Stephen finally gave up, shrugged, and knocked back the glass of bourbon on the rocks he held in his hand.

Sandra noticed a barely perceptible hint of regret on his face and wondered if Stephen was kicking himself for not trying harder to avoid the domestic mess they now found themselves in.

Someone behind them finally interrupted the tension.

"Good evening, Senator, Mrs. Wallage."

Sandra and Stephen both turned around to find Henry Yang.

Yang looked disconcertingly handsome in a casual Tom Ford gray blazer, an open white collar shirt and blue jeans.

"Henry . . ." Stephen said coldly. "I'm glad you could come out tonight and support Elisabeth."

"Not sure why she's even bothering with the fiery speeches and cheap champagne. I've seen the latest polling. It's going to be a cakewalk to reelection."

Stephen held up his right hand. "Please, don't jinx it."

One of Dooley's aides, a sweaty, overstimulated young man, suddenly appeared. "Senator Wallage, Senator Dooley would like you to come over to say hello to Bill Warburton from the Senate Majority PAC."

Sandra knew Warburton was a big deal, running an organization solely dedicated to building a Democratic majority in the Senate.

But Stephen didn't make a move to rush off.

He was squarely focused on glaring at Henry, who he obviously felt had rudely disrupted his private moment with his wife. Sandra could not help but believe that if anyone else, besides Henry Yang, had inserted themselves into their conversation, it would not have been nearly as offensive to her husband.

Even though Stephen was glowering at him in what could have been perceived as a menacing manner, Henry remained poised and unflustered.

"Senator?" the now near-panicked aide asked in a strained tone.

Stephen finally snapped out of his trance and gave the aide a withering look. "Yes?"

"Mr. Warburton is here," he said, even more strain in his voice. He didn't want to beg.

"Excuse me," Stephen said, glancing back and forth between Sandra and Yang, reluctant to leave them alone together but basically having no choice.

He moved off, and Henry seized the opportunity to slide in front of Sandra. "You look gorgeous."

"Thanks," Sandra replied brusquely.

"I'm glad to see you here because there's something I've been wanting to talk to you about since the other night."

"Okay," Sandra said, flicking her eyes over in Stephen's direction to see him chatting with the deep-pocket donor Astrof and Warburton while stealing glances at her and Henry, clearly dying to know what they were saying to each other.

"I believe I gave you the wrong impression. I never meant to say I didn't approve of the work you're doing with . . ."

"Maya. Maya Kendrick. My partner."

She made sure to hit the word *partner*.

"Yes, Mrs. Kendrick. Sandra, I like to think I don't judge people, especially the work they do. And anyone who wants to make a difference and help people, my hat is off to them. I admire you for taking on this investigator role. I really do. I guess I was just thinking out loud, processing my thoughts in real time, and I may have come off as unenlightened, if I'm being generous. You may prefer other words like chauvinistic, pigheaded and ignorant, for example."

Sandra couldn't help but crack a smile.

"I don't want to be *that* guy," Henry said. "That's not who I am. That's why I sued the paper that claimed I had fired one of my vice presidents when she became pregnant. It was a false story, not a shred of truth to it. My reputation is important to me, both publicly and personally. So I want to be absolutely clear with you. If things between us progress, if we decide to move forward together, I wholeheartedly support you in whatever you choose to do."

It was a lot to take in. She still wasn't sure she was up for a third date, let alone a journey forward together as a couple.

But she did appreciate the sentiment.

Henry leaned in and whispered in her ear, "Plus, I can't stop picturing you in a leather suit karate-chopping the bad guys like Diana Rigg in that old British show from the sixties. . . . What was it called?"

"*The Avengers*," Sandra answered.

"Yeah, that," Henry said, winking.

His attempt at flirting was clunky at best, but she couldn't fault him for trying.

And it did make her feel good.

Stephen was back with a protective arm around her waist. "Darling, I have some people who are dying to say hello to you."

He didn't name names because he probably didn't have any. He just wanted to get her away from Henry Yang.

"It was nice talking to you, Henry," Sandra said.

"I'll call you," Henry said with an inviting smile, which caused Stephen to bristle.

He then quickly whisked Sandra away.

"I know Yang's donated a lot of money to our cause, but I have to be honest, Sandra, I don't like him."

"Of course you don't."

"This isn't jealousy talking—"

"No, I'm sure it isn't."

Stephen pouted. "You don't have to be condescending."

"It's what this conversation deserves," Sandra said before turning and throwing on a bright smile. "Gloria, how lovely to see you!"

Sandra happily hugged the wife of Gordon Astrof, who was drowning in Tiffany jewelry, weighing down her entire body with the exception of her heavily Botoxed, pulled up, expressionless face.

Chapter Twenty-Seven

"Care to comment on your relationship with Henry Yang?" a woman's smooth voice purred from behind Sandra.

She was suddenly filled with a sense of dread. She probably should have expected to get this specific question tonight. Why she thought for a minute that she might escape the reach of the hungry press at a political fundraiser seemed silly now.

Collecting her thoughts, she spun around to face the reporter when a wave of relief rapidly washed over her.

It wasn't just any reporter.

It was Zoe Rush of the *Portland Press Herald*, a frizzy-haired, fiery, tiny ball of energy, and a former classmate of Sandra's at Bates College. Zoe was a friend first, a reporter second.

Sandra relaxed. "We're registered at Tiffany's if you want to buy us some sterling-silver salt and pepper shakers," she deadpanned.

Zoe cracked a smile. "A romantic dinner in New York City. You certainly do get around, Sandy."

"That whole night was his idea. I was totally taken by surprise. I couldn't exactly tell him to take me home when we pulled up on the tarmac next to a private jet."

"Well, congratulations. You and the ubiquitous Mr. Yang are trending on Twitter."

"I know." Sandra groaned.

"What are you planning to do about your sudden turn in the spotlight?" Zoe inquired, leaning in closer.

"Off the record?"

Zoe nodded.

"I'm still trying to figure it all out. I like Henry. He's got some opinions that worry me, but he's a decent guy from what I can tell. He certainly loves his son and would do anything for him. I'm just not sure how I fit into his life or how he fits into mine."

"And how does Stephen feel?"

"You know him well enough to already know the answer to that," Sandra said with a wry smile.

Zoe thought about it for a second before nodding in agreement. Then she stepped back to inspect Sandra's cocktail attire. "Pretty dress. Looks expensive. How much did that set you back?"

Sandra glanced down at her red sheath number. "I like it. I don't remember how much I paid for it."

Zoe grabbed the sides of her own outfit. "See, that's how different we are. I can tell you exactly how much I spent on this Jaclyn Smith black velour dress I got off the rack at K-Mart. Twenty-nine ninety-eight plus tax."

Sandra laughed. "Well, you look lovely in it. Now, what about you? Are you seeing anyone?"

Zoe scoffed. "Um, no. According to my ex-boyfriend, not only does he find me too abrasive and annoying to be around, most men in general, at least the ones he knows, are of the same opinion. And because women don't do it for me, although for some reason most people automatically assume I'm a lesbian, I've decided to date myself."

Sandra raised an eyebrow. "And how does that work?"

"Saturday night is date night. I cook myself a meal, relax with a bottle of wine and just chill with a movie. I have to say, I find myself utterly charming and fun to be around."

"I think I might really enjoy that. Dating myself, not you. And on the record, your ex-boyfriend is dead wrong, and so are his awful friends."

"You've always been so nice to me, ever since college," Zoe said. "That's why I never write any nasty stories about you."

"Well, I do appreciate it, Zoe," Sandra said before casually scanning the crowd. "So, who do you have in your crosshairs tonight?"

"Why can't I just be here as a registered undecided voter?"

"Because just getting in the door costs a thousand dollars, and I do not believe you would spend that much money just to show off your lovely Jaclyn Smith dress and hear Senator Dooley speak."

Zoe grabbed a glass of white wine from a passing waiter's tray and took a gulp. "You're right. I'm here following a few leads, which I believe might develop into a whopper of a story. Obviously I can't talk about it."

"Obviously," Sandra said dryly. "Would you tell me if it involved Stephen?"

"No, I wouldn't."

Sandra knew the game. "Would you nod if it involved Stephen?"

Zoe took another sip of her white wine. She didn't nod.

"So, I'm going to assume you're not here about something Stephen did or anything to do with his personal life."

"Sandra, I know about Stephen's relationship with Deborah Crowley."

Sandra reared back, surprised. "You do?"

"*Everybody* does," Zoe said pointedly.

"Then it's true. Why hasn't anyone written about it?"

"Because it's not remotely interesting. You and Stephen announced your separation, so nobody's going to be shocked if one of you starts seeing someone new. Deborah Crowley, although she has good intentions at the Commonwealth Fund, is basically a political hack. There is nothing special about Stephen dating her. Now, a drop-dead gorgeous tech billionaire with a household name, that's a scoop."

Sandra groaned. What had she gotten herself into?

"But I'm here about something much bigger than covering your sex life."

"Please don't say it like that," Sandra begged. "There has been no sex. None. Zero. Two dinners. That's it. No making out. No heavy petting. Nothing."

Sandra looked around the room. "Are you following a story about one of the donors?"

"Nope," Zoe said, shaking her head.

"Well, if the story is as big as you say, and it doesn't involve Stephen or any of the big donors, that only leaves one person."

Zoe wasn't going to say the name. She just waited for it to come out of Sandra's mouth.

"Senator Dooley?" Sandra whispered.

"I can neither confirm nor deny," Zoe said emphatically.

"Which is Zoe-speak for, 'It's *absolutely* about Senator Dooley.' What kind of scandal is it?"

"Take your pick," Zoe said under her breath. "There's a minefield of scandals she's traipsing around right now, including the usual cronyism, a handful of ethics violations. My focus, however, is on one in particular of a more personal nature. And boy, it's a doozy." Zoe was practically biting her tongue not to spill more details. Sandra could tell she wanted to. Her mind started racing.

Stephen certainly would not be happy to hear that Senator Dooley was about to be publicly embroiled in a scandal of any kind. He didn't want anything to risk Dooley's reelection. They were from the same party. Her losing the race would put the senate majority in play in the next presidential election.

"Does Elisabeth know what's coming?"

"No, not yet. But she will soon. The good news for you is that your adorably innocent tête-à-tête with Yang will definitely fall off everybody's radar once this breaks."

Sandra didn't need to hear any more clues.

"So I'm guessing she's having an affair . . . behind her husband's back," Sandra said flatly, disappointed if her theory was true. Elisabeth Dooley and her husband Lou had always seemed like a happy couple, and they made a great team.

"Maybe," Zoe said in a singsong voice. She looked like the proverbial cat who'd swallowed the canary and was enjoying herself immensely as she stoked Sandra's curiosity.

Sandra took a stab at a name. "Senator Hitchens? Stephen said he and Elisabeth seemed rather chummy on a congressional trip to Afghanistan last year."

Zoe shook her head. "Not a politician."

"Someone from the media? Oh, please don't tell me she's having an affair with Chris Cuomo. I don't want to have to stop watching him," Sandra moaned.

"He's not from the media."

"So is Mr. X a public figure?"

"Nope."

"Does he live in Washington?"

"Nope."

"Then he lives here in Maine."

No answer.

"And he's not famous."

No answer.

The silence meant she was only getting warmer.

"Does he work in politics?"

Zoe cleared her throat. "No, he does not."

Sandra threw her hands in the air. "Then it could be anyone. A personal trainer, a Starbucks barista, her mailman for all I know. . . ."

Zoe glanced around to make sure no one was surreptitiously eavesdropping on their conversation and then said softly, "Ask me if you know him."

"Do I know him?"

No answer.

That meant yes. Sandra knew him.

But she and Elisabeth Dooley rarely moved in the same social circles. They only really interacted at political events, and Zoe had been quite clear that Mr. X was not involved in politics, at least as far as she knew.

The only other thing she could think of that they had in common was . . .

"Someone at the high school her daughter attends?"

Zoe folded her arms, trying not to look too excited or yell out *Bingo!*

Sandra knew she was closing in on a name.

"A teacher? Please don't tell me it was the Spanish teacher Diego Sanchez!" Sandra gasped, bracing herself.

"No, not him."

"Well, Kendra's in a lot of Ryan's classes, and most of their other subjects are taught by women. . . . Is it a *woman*?"

"No. Senator Dooley is aggressively heterosexual."

If it wasn't a teacher, that only left the janitorial staff or a school bus driver or . . . Kendra's extracurricular activities. She wasn't aware that Kendra played on any sports teams at SoPo High, but that was not proof that she didn't.

"A coach?"

Zoe playfully tapped the bridge of her nose.

"Coach Cooper? Is that why he resigned?"

Zoe was bored playing their little guessing game.

"No, the new guy. The one who coaches her field hockey team."

"Josh Kirby?"

Zoe nodded in the affirmative. "I have a few reliable sources that tell me that the senator and the coach—which sounds like the title of a 1980s' sitcom, by the way—they've been spotted together off school grounds, at a few quiet locations, meeting on the down low."

Senator Dooley and Josh Kirby, who had to be at least twenty years younger. No wonder Zoe had been doggedly pursuing this story. An exposé revealing an affair between them would be explosive and a real boost to her career.

Many politicians had survived scandals like this in the

past. However, this one would undoubtedly strike many as particularly odious because the other party was her daughter's field hockey coach. And that might be seen by many voters as unseemly and, more importantly, unforgivable.

Not good so close to Election Day.

Chapter Twenty-Eight

Stephen's face paled as he listened to Sandra recount what she had just heard from Zoe Rush. His mind seemed to wander while his wife was still talking as he shifted into damage control mode.

He scratched his chin, thinking hard. "When's the story coming out?"

"Zoe didn't say," Sandra answered coolly.

"Okay, we can probably get ahead of this. We just need to come up with a quick game plan."

"So you think it's true?"

"It doesn't matter what I think. It matters what the voters think. And in this political climate, a whole lot of them will probably believe what they hear, whether it's true or not."

"That's a depressing thought." Sandra sighed.

"It's the new reality, I'm afraid."

Stephen searched the room, zeroing in on Senator Dooley, who was busy hobnobbing with a gaggle of donors alongside her dutiful husband.

"She needs a heads-up about what's coming. You should go talk to her," Stephen advised.

Sandra's eyes widened. "*Me?* Why should I do it?"

"It'll be better coming from you. Trust me."

"But she's *your* colleague."

Stephen sighed, obviously annoyed that he had to try and convince her. There had been a time when Sandra would simply obey a request from him with no questions asked. But all that had changed. "Honey, if I do it, all hell will break loose. Elisabeth will figure if I know, my staff knows, the party knows, all of Washington knows. If you do it, you're just casually letting her know about a rumor that's out there, woman to woman, you're just watching her back, that sort of thing."

"Well, if I know, won't she assume you know too?"

"Not necessarily. She knows we rarely talk."

So, Stephen had been lamenting to his fellow senator about the state of his marriage. She should not have been surprised. But she was. She threw him an exasperated look and made a beeline over to where Senator Dooley was at present holding court.

The senator noticed Sandra hovering to her left out of the corner of her eye. She smiled to the donors. "Have your people talk to Sally about setting up that event in Kennebunkport. So nice to see you all. Excuse me."

Dooley shook everybody's hand before they dispersed, and with her husband Lou shadowing her, turned and joined Sandra, leaning into her and whispering, "Thanks for rescuing me. I thought I'd never escape from that coma-inducing conversation. How can people with that much money be so utterly uninteresting?"

"Lower your voice, dear; the old codger told me he's got a new, stronger hearing aid that's jacked to the max, so he might be able to hear you," Lou warned.

Dooley waited for the donor and his family to move all

the way across the room before turning back to Sandra. "Now we can really dish. I've been hearing things about you."

How ironic.

Sandra blinked at her.

Dooley glanced around to make sure no one had wandered over to eavesdrop and then whispered, "Henry Yang?"

Sandra shook her head slightly. "I'm sure what you've heard is much more exciting than the actual truth."

"Well, according to my sources, he's *very* sweet on you," Dooley said, while her husband slid an arm around her and pulled her closer to him, almost possessively, as if she was talking about herself and not Sandra.

"Like I told Zoe Rush, we're talking about two very innocent dinners. That's it," Sandra proclaimed emphatically, waving a hand in front of her.

"I know Henry," Senator Dooley said with a knowing smile. "He never does anything innocently. And I mean that in the best possible way."

Lou chortled appreciatively.

Dooley's jocular air faded as she seemed to get more serious. "Is your dating life Zoe Rush's latest obsession? She's never happy unless she's pinning down and dissecting someone like a seventh-grade science class does to a poor butterfly."

Sandra marveled at how Senator Dooley herself had just so easily provided the perfect segue. "Yes. Among other topics of interest."

The senator was intrigued. "Such as?"

Sandra furtively glanced to Lou, who also appeared keenly interested in what she was about to say. Sandra offered him a pleasant smile, and then casually turned her attention back to Senator Dooley. "Do you have a moment to speak with me privately?"

"Of course."

Lou didn't budge.

Sandra hesitated.

Finally, Senator Dooley registered her apprehension. "Sandra, whatever it is, you can speak candidly in front of Lou. Believe me, the few times I have tried hiding anything from my husband, he already knew."

Sandra still wavered. "It's just that what I have to say is of a very sensitive nature. . . ."

Dooley touched Sandra's arm and gave her an encouraging smile. "It's fine, really. Lou won't melt. I promise. Go on."

Sandra glanced at Lou again. His expression was so stoic and stone-faced, his profile could have been found on the side of Mount Rushmore.

Sandra took a deep breath and decided to go for it. "Zoe is pursuing a story about you."

Senator Dooley didn't flinch.

Neither did Lou.

"It involves an extramarital affair."

Dooley appeared genuinely stunned. "I beg your pardon?"

Lou flushed with anger and hissed, "Zoe Rush is a vile, despicable woman who cares nothing about the truth. She's a muckraking disgrace who should never have been legitimized with a press pass."

Sandra noticed spittle on the sides of Lou's lips, as if he was a rabid dog foaming at the mouth.

"Lou, *please* . . ." Dooley scolded before turning back to Sandra. "And with whom am I supposed to be cavorting in this tale of a torrid affair?"

"A man by the name of Josh Kirby."

This time Senator Dooley definitely did flinch.

Her husband just looked confused.

"Do you know who he is?" Sandra asked carefully.

"Of course I do," Senator Dooley said. "He's Kendra's new field hockey coach."

"That's right," Sandra said. "He just replaced Coach Cooper, who is moving to Chicago."

Senator Dooley nervously tucked some of her hair behind one ear. Her hand shook slightly, as if she suddenly had been thrown off guard. "Where on earth did she get this ridiculous story? I mean, if she didn't make it up out of whole cloth?"

"Apparently she has a couple of sources who have seen you and Mr. Kirby together on several occasions. . . ."

"He's my daughter's new coach. I wanted to meet him and advocate for my daughter on her behalf. There is nothing wrong with that," Dooley insisted.

"No, of course not. I guess the red flags were raised when the sources spotted the two of you meeting off school grounds, at what some might suggest were out-of-the-way locations?"

Dooley bristled.

Lou's stoic demeanor seemed to melt away and he numbly stared at his wife, anxiously waiting to hear more.

She could sense her husband's rising panic but chose to ignore it for the time being and keep her focus squarely on Sandra. "I am *not* cheating on my husband."

"What was wrong with just meeting him at the high school?" Lou asked warily.

"Because I have been accused by some parents of badgering teachers and staff at SoPo High, making everything about Kendra, and maybe there's some truth to that, but you can't fault me for wanting the best educational experience possible for my only child. So, in order to avoid people criticizing me for stalking the halls of the high school, fighting for Kendra once again, I simply asked Coach Kirby to meet me off campus in a less public setting."

"More than once?" Lou asked with a raised eyebrow.

Senator Dooley shot her husband a sharp look. "Yes, Lou. We had a lot to discuss because it's no secret to anyone, especially you, that I take a very active interest in my daughter's life. Her success is very important to me."

The implication was clear to Sandra that the senator was suggesting her husband wasn't as enthusiastic an advocate as she was.

Lou got the message and quickly backed off.

Dooley turned away from him and moved closer to Sandra, invading her personal space to the point where Sandra took a tiny step back so they weren't nose to nose. "So, you can inform Zoe Rush that I may have met Kendra's coach a couple of times, but there was nothing sordid about it. I like to think I set a good example for my daughter. I would never commit adultery. And if Zoe feels the burning desire to say otherwise in one of her salacious, unsubstantiated Sunday pieces, I would be more than happy to slap a libel suit on her and that miserable paper that was stupid enough to hire her."

"I'll be sure to let her know," Sandra said.

"What a lovely dress," Senator Dooley observed, suddenly shifting gears. "How I wish red was my color."

And then she floated away, warmly greeting some new

arrivals bearing checkbooks, the seasoned politician back at work.

Sandra was left standing awkwardly with Lou, who on the surface appeared calm and unfettered, a benign smile plastered on his face. And yet it was not difficult for Sandra to guess from his stiff body language that behind his serene mask, a tumultuous storm was brewing.

Chapter Twenty-Nine

Vanessa had been understandably quiet on the car ride to the Maine correctional facility that housed her father. Maya, who zipped her Chevy Bolt through an early morning wet, heavy fog, knew Vanessa was frustrated that her mother and Sandra had made relatively little progress on the case to find her teacher's murderer despite many already assuming Melanie Tate was the killer.

The fact that Sandra was currently all over the internet as Henry Yang's latest love only complicated matters. Vanessa never said it, but the impression she got from all the publicity was that Sandra was more concerned with her social life than solving the case. Maya knew that could not have been further from the truth, but she just did not have the energy to argue with her daughter, especially because Vanessa wasn't saying it out loud. Maya knew her daughter well enough to be keenly aware of what was going on in her mind.

Maya flipped on her turn signal and veered right onto River Road, which would lead them to the correctional facility in Windham. Mother and daughter drove in silence until they parked the car and were waiting in the security line to be processed. Vanessa mumbled something about getting together with Ryan later and Maya nodded with no objection.

Twenty minutes later they were in the visiting room, sitting at a familiar, scratched Formica table waiting for Max. The inmates began to be paraded in, led by two security officers. Max was one of the last in line, looking a little gaunt and tired in his prison-issue, hunter-green jumpsuit. He brightened at the sight of Vanessa, who popped up from the table to give her father a hug under the watchful eyes of the guards.

Maya remained seated, acknowledging Max with a slight smile as he plopped down across from them. He was focused on Vanessa.

"How's school, baby?"

Vanessa shrugged. "Weird. Sad. Nothing's been the same since Mr. Sanchez died."

There was some small talk about her other classes. An English lit assignment on Thomas Hardy that was causing her some consternation. Complaints about her lab partner in a science project who was leaving all the heavy lifting to her. The only time she cracked a smile was when Max casually asked about "the boyfriend."

"He's fine" was all she offered for an answer, although it was clear the relationship was on pretty solid ground, considering she was still smiling.

Max leaned back in his chair and folded his arms. "His mother seems to be doing fine too. Dating a billionaire."

Maya cocked an eyebrow.

Max instantly noticed her surprise. "I get one-hour-a-day internet access, that's it. So I only have time to see the big headlines to know what's going on in the world. And yesterday, every page I went to, there was your friend with Henry Yang."

Vanessa sighed loudly, noting her disapproval. She had obviously heard Ryan's view of the relationship, and as a dutiful and supportive girlfriend, did not hesitate to firmly take his side.

Maya couldn't believe Max had taken only two minutes to bring up a sore subject. He was the master of stirring the pot and causing tension between Maya and Vanessa, even if unintentionally.

Max glanced from Maya to Vanessa, clearly sensing the battle lines being drawn. "Did I say something wrong?"

"No, it's just that Sandra's my friend and business partner, and I want to support her—"

"Do you even know what Henry Yang stands for?" Vanessa snapped.

Maya raised a hand. "I've heard all the stories. Let's not get into this right now, please, Vanessa, okay?"

"Sorry. I didn't mean to cause trouble," Max said apologetically.

Sometimes Maya wondered if that was true.

"It's just that I heard . . ." He stopped himself.

Vanessa noticed instantly and sat up in her chair. "What?"

"Nothing, forget it," he said with a shrug.

Maya knew exactly what he was doing.

Whenever Max had something he wanted to get out, he'd drop a hint and then pretend to wrestle with whether he should go on or not. It was a tried-and-true tactic and it always worked because now Maya was also curious to find out what he had heard.

"You've already teased us, Max, you might as well just come out with it," Maya said with a wave of her hand.

"Henry Yang is a grade A d-bag and a criminal. I recently talked to a few buddies of mine from the FBI field office in Boston. We've stayed friendly, even after all this," Max said, gesturing toward his prison jumpsuit. Then he leaned in to his wife and daughter. "They tell me Yang is under investigation."

"For what?" Vanessa gasped.

"You name it. We've all heard the rumors, read the press accounts. He's one of the most corrupt businessmen in America and he should go to prison," Max declared before the irony of his statement sank in and he couldn't help but flash a knowing grin.

"First of all," Maya said evenly, "isn't it illegal for your FBI pals to be telling you *anything* about an ongoing investigation, and isn't it a crime for you to be leaking that information?"

Max chortled and looked around at his surroundings. "What are they going to do to me, send me to prison?"

"They could tack on some more time if you break the law," Maya said matter-of-factly.

This appeared to sober Max up a little bit.

"Look, I get how funny it is that I'm the guy blowing the whistle on someone else for corruption, but I just thought your friend Sandra might want to know," Max said, leaning back and interlocking his fingers behind his head. "I'm just the messenger."

Vanessa swiveled around to her mother. "We have to tell her."

"*We* do not have to do anything. Sandra is my friend and I will be the one to decide whether to tell her or not," Maya said evenly.

"What's to decide? Mom, the FBI—"

Maya slapped a hand down hard on the table, which quickly silenced Vanessa.

"You are not to say a word to Ryan about this, do you hear me? Give me a chance to check out a few things, find out more before we charge headfirst into Sandra's private life."

Vanessa shifted in her seat, looking peeved and stifled.

"Your mom's right. You should listen to her," Max said, surprising Maya. "These FBI guys, they like to talk, they may be making more out of this than there actually is. It's good to be cautious."

Vanessa looked to her father, then her mother. Finally, she slumped down, defeated. "Okay, I won't say anything," she sighed, punctuating it with a pronounced pout.

Maya appreciated Max's support, for once, but that didn't make her feel any better. Because she knew her daughter. And out of a sense of justice, at least in her own mind, she would go straight to Ryan and unburden herself by telling him every word of what her father had just revealed.

"Can we change the subject? We only have a few minutes left together," Max pleaded before turning to Maya and giving her a wink. "Let's talk about how beautiful your mother looks today."

He was definitely conning her. She was in a frumpy gray sweater, mom jeans, no makeup, and her hair was a rat's nest.

"You can stop right there," Maya scoffed.

"But you do," Max insisted before whispering under his breath, "You always do."

Maya told herself to keep up her guard. Max could be irresistibly charming. She had fallen for it countless times. And now here they were. Max was in prison and Maya was raising their kid all on her own. She had to keep reminding herself whenever they came to the prison for a visit that Max had betrayed them, caused them all so much pain, uprooted their lives.

Yes, he could be forgiven. Vanessa already had forgiven him. Almost from the moment he was convicted. Maya didn't blame her daughter. Max was her father. She loved him. And she would always stand by him.

Maya had beaten herself up bad for being so gullible. She should have seen what was going on, Max's rampant corruption as a police captain, and she should have done more to stop it. She might have saved her family from all this.

She had tried to move on by asking for a divorce. But she still had not turned the signed paperwork in to the lawyers for final processing by the court.

Why was she dragging her heels on this?

Why couldn't she just finally cut ties and be free?

Whenever Maya asked herself these questions, she always found an excuse to think about something else so she wouldn't have to actually answer them.

Chapter Thirty

It was already dusk the following Monday afternoon when Maya and Sandra arranged to meet outside the school gym. Sandra had requested that Jack text her once football practice finished so she and Maya could rendezvous and talk to SoPo High's new head coach, Josh Kirby.

By the time Jack remembered to text his mother, it was already a few minutes past six o'clock. Sandra feared they might miss Kirby, who by now could have driven off to parts unknown in his brand-new Tesla. But luckily, as Sandra pulled into the school parking lot, she spotted Kirby's expensive wheels parked in his designated space, which had once belonged to Coach Vinnie Cooper's far less flashy Toyota Corolla Hatchback.

Maya was by the gym entrance waiting for her, rubbing her hands together to keep them warm in the chilly, late autumn Maine temperature. "I saw most of the football team leave, so I'm betting we can catch him alone."

Sandra whipped open the door and they headed inside. The building was eerily empty except for a janitor mopping the hallway floor from one side to the other. Maya and

Sandra acknowledged him with a friendly wave before veering off to the gymnasium and athletic office. A couple of boys were playing basketball on the court, one with the ball waiting for the opportunity to make a clean shot, the other, hands out, trying to block him. The boy dribbling the basketball got distracted by the two pretty moms, allowing his opponent to steal the ball away from him and charge down to the opposite end of the court and make a layup, the ball swishing through the net.

"Hi, Mrs. Wallage," the boy who'd lost the ball said dreamily with a goofy smile.

"Hello, Peter," Sandra said, ignoring his rapt attention toward her. "Is Coach Kirby in his office?"

"He should be," the boy, Peter, answered, unable to wipe off that silly smile from his face.

The other boy hurled the ball back to him, but he didn't see it coming and it bounced off his head.

The other boy burst out laughing. "Dude, focus!"

Peter's face reddened with embarrassment and he quickly chased after the ball, pretending he wasn't the least bit enamored with the mother of one of his classmates.

"You're such a heartbreaker," Maya cracked as they made their way down to the far end of the gym, which housed the coach's office, leaving the two boys to resume their scrimmage.

Sandra willfully ignored Maya's comment.

The door to Kirby's office was closed, so Maya knocked on the frosted glass. There was no answer. She tried the door handle and turned to Sandra. "It's unlocked. Shall we?"

Before Sandra had the chance to respond, Maya swung open the door with a flourish.

No one was there.

"Well, we know he couldn't have gone home. His car is still outside," Sandra reminded her.

Maya poked her head inside and looked around. "Maybe he's in a meeting with the principal. Should we sit down in his office and wait for him to come back?"

Sandra wasn't sure they should make themselves comfortable in Kirby's office because they had not been invited, but Maya was already behind his desk, casually glancing down at the papers in his in-box, quickly opening the side drawers.

Sandra envied Maya's fearlessness, her strength, her dogged resolve when she was focused on a mission. Maya bent over and tapped some keys on his computer. "His calendar just came up. There is nothing about a meeting today. Just football practice until five thirty."

Sandra, who was still hovering out in the hall, not quite brave enough to enter yet, suddenly heard something. She spun around and cocked an ear. She waited for the sound to come again but heard nothing.

In the office, Maya was scrolling down the calendar on Kirby's computer. "Did your reporter friend mention where Kirby met up with Senator Dooley?"

"Not specifically; why?"

"Because he seems to keep a detailed log of his dentist appointments, visits to the Tesla dealership, dinner with some old fraternity brothers, but there are a handful of late-night meetings when he doesn't say who he is seeing, just a time and a place, which strikes me as odd."

Sandra suddenly heard the strange noise again.

It sounded like a ghostly moan.

Like a tortured spirit roaming the halls.

"He's so specific in some cases and purposely vague in others, which makes me think—"

"Shhh!"

Maya looked up from the computer, concerned. "Is he coming back?"

Sandra shook her head as she held a finger to her lips, listening intently. She finally heard the noise again. She scurried out the door and down the hall in the direction of the sound, stopping abruptly outside the door to the boys' locker room.

Maya had circled back around from behind the desk and followed her. By the time she reached Sandra, she had already pushed open the swinging door to the locker room and called inside, "Hello?"

Another moan. This one more distinctive.

Like someone in pain.

Sandra burst into the locker room, Maya close on her heels. She rounded the corner until she had a clear view of the shower room. She gasped. A man wearing just a white towel wrapped around his waist, was crumpled up on the floor, his face bloodied.

It was Coach Kirby.

Sandra rushed over to him and knelt down, tentatively touching his bare arm. "Josh, are you okay? What happened?"

Josh strained to sit up. "Yeah . . . I'm fine. . . ." He winced as he moved. Sandra and Maya positioned themselves on either side of him to help lift him up on his feet.

"Did you slip and fall?" Sandra asked, although she already knew the answer.

Josh shook his head, holding a hand to his rib cage. Sandra and Maya gingerly led him over to a bench dividing two rows of lockers and lowered him down so he could sit as he spoke. "I was doing some paperwork in my office after practice, and once I knew the team had all left, I came in here to take a quick shower. I barely had time to turn on the water when someone rushed me from behind and started beating me senseless."

"Did you get a look at who attacked you?" Maya asked.

Josh shook his head again. "It all happened so fast. Whoever it was had a baseball bat or something, because there were a lot of fast blows to the neck and back. One got me in the face as I tried to turn around and nearly broke my nose. Before I even knew what was happening, it was over and he was gone and I found myself sprawled out here on the floor."

"Why would anyone want to do something like that to you?" Sandra asked.

Josh shrugged. "I have no idea."

Sandra noted Maya's blank expression, which was always a dead giveaway that she suspected a person wasn't telling the truth but didn't want him or her to see what she was really thinking.

Sandra whipped out her phone. "I'm calling the police."

Josh nearly jumped out of his naked skin. "No! I'm fine. Really. There's no need to drag the police into this."

"But you were attacked," Sandra protested. Her finger was poised to punch the numbers on her phone screen.

Josh nearly shot out a hand to grab her phone away to stop her but resisted the urge.

"Seriously, it's okay," he insisted.

"Well, we should at least get you to the hospital so a doctor can check you out," Sandra said.

Determined to show them he was not injured, Josh managed to stand up, clutching the white towel to make

sure it didn't fall and expose too much of himself to the
ladies. "See? No permanent damage. I'd rather deal with
this my own way instead of dragging the cops into it."

"How are you going to deal with it? You didn't even
see who it was who came at you!" Maya scoffed.

Josh ran a shaky hand through his wavy hair. "I appreciate your concern, I really do, but this is a private matter."

"So you *do* have some idea who your assailant was,"
Maya said evenly.

Josh pretended he didn't hear her. "Sandra, would you
mind picking up my gym bag from the floor? It must have
gotten knocked over during the scuffle."

Sandra zeroed in on an unzipped gym bag by a row of
lockers. "Of course." She walked over and picked it up,
carried it back over to Josh and handed it to him. He
smiled gratefully and then rummaged through the bag for
a shirt to put on.

Sandra noticed Maya staring at something on the floor
that had presumably fallen out of the bag. It was a slip of
paper. Maya bent over and picked it up. As she turned it
over to read what was on it, Josh suddenly saw what she
was holding, and his face slowly lost its color.

"What is that?" Sandra asked.

Maya held it up for them to see. "It's a check. Made
out to Josh. In the amount of five thousand dollars."

"I had an aunt who died recently. . . . She left me some
money. . ." Josh squeaked.

The lie was laughable. And he knew it.

So he decided to shut his mouth and not say anything else.

Maya studied the check. "The payer is an LLC corporation, the Wagner Group. So if we follow up with the
state to find out what kind of company this is, you're

saying we'll discover the Wagner Group is some kind of law firm handling your dear departed aunt's estate, is that correct?"

Josh hesitated, his mind racing.

Sandra could tell he was struggling because if he answered in the affirmative, he just might be caught in an even deeper lie.

"Josh?" Maya asked with a rapacious smile, like a hungry cat that had just cornered a frightened, confused mouse.

Josh gripped the towel around his waist even tighter, his knuckles whitening, fearing more exposure than just his naked body. Finally, he expelled a sigh, defeated, and said quietly, "The Wagner Group is a shell corporation for someone I had some business dealings with. . . ." He knew he had to offer more but paused, almost praying for some divine intervention that would save him from having to come clean.

But there was none.

It was just him standing, wearing a towel, feeling vulnerable and quite literally beaten up, with two very curious, very determined, very pugnacious women determined to hear what he had to say.

"Who does the Wagner Group belong to?" Maya pressed.

"Ed Brady."

"Kelton's father?" Sandra asked, surprised.

Kelton Brady was in Jack's class. He had been cut from the football team earlier that fall during tryouts. His father, reportedly, was apoplectic, Kelton not so much because he only tried out for the team to please his demanding father and had little to no interest in the sport.

"Why is the parent of a student writing you a check for

five thousand dollars?" Maya demanded to know, waving the check around.

Josh dithered some more, hemming and hawing.

Sandra decided to play good cop. "Josh, we want to help you."

Maya snorted. Sandra could tell that Maya had no interest in helping Coach Kirby because they both already had a pretty good idea of what was really going on here, and Maya was resoundingly unsympathetic.

"A few parents have paid me to help their kids get a leg up in the college admissions process. . . . It can be very stressful for all involved, and they just want their kids to get a fair shot."

"Fair shot?" Maya snapped scornfully. "By fudging their application? Let me guess. You wrote a glowing report on how Kelton Brady is your star quarterback even though in reality you cut him from the team because he was a terrible athlete! Did you suit him up in a uniform and take pictures of him running around the field carrying a football?"

Josh didn't answer her.

He didn't have to. The answer was written all over his face.

"I've heard of this before. It's a despicable practice. You're hurting the kids who work hard and deserve the scholarships and admission into good schools that these rich parents are stealing from them!" Maya raged.

Sandra instinctively knew how offended Maya had to be because she was a far cry from those wealthy parents who could so easily scribble out a fat check to cut the line and bypass everyone else, essentially knocking kids like her daughter out of the way to make room for their own overprivileged, less-deserving offspring. It was sickening and grossly unfair.

"How many parents have paid you?" Maya asked.

Josh sat back down on the bench, his head bowed.

Maya stepped forward, fists clenched. "How many, Josh?"

"Five, maybe six," he whispered.

"I assume enough money to buy that fancy Tesla parked outside," Maya seethed.

Josh nodded, eyes glued to the floor, humiliated. Then he raised his head. "I've been tortured by what I've done. It's been eating me up inside. I called a few of the parents to let them know I was thinking of contacting the deans of admissions at all the colleges I defrauded to come clean. Well, as you can imagine, that didn't exactly go down well with any of them. They got very nervous. Some even threatened me, physically, if I talked. . . ."

"Do you think that's why you were attacked today?" Sandra gasped.

Josh shrugged. "I can't be sure, but it may have been some kind of a warning."

"Who are the other parents?" Maya asked.

"I-I can't tell you that," Josh stammered, panicking. "They'll come after me. These are very important, powerful people."

"It's going to come out eventually," Maya said flatly.

But Josh kept mum, undoubtedly fearing he might further endanger himself.

Maya stood glaring at him, fuming.

Something dawned on Sandra.

"Josh, you should know, the reason Maya and I are here had nothing to do with any college admissions scandals. We wanted to talk to you about a whole different kind of scandal that's got the press sniffing around, and it involves you—"

"*Me?*" Josh wailed.

"You and Senator Elisabeth Dooley."

Josh's lip quivered. "What about her?"

"There is a rumor going around that you and the senator are embroiled in an extramarital affair," Maya said coldly. "I'd ask if it was true, but it would be hard for me to believe anything you say at this point."

"It's not true, I swear!" Josh howled. "There is absolutely *nothing* going on between us! She's a married woman! I would never—"

Maya, skeptical, stared daggers at him. "Yes, you've shown us your indubitable moral compass."

Sandra, on the other hand, tended to believe Josh's fervent denial of an affair because now there was another very clear reason for Josh and Elisabeth's clandestine, late-night meetings that had suddenly floated to the surface. "She's one of the parents, isn't she?"

Josh flicked his eyes away from Sandra, perhaps not quite having the nerve to sell out a sitting US senator.

"Her daughter, Kendra, isn't even on the field hockey team. You just said she was to ensure she was admitted to the school of her choice. Which one is she going for? Princeton? Stanford? Harvard?"

Josh buried his face in the shirt he still held in his hand. He appeared defeated, yet almost relieved that he was done keeping this big, dark, overwhelming secret to himself. Then, after a few silent moments, he shook out the shirt and, with a pained expression on his face, pulled it over his head and slid it on, slowly, creakily, wincing. He was still very much hurting from the attack. "Give me some time. I will make this right."

Maya snorted, again punctuating her skepticism.

Sandra continued adopting a more diplomatic approach. "Would you like us to step outside and wait for you to get dressed, and then help you to your car?"

"No, thank you," Josh said, no doubt afraid to accept any help from Maya, who looked ready to punch him in the face. He'd surely had enough of that for one day. "I'll manage."

Maya shoved the check in front of Josh's face and said, her voice dripping with disdain, "Don't forget your five thousand dollars for services rendered."

Josh swatted it away. "I don't want that anymore."

Maya aggressively waved it in front of him. "You might need it to hire yourself a good lawyer."

Then she dropped it, watching it slowly float to the floor, landing an inch from his big toe.

Maya dramatically turned and stormed out of the locker room.

"We'll be in touch," Sandra said, as kindly as possible. She felt a little sorry for Coach Kirby. He had broken laws, not to mention a serious code of conduct. He would pay dearly. And he had gotten beaten up over it. But from the crushed look on the young coach's face, she could tell that most of the pain he was suffering emotionally would have far more devastating effects on him than the physical bruising of his body.

Chapter Thirty-One

As the Chevy Bolt silently zipped along the slick, wet road after a brief rainfall, Maya gripped the wheel, eyes fixed on the road, her mind all over the place after their confrontation with Josh Kirby, as Sandra sat quietly in the passenger seat next to her.

Maya glanced over at her a couple of times.

Sandra stared out the side window, seemingly a million miles away.

"You okay?" Maya asked, concerned.

Sandra sat up, suddenly snapping back into reality. "Yes, fine. Sorry."

"Don't apologize. You just seem a little preoccupied."

"It's nothing," Sandra said, brushing it off.

Maya could tell she was lying. She suspected Sandra was thinking about her marriage, or the possible end of her marriage. She had spent enough time with her over the past year to know what was on her mind because Sandra was pretty much an open book. There were not a lot of subterfuge or hidden secrets with her. Maya, on the other hand, was much harder to read, or at least that was what she liked to believe. She wasn't keen on sharing too much with anyone, but had been surprised at how Sandra had managed to break through to her and somehow get her to open up in their free moments together. Maya had been betrayed before, so she often eschewed friendships, kept a safe distance from everyone other than her daughter.

But Sandra was different. Sandra had found a way to burrow into Maya's heart, although she loathed to admit it. So it was disconcerting to see Sandra so uncommunicative, unwilling to share what was on her mind.

Maya hoped that would change.

"So, I've been thinking," Maya finally said, to let Sandra off the hook, at least for now. "What if Diego was never the target at all?"

Sandra turned toward her and cocked an eyebrow. "How do you mean?"

Maya huffed at a slow-moving car in front of them, then jerked the wheel and swerved around it, fast and recklessly, as Sandra slammed the palm of her hand down on the dashboard in front of her.

After Maya was safely back in her rightful lane, leaving the other car far behind them, headlights disappearing in the heavy mist, she turned toward Sandra. "Josh Kirby told us he was threatening to go to the authorities and come clean about what he was doing. What if one of the wealthy parents he was working for on the side panicked, got scared he was going to expose what was going on, put them in legal jeopardy; what if they decided to shut him up before he had a chance to report his actions to the school board, or worse, the feds? Maybe the poisoned cookie was meant for Josh, but because of some mix-up, it somehow wound up in Diego's box of cookies by accident."

Maya looked to Sandra for a reaction to her theory, but Sandra seemed more concerned that the Bolt was drifting across the yellow line in the center of the street to the other side. "Eyes on the road, Maya."

Maya quickly turned back her head and jerked the wheel to the right. She flipped on the wipers as rain pelted the windshield.

"I suppose that's possible, especially if one of those rich parents wanted to avoid a scandal that would adversely affect his or her business or reputation," Sandra said.

"It's a theory at least," Maya said softly as she pulled her car into Sandra's driveway, stopping a few inches behind her Mercedes.

It was usually Sandra who excitedly burst forth with her Agatha Christie–inspired suppositions. But not today. Something was obviously on her mind, and Maya finally decided to broach the topic she suspected it might be.

"Do you have plans to see Henry Yang again?"

That snapped Sandra to attention. She blinked at Maya, clearly debating with herself whether or not this was going to be a topic she was willing to discuss with her. After a brief moment, Sandra shrugged. "I don't know."

Maya kept mum, not wanting to pressure her into confessing whatever was on her mind.

There was an uncomfortable pause before Sandra spoke again. "I've had some doubts recently, but I think he's a good man. He obviously likes me, and frankly, it's nice to have someone interested in me, with Stephen absent for a while now, emotionally and physically."

Maya opened her mouth to say something, but thought better of it and demurred.

Sandra noticed instantly. "What?"

"Nothing," Maya said.

Now it was her turn to brush things off. Sandra studied her. "You were going to say something."

"No, I wasn't," Maya said quietly and firmly, so Sandra would stop asking.

But Sandra was right. Maya was going to have to spill what she had heard about Henry Yang. But she just didn't have the heart to break the news. At least not yet. It was hearsay. And it was coming from Max. Yes, she trusted him, but why should Sandra? Max was a convicted felon. She wanted some hard proof to present before she went ahead and insinuated herself into Sandra's dating life. And that meant looking into the matter on her own, starting a little side investigation to see if there was any merit to Max's claim, before dumping any bad news on her new friend's doorstep.

"Good night," Sandra said, trying to be chipper as she opened the passenger side door and hopped out in the drizzling evening rain.

"See you tomorrow," Maya said with a smile.

Sandra slammed the car door shut and scurried up the walk to her front door, balancing her bag on top of her head to keep her hair from getting too wet.

Maya watched her disappear inside the house.

She sat in the driveway another minute, staring at the house.

She asked herself whether she should get involved in this.

She needed to think about it.

Like Sandra, Maya was reluctant to jump into the dating pool again after so many years. It was complicated and messy and scary, all at the same time.

But at least when it came to Sandra's first time out, she only had to deal with an enigmatic and possibly morally compromised billionaire. In Maya's case, her maiden effort had ended with finding her date dead.

Chapter Thirty-Two

When Sandra entered the house, she immediately froze in the foyer at the sound of Stephen's deep baritone and commanding voice.

What was he doing here?

She could hear him chatting with the boys in the kitchen, no doubt as he stirred a pot of his homemade marinara sauce, his specialty, actually the only half-decent dish he could be counted on to whip up when he was home in Maine. She shed her coat and marched into the kitchen, where the image in her mind matched exactly what was happening.

Stephen was holding out a wooden spoonful of sauce for Jack to taste. Jack slurped it off the spoon and nodded his approval. Ryan was rummaging through the utensil drawer for some forks and spoons. How Stephen had managed to enlist their help was beyond her. Whenever she asked the boys to assist her in setting the table, there were always a litany of moans and excuses. But having their dad home was always a special occasion, so they were a little more amenable to getting off the couch or coming down the stairs from their rooms.

"What's this?" Sandra asked because none of them had noticed her yet.

They all turned toward her.

"Hey, Mom," Jack said casually as he stepped away from the stove and bumped into Ryan, who grumbled, annoyed, as he gripped the silverware in one hand while slamming the drawer shut with the other.

Stephen offered her a sheepish grin. "Surprise."

"Yes, it is. Why aren't you in DC?" Sandra said in a clipped tone, one that obviously irritated the boys and she quickly regretted.

"Senate's in recess, so I thought I'd fly up here and spend some time with the boys and hold a couple of town halls, get my face back out in front of my constituents," Stephen said before swiveling around to check on the sauce bubbling in the pot.

"Why didn't you call to let us know you were coming?" Sandra asked evenly.

"I did," Stephen said, adding a pinch more oregano to his sauce.

Sandra fished her phone out of her bag to check. Sure enough, there was a voice-mail message from Stephen. "Sorry, I've been working." She dropped the phone back in the bag and shifted to one side, irked.

"Well, I'm glad you're home, Dad," Jack said, shooting a sore look at his mother before strolling out of the room. "I'll be upstairs in my room. Call me when it's time to eat."

Jack knew an argument was coming and didn't want to hang around to hear it. Ryan was hyperaware of the tension as well and wandered into the dining room to set out the dinner utensils.

Sandra waited for them to be gone before she spoke. "Stephen . . ."

He held up a hand. "I know what you're going to say. I should not be just showing up here whenever I want to."

"Yes, you keep playing fast and loose with the rules of an official separation."

"Tell me, what *are* the rules of an official separation?"

"Usually that means the two parties don't cohabitate."

"I'm only here for a few days," Stephen huffed. "Look, I've already made up the guest room. I promise not to be underfoot. I'll hardly be around anyway."

"That's not the point—"

"When I got here, the boys practically begged me to make my famous marinara sauce for dinner. I barely get to spend time with them anymore. How could I say no?"

He was right.

She knew he missed his sons desperately when he was down in Washington.

It had been her decision not to yank the boys out of school and move the whole family to DC before the separation. Stephen just went along, but it was obvious he would have preferred they all come to be with him. Maybe that was why the marriage had soured.

She stopped herself.

No. That was not the reason.

Or at least not the only reason.

Stephen's infidelities had played a major part in the crumbling of their happy marriage. She had to keep telling herself that because she tended to blame herself for her husband straying, and that wasn't fair to her. Stephen had willfully breached her trust. And that was why they were now in the predicament they found themselves in.

"You still seeing Daddy Warbucks?"

Sandra suddenly was jolted out of her thoughts. "What?"

"Henry Yang. Are you still dating him?"

Sandra stiffened. "That's none of your business."

"You can tell me. I'll admit, I'm a little weirded out by the whole thing, but I promise not to fly into some jealous rage," Stephen promised with a tight smile.

"Are you still seeing Deborah Crowley?" Sandra asked pointedly.

That caught him by surprise. "Who told you that?"

"I've suspected for a while now."

"Well, it's not true—"

"Oh, Stephen, please."

"I'm telling you—"

"Your own son says you two are romantically involved."

"Jack?"

Sandra nodded.

"Jack saw us together when he was down visiting me and just assumed we were dating. I never said anything to him. Deborah and I have been working day and night on some legislation, and yes, I'm rather fond of her, but there is nothing physical between us."

"So Jack is wrong, and Zoe Rush is wrong?"

"Zoe Rush? What does she have to do with anything?"

"She also thinks your relationship with Deborah Crowley is more than just a professional one."

"Zoe Rush is a political hack who would lie about her own mother if it got her some clickbait on her paper's website. And let's not forget she was wrong about Elisabeth cheating on Lou." He took a deep breath. "I'm not sleeping with Deborah."

Sandra eyed him suspiciously. As a consummate politician, he was frustratingly adept at talking his way out of any uncomfortable situation. It had always been difficult for her to tell if he was being totally honest with her, even back when they were idealistic college kids chasing after the same causes, which should have been the first clue that their marriage would have mountainous challenges. The more Stephen gained power in Washington, the better he became at talking a good game.

Still, there was a chance he was telling her the truth.

She just wasn't ready to take him at his word. Which was why they weren't still playing house together.

"Elisabeth called me a few minutes before you got home," Stephen said nonchalantly, almost as an afterthought.

Sandra perked up. "About what?"

"Are you and your friend, what's her name again—?"

"Maya." Sandra sighed. "I've mentioned her to you dozens of times, Stephen."

"I'm sorry, you know how I am with names. Anyway, are you and Maya investigating her for some reason? Because she has sworn to me over and over that she's been faithful in her marriage, and I believe her."

Sandra suddenly felt herself on guard. She didn't want to share anything about what they had learned about Senator Dooley's connection to Josh Kirby and the brewing college admissions scandal. But how did he already know this? She had just come from meeting Kirby at the high school. It was downright scary how he was so tuned in. "I can't talk about cases we're working on."

"Oh, come on, you and Maya aren't the FBI," he scoffed. "And I'm not some senate oversight committee. It's me you're talking to."

"I know, and you and Elisabeth Dooley are very close. I don't want to risk anything somehow getting back to her. At least not yet."

Stephen took great pains to act low-key and unruffled, but he was clearly curious and laser-focused on finding out exactly what was going on. She didn't blame him for it. Senator Dooley was an important partner in the legislative goals he had set for the state of Maine, not to mention the whole country.

"I see," Stephen whispered. "Is it bad?"

Sandra slowly nodded.

She could tell Stephen's brain was now working in overdrive as he contemplated what the senior senator might be involved in. After a few moments, he glanced back at his wife, choosing to toe the party line. "Elisabeth is a good progressive, working very hard to better the lives of the American people."

"You can spare me the stump speech, Stephen."

His face reddened. He didn't like being called out. "All I'm saying is, I'd hate to see her chased out of Washington because of some personal failing."

"It may be a little more than that. Maya and I found the new coach at the high school in the boys' locker room beaten up pretty bad."

"And you think Elisabeth slapped him around for giving her precious daughter Kendra a B plus in PE?"

Sandra ignored the question.

She was done offering him any more information.

And that just stoked his curiosity, but he knew better than to press her any further. Stephen turned back around and stared at the red sauce still bubbling on the stove. He turned down the heat on the burner. "I'd better start boiling the pasta."

As Stephen opened a cupboard to retrieve a bag of fettucine, Sandra backed out of the kitchen and headed upstairs to change.

She was fairly certain that Senator Dooley had called Stephen knowing Sandra had been asking Josh Kirby questions relating to her. Which meant Kirby must have called to warn her.

And she, in turn, had contacted Stephen with the express desire of having him put a muzzle on his nosy wife.

But it was too late for that because Sandra was not about to stop until everything was out in the open, and the identity of Diego Sanchez's killer was finally known.

Even if it turned out to be a sitting US senator.

Chapter Thirty-Three

Maya had an uneasy feeling she was being watched. She sat in her Bolt outside the high school as Vanessa stuffed her iPad in her backpack and flung open the passenger side door.

"Have a good day," Maya chirped.

"You too," Vanessa called back curtly as she slammed the door and joined a gaggle of her friends, clinging together in a tight circle, gossiping.

Maya glanced up at the rearview mirror. Behind her was the mother of one of Vanessa's classmates, whom she recognized from various school functions, including the bake sale. Maya specifically remembered her because she'd stopped by Maya's table and turned up her nose at Maya's batch of homemade cookies. Maya had made a mental note that she wasn't a fan of this woman. A few cars back, jammed into a fire-red Kia Optima, was a hulk of a man: big muscles, wide frame, like a wrestler, with a shaved head and a black goatee speckled with bits of gray, probably in his midforties. She couldn't get too good a look because the sun was reflecting off the windshield of his car, but he seemed to be focused on her.

Maya waited for Vanessa to make her way inside the building before pulling away from the curb into the heavy traffic of parents dropping off their kids, students arriving in their own cars and a long line of yellow school buses arriving to unload their dozens of chattering teenage passengers.

Maya rolled along, stopping at a crosswalk to wait for a group of kids to saunter past while a heavy, sweaty, weary-eyed man, around retirement age, wearing an orange crossing guard vest while half-heartedly holding up a stop sign, acknowledged Maya with a curt nod and a half smile. Maya gave him a polite wave and then glanced back up at the mirror. The brute in the Kia was directly behind her. She had a clearer view of him now. He reminded her of the actor from those *Guardians of the Galaxy* movies, the former wrestler. Dave something. Vanessa loved him. Bowers. Barista. Something like that. It didn't matter. Bautista. That was it. The guy was a dead ringer.

After the last student scooted by and was safely on school grounds, the crossing guard lowered his sign and trudged back to the other side of the street, allowing Maya to drive forward. Once she was past the school and turning onto the main road, traffic lightened considerably and she was able to tamp down on the gas pedal and pick up more speed.

The Kia was following her.

Maya tried to recall if she had seen him tailing her when she was on her way to the high school with Vanessa but couldn't quite remember.

Maya turned right.

The Bautista look-alike followed suit.

He was starting to make Maya nervous. Who was he? Why was he following her?

Or was this just a coincidence and they both were just coincidentally driving in the same direction?

There was one way to find out.

Maya jerked the wheel, taking a sharp turn down a side street. Sure enough, the Kia did the same. He was close enough to her rear bumper that she could see his big, meaty hands gripping the steering wheel of the Kia up close.

Maya was going to try to lose him, but when she pulled into a parking lot next to a Starbucks the Kia kept going.

Maybe she had imagined the whole thing. After all, it was in her nature to be suspicious.

She parked her Bolt and headed inside, where she waited in line to order a Caffè Latte. After paying with her phone, which she held up to the scanner next to the register, Maya moved down to the pickup area and waited for her drink. The store was unusually busy this morning.

She checked her watch.

Almost eight thirty.

The barista finally called her name, and Maya grabbed the grande paper cup and spun around to leave. She nearly collided with a giant man standing uncomfortably close behind her.

It was him.

The guy in the Kia.

He was a giant and had a deep scar down the side of his left cheek, as if someone had slashed him with a knife at some point. His eyes were dead as he gazed at her. A slight, crooked smile on his ruddy face was the only thing that indicated he had a pulse.

Maya considered confronting him, demanding to know

why he had been following her, but she wasn't certain he had. Instead, she stared at him for a few moments, then nodded and pushed past him. "Excuse me."

He didn't say a word.

She hurried out to her Bolt, a bit rattled by the encounter, but still not sure if she had any reason to be.

Maya drove the rest of the way to the office keeping a watchful eye on her side mirror to make sure he wasn't still following her, but she never caught sight of the Kia again.

She parked her car on the street outside her building, and as she entered, she took one last look back to make sure the brute wasn't lurking around somewhere.

Nothing.

Maybe he was still at Starbucks, waiting for his coffee.

Maya made her way up to the second floor, and as she rummaged for her key to the office, she heard the phone ringing inside. She quickly unlocked the door and rushed in to snatch up the phone.

"Maya Kendrick Investigations, how may I help you?" she said, adopting a professional, reassuring tone.

Sandra always answered the phone with a much more chipper and inclusive, "Good morning, Maya and Sandra Investigations," but Sandra wasn't there yet.

"Hello, my name is Carolyn Simpson and I own a bakery in the Old Port, and recently, I hired a part-time worker and I'm not sure I trust him. . . ."

"Why not?" Maya asked, searching her desk for a pen and some paper.

"It's just a feeling I have. I was wondering if you do employee background checks?"

"Yes, that's definitely a service we provide, if you could just—" Maya stopped suddenly in midsentence. Her eyes fell upon the big, brawny, faux Dave Bautista filling up the doorway to the office. She suppressed a gasp, not wanting him to know just how rattled she was by his sudden appearance.

"Hello? Are you still there?" Carolyn Simpson, the potential client asked, confused.

"Hold on. I'll be right with you," Maya said as she slowly put down the phone.

He took a step inside the office. Up close he looked less like Dave Bautista and more like Brutus from the old "Popeye" cartoons.

Maya instinctively stood up. There was no point in pretending she didn't know he had been stalking her all morning. "What do you want?"

He didn't answer her.

He just advanced, ever so slowly, with those dead eyes and that off-putting, crooked, half smile.

Maya's mind raced.

She had left her gun locked up at home and had no way to defend herself if she had to.

"If you have a case you'd like to discuss, you're going to have to make an appointment," she said soberly.

"I don't have a case," he muttered in a deep, gravelly voice.

"Then I'm going to have to ask you to leave—"

"I have a message."

"From whom?" Maya asked, backing away from her desk until she was almost flat up against the wall.

Then, with unexpected agility for a man his size, he circled the desk and pounced.

Maya managed to grab her office chair and hurl it at him to slow down the attack. It banged him in the knee but didn't do any damage. It did allow her to bolt around the other side of the desk and make a run for the door.

She didn't make it.

Suddenly, she felt two massive paws wrap around her neck, cutting off her air supply. With one of his size-twelve feet, he kicked the door to the office closed. Maya used her fingernails to try to claw the big mitts choking her. She drew blood that trickled down the sides of his hands, but her efforts didn't loosen his iron-tight grip.

She thought she was going to pass out. He dragged her across the office like he was carrying a tiny kitten hanging ten and slammed her down on top of the desk.

Maya's eyes widened, fearing he was going to strangle her to death in that moment.

"For what it's worth," he growled, "I don't like messing up pretty ladies, but it just comes with the job."

Then he formed a fist with one of his gargantuan hands and was about to punch her squarely in the face.

Maya closed her eyes, anticipating the worst.

But then, in an instant, she heard a sound like a thunder crack and constant clicking, and heard Brutus howling in pain. He withdrew his hands from Maya's throat and she popped open her eyes.

He was blindly swinging at someone else in the room that his body blocked from Maya's view. His whole body was spasming and he was panicking. Then he sank to the floor, subdued, moaning softly, only half-conscious.

Sandra suddenly was standing there, bent over, heaving, clutching something in her hand. It took her a few seconds to catch her breath so she could speak. "Who the hell is that?" She got up, pointing at the unconscious gorilla lying on the floor.

Maya slid off the desk, a hand to her throat, which was

surely going to bruise badly, and shook her head. "I-I don't know . . ." she sputtered. "What did you use on him to knock him down like that?"

Sandra held up a small gold container. "Lipstick taser. I got it on Amazon."

Maya gave her a quizzical look as she snatched her phone from the desk to call the police.

Sandra screwed the top back on the lipstick. "What? You won't let me buy a gun yet, and I figured in the mean-time I needed some kind of weapon to defend myself now that I'm a private eye, so I did a little research online."

And Maya was grateful that she had because it was that kind of resourcefulness that had saved her life today.

Maybe this odd partnership was going to work out after all.

Chapter Thirty-Four

Lieutenant Beth Hart greeted Maya and Sandra in the reception area of the Portland police station, where they sat in a couple of rickety metal chairs awaiting word following their assailant's arrest at their office earlier that morning. Maya sprang to her feet first and hustled over to Lieutenant Hart for an update.

"What's the word?" Maya asked as Sandra popped up behind her and scooted over, not wanting to be left out of the conversation.

"His name is Cole Perry. He's a two-bit thug with a long rap sheet. We've had him in here before, many times in fact," Lieutenant Hart said.

"Any clue why he was following me around?" Maya asked.

Lieutenant Hart shrugged. "Not yet. But I have one of our detectives questioning him."

Maya's eyed narrowed. "Who?"

"Detective Marino," Hart answered.

Maya grimaced.

Hart raised an eyebrow. "Know him?"

"Yeah, I know him," Maya spat out bitterly.

"I take it you're not a fan," Hart said.

Maya shook her head. "He didn't exactly rally around me to show his support when Max got arrested."

In fact, he had been one of the cops who had made her life at the station unbearable post-Max, out of suspicion that she had somehow been involved with her husband's illegal activities. He had refused to believe that Max had kept her in the dark the whole time, which was the honest truth. Besides, he had told her at the time, if she had been clueless, she was a lousy cop. Maya had hated him for saying it, but couldn't help but feel that, deep down on some level, he was right. It had haunted her for months, long after Max was convicted and sent to prison, up until the day she finally resigned from the force to preserve a little slice of her sanity. Only after starting her own detective agency a year later had she finally managed to build up her confidence again when it came to investigative work.

"I get it," Hart said, reaching up and gently squeezing Maya's arm with her hand. "But he's one of my best interrogators."

"Mind if I watch?" Maya asked.

"Me too," Sandra piped in.

Lieutenant Hart hesitated, then shook her head with an apologetic smile. "I'm afraid not. But I promise to call you as soon as we know something." Hart noticed the discouraged look on Maya's face. "Look, Maya, I understand this used to be your old stomping ground, but I'm afraid I have to follow procedure."

"I understand," Maya said in a clipped tone, not really understanding at all.

"Trust me, I will keep you both in the loop," Hart promised before turning around and heading off, leaving them standing there. Sandra had to step aside to avoid being bumped by a boisterous, handcuffed drunk two officers were busy hauling to the booking room.

Maya debated with herself, then made a decision and turned around to Sandra. "Wait here. I'll be right back."

"Where are you going?"

"To see an old friend."

Sandra seemed to buy it. She sat back down in the uncomfortable metal chair and checked her phone for messages.

Maya waited for the desk sergeant to answer a phone call that conveniently distracted him long enough not to notice her slip by and disappear down the hall. Maya walked at a brisk pace, eyes straight ahead, pretending she absolutely belonged. She was intimately familiar with the station's layout, so it was an easy trick to pull off.

She rounded a corner, nodding to a junior officer who passed by with a file. He eyed her as if he was trying to figure out who she was but he was too wet behind the ears to actually stop to ask her.

Maya powered on assuredly until she reached a tiny office near the end of the hall. This was the cybercrimes unit, manned by her old buddy Oscar Dunford, a young, eager detective with impressive technological know-how when it came to computers. The captain had decided to give him an important-sounding sign to hang on the door, CYBERCRIMES UNIT, but most of the officers at the station just referred to him as "the IT guy."

Sensing a presence standing in the doorway, Oscar glanced up from his desktop computer and melted at the sight of Maya, a big, dopey grin nearly swallowing up the rest of his face. "Hello, gorgeous."

Oscar had always had a huge crush on Maya, which she was not above exploiting.

Maya flicked her eyes to the hallway to make sure no one else was around and then slipped inside Oscar's office and closed the door.

"I must be dreaming." Oscar sighed, blinking. "Seriously, I had a dream the other night just like this, where you showed up here and we ended up naked, making pottery."

"Pottery?"

"I was watching that old movie *Ghost* on Netflix before I drifted off. . . ."

Oscar was also a big movie buff.

"I don't remember Patrick Swayze and Demi Moore being naked in that scene," Maya remarked.

"They weren't. I just like to add my own spin to my dreams."

"You're naughty."

"Oh, you have no idea how naughty I can be."

Maya laughed. She knew Oscar was all talk. If one day she actually called his bluff and made a move on him, she was fairly certain he would panic and faint dead away.

"I know it's inappropriate, saying that in the workplace," Oscar said. "We all had to take a sexual harassment training course a couple of months ago, but you don't work here anymore, so I think I'm okay, right?"

"You're good. Oscar, I need a favor."

"You want me to sneak you down to the interrogation room so you can eavesdrop on the guy who attacked you this morning?"

"Word gets around."

"I heard Lieutenant Hart talking to that a-hole Marino earlier when I was getting coffee. You know my ears perk up whenever I hear my beloved's name roll off anyone's tongue."

"Okay, don't get weird," Maya said, holding up a hand.

Oscar stood up, knocking over his coffee cup and spilling it all over the floor. He just ignored it, pretending it never happened, and then grabbed a file folder off his desk with one hand, took Maya's hand in his other and led her down the hall. He stopped at the corner, poked his head around to make sure the coast was clear and then quickly dragged her down another hallway, sharply veering right. They both came to a screeching halt.

Lieutenant Hart was stamping down the hall toward them, conferring with one of her officers. Oscar quickly pushed Maya against the wall and opened the file folder, lifting it up in front of them as if they were discussing the contents. Maya held her breath.

As Hart passed, Oscar said from behind the file folder, "Morning, Lieutenant."

Hart never paused or even glanced his way. "Hey, Oscar," she said brusquely before resuming her conversation with the officer.

Once she was gone, Oscar slapped shut the folder and grabbed Maya's hand.

"I think I can make it the rest of the way without you holding my hand, Oscar."

"I know, but I'm taking a risk here, so I should get something out of it," he said, trying on a lascivious smile but coming off more like a little kid playing Don Juan in a middle school play.

Maya shook her hand free from him and gave him an admonishing look, and he gave up and led her the rest of the way to the interrogation room. No one was outside in the hallway watching through the two-way mirror, so they were safe to listen, at least for now.

Inside, Cole Perry, the gorilla who had stalked and tried to beat Maya senseless, sat hunched over in a chair, one wrist handcuffed to a table. Across from him was Detective Roman Marino, cocky, aggressive, admittedly handsome, but older than Maya had remembered, now in his midforties, temples starting to gray just a bit.

Marino leaned back in his chair and folded his muscled arms, which he spent hours at the gym every day sculpting. "You tell us who hired you to go after Mrs. Kendrick, things will go a lot easier for you."

Perry appeared defiant, ticked off and uncommunicative.

"Cole, it's past my lunch break. I'm starving. Tell you what: give me something, anything, I'll come back with a double quarter pounder with cheese. I'll even throw in some fries, maybe an apple pie? What do you say?"

Perry didn't budge, keeping his eyes glued to the floor.

"I know you're working for someone. You're too dumb to do much of anything on your own."

Maya noticed Perry clenching his handcuffed fist.

Marino was getting to him.

But so far, the thug was refusing to break.

Marino tried another tactic. He started chuckling, softly at first, then a little louder, until he was laughing hard enough for Perry to reluctantly lift his eyes off the floor and stare at him, wondering what was so funny.

Marino slapped down a hand on the table. "Sorry, I just find it hilarious that you got your ass whooped by two suburban mommies!"

Perry bit his bottom lip, rage building up inside him.

"I mean a big bear like you taken down like that? Just a tiny little lipstick, and bam, they send you right into hibernation for the winter."

Maya could tell Perry was dying to say something.

But he thought better of it and kept his mouth shut.

Marino taunted him some more, called him a few derogatory names, trying to get a rise out of him, hoping he would blurt out something, anything that might prove useful, but Perry remained frustratingly tight-lipped.

Finally, after another ten minutes of badgering and threatening, detailing the massive amount of jail time Perry was facing for attempted murder, Marino finally stood up, incensed he wasn't getting anywhere and stormed out, leaving Perry to stew about his current predicament.

Maya and Oscar didn't have enough time to slip away before Marino banged out of the interrogation room, stopping in his tracks at the sight of Maya. He stared at her glumly, then focused on Oscar. "What is *she* doing here?"

"She's my guest," Oscar squeaked out.

"Hart's going to hear about this," Marino hissed.

"Hart already knows she's here. She's fine with it," Oscar bluffed, standing toe to toe with Marino.

The detective seemed to buy it and turned his attention back to Maya, sneering, "Give your dirty cop husband my best, Maya, the next time you visit him in the big house." And then he gave her a wink and sauntered away.

Maya didn't let him get to her. She knew Max's betrayal had adversely affected the whole department, turned them all against the name Kendrick.

She had no interest in engaging with Detective Marino. He had no hold or influence over her. She didn't care one whit whether he liked her or not.

What she really wanted was to get inside that interrogation room and question Cole Perry herself, one-on-one. She knew in her bones she would get a lot further than the blunt, sledgehammer approach of Marino.

But she also knew it was too big of an ask.

Eavesdropping was one thing. Taking over an interrogation when you were no longer a cop was quite another.

Chapter Thirty-Five

Maya and Oscar blew into the reception area, where they found Sandra still sitting in that hard metal chair, her Gucci bag perched on her lap.

Maya made a big show of introducing Sandra to her friend in front of the young officer manning the reception desk. "Sandra, this is Oscar Dunford, head of the Cyber-crimes Unit."

She could hear the officer behind her at the desk snickering over her using such a big, fancy-sounding title to describe Oscar's job.

Oscar ignored him.

Sandra extended a hand. "Pleased to meet you, Oscar."

"Likewise," Oscar said, grinning. "Would you like a tour of the precinct?"

Sandra looked at both of them, confused. "What? You mean now?"

"Sure, come on," Oscar said cheerily with a wave, leading them back past the reception desk.

The young officer looked up, craning his neck, not sure if he should object, but Maya calculated he would keep his mouth shut because Oscar technically had a higher rank, and she was right. The officer let them pass and buried his head back down, scribbling on some paperwork.

Oscar led Maya and Sandra down the hall to his office and quickly ushered them inside. "Make yourselves comfortable. I'll go get us some coffee."

"Oh no, I'm fine. I already had two cups—" Sandra started to say.

"Cream, no sugar, thanks, Oscar!" Maya shouted over her as he hustled back out, leaving them alone.

Sandra turned to Maya. "I really don't want coffee—"

"Good, because he's not getting us any," Maya said under her breath.

"He's not? Then where is he going?"

"Keep your voice down," Maya urged. "He's helping us."

"With what?"

"Patience, Sandra."

Sandra shrugged and decided to just stop asking questions.

A few minutes later Oscar returned, furtively looking behind him to make sure no one was following him. He closed the door to the office and locked it. Then he yanked a cell phone out of the back pocket of his khaki pants and sat down at his desk, plugging it into his computer.

Sandra could not resist asking one more question. "Who's phone is that?"

"It belongs to the guy you took down with your lipstick taser," Maya said, hovering behind Oscar's shoulders as he typed furiously on his computer.

"Where did you get it?" Sandra asked.

"The property clerk's office. They confiscated it when he was booked."

"Are you allowed to have that?" Sandra asked, wide-eyed.

Oscar shot Sandra a withering look. "No. Are you going to tattle on me to the teacher?"

Sandra took a step back, held up a hand. "No, I'm not that girl. Well, I used to be in middle school, but not anymore."

"You were like that in high school too, as I recall," Maya scoffed.

"Okay, I may have once been a Goody Two-shoes, but my moral character has decayed a bit after being married to a politician for almost twenty years. So go ahead, have at it."

Maya leaned down, peering at the desktop computer screen over Oscar's left shoulder. "I'm sure the phone has touch ID or a passcode, how are you going to—?"

Now it was Maya's turn to be on the receiving end of Oscar's withering look.

Maya smiled. "Sorry. I should know by now to just shut up and let you do your thing."

With his right index finger poised in the air, ready to click on the keyboard, Oscar swiveled his head around to face Maya. "Now, before I do this, are you going to tell me what's in it for me?"

"My enduring appreciation and the knowledge you helped bring the man who tried to hurt me to justice?" Maya offered.

"Nope, not good enough," Oscar said, shaking his head.

"Then what do you want?" Maya asked.

"Dinner," he said bluntly.

"Oscar, we've had dinner together dozens of time. . . ." Maya sighed.

"Yes, pizza and Chinese food here in my office while you have me do your bidding. I want real food. A real restaurant. With Michelin stars and a two-year wait to get a reservation."

"I can't afford a place like that," Maya protested.

"I can," Sandra said firmly.

Oscar suddenly perked up.

"I promise to get you two lovebirds into a nice place, and I will personally pay for the meal myself," Sandra said.

Oscar broke into a satisfied smile. "I want a romantic corner table with candles and maybe flowers, and pick a place that has bread pudding for dessert. I love bread pudding."

"Done," Sandra said.

"Don't I get a say in this?" Maya asked.

"No. Don't you worry, Oscar. I'll make sure she shows up. You can count on me. Now, go on, work your magic," Sandra said with a wave of her hand.

Maya shot Sandra an annoyed look.

Sandra sighed. "It's just one dinner. No one's asking you to marry him."

"Not yet," Oscar said with a sly smile.

He happily spun back around and dropped his finger down on a key, opening a cache of personal information on Cole Perry. As he poured over his apps, emails and texts, Maya and Sandra bunched together behind Oscar to take everything in. He was scrolling fast, almost too fast to absorb all the names and numbers stored in Perry's phone.

"Wait, stop!" Sandra cried as Oscar explored a spate of calls Perry had recently made.

Oscar withdrew his hands from the keyboard and they all stared at a long list of numbers. Sandra pointed to one number Perry had called at least six times.

"Do you recognize that number?" Maya asked.

"Maybe," Sandra said, studying it.

Sandra hunted inside her Gucci bag for her phone, found it and then typed in her passcode. She hastily typed the number into her list of contacts. She held up the phone in front of her face as her mouth dropped open in shock.

"Yes. I've called it on many occasions when we've had to team up to stump for our spouses."

"Well, who does it belong to?" Maya asked.

"Lou Dooley," Sandra said, still not quite believing it.

"Who's that?" Oscar asked, clueless.

Maya already knew the answer and was as stunned as Sandra. She turned to Oscar. "Senator Elisabeth Dooley's husband."

Chapter Thirty-Six

The State Theatre, located on Congress Street, boasting a combination of Moorish and Art Deco architecture, had been a go-to performing arts venue since 2010, but tonight this historic building was hosting a pep rally for enthusiastic voters supporting the reelection of their beloved Senate representative in Washington, Elisabeth Dooley.

The nearly nineteen hundred seats in the theater were filled and it was standing room only in the back as a popular, three-term congressman from Maine's second congressional district, a vet of the Afghanistan and Iraq wars, young, energetic and handsome, stood behind the podium on stage, praising the litany of impressive accomplishments Maine had enjoyed under the stalwart leadership of Senator Dooley.

Backstage, Sandra and Maya stood in the wings, watching Senator Dooley, who was at the moment confabbing with a few of her staff as well as her fellow senator, Stephen Wallage, who was on deck to introduce her from the podium once the young, movie-star handsome congressman wrapped up his rousing speech.

After Sandra did some fast checking and discovered

that Senator Dooley had a rally tonight at the State Theatre, where her loyal, puppy dog of a husband Lou would surely be in attendance, Maya and Sandra had swung by the Wallage house for a quick change of clothes. Sandra was still technically a senator's wife, and there were unwritten rules about her appearance. She could not necessarily show up in a pair of jeans and a ragg wool sweater from L.L.Bean, so she had shed her clothes and slipped into a stylish rose, knot-front kimono dress and high heels. This had made Maya feel supremely underdressed, so Sandra had lent her a lovely pink, leopard-print, long-sleeved satin midi Leith wrap dress Sandra had ordered from Nordstrom but turned out to be too big for her. Maya filled it out perfectly. As Sandra fussed with Maya's hair and perused lipstick shades to draw on her face, Maya felt the need to remind Sandra that she was not suddenly Sandra's makeover project.

Once Sandra was satisfied, they headed off to the rally, where they turned heads as they bypassed security thanks to Sandra's VIP status and watched the rally from back-stage, hoping to locate and corner Lou Dooley the first chance they got.

Hot congressman from the second district had just finished his speech to rapturous applause. As he glided off the stage, waving to the adoring crowd, his eyes settled on Maya, and he lit up, obviously dazzled. He slowed down, about to introduce himself, but before he had the chance, one of Senator Dooley's staffers whisked him away to talk to a reporter. He managed to get a quick wink out to Maya before he passed by.

Sandra nudged Maya. "See, I told you. You look stunning in that dress."

"We're not here to get me a date, okay? Any sign of him?" Maya asked, glancing around.

Sandra shook her head. "Not yet."

It was Stephen's turn to speak.

He shook off his blazer, rolled up his sleeves and loosened his tie, going for his reliable, man-of-the-people look. Then, he marched confidently toward the stage, stopping only to acknowledge his wife, who he was seeing for the first time that day.

"I didn't think you were going to come," he said to Sandra, genuinely surprised.

"I changed my mind," Sandra said.

He noticed her dress. "You look beautiful."

"Thank you."

He turned to Maya. "You too, Maya."

Maya shifted uncomfortably, never one to easily accept compliments. She just nodded with a tight smile. She had only met Stephen once, when he was up from DC to see the boys, shortly after she and Sandra had begun working together.

"Showtime," Stephen said with a smile as he bounded out on the stage. The audience erupted in shouts and applause. It was a friendly crowd, mostly made up of party faithfuls.

Sandra scanned everyone jammed backstage and saw Lou Dooley hovering near his wife, who was now giving a quick interview to a local reporter. "There he is."

Lou was not a charismatic man. If he had not been wearing a daring botanical-print blazer, he might have faded into the backstage wallpaper. Lou had always claimed to be content to allow his far-more-magnetic wife to take center stage. He seemed happiest standing off to the side, soaking up a few of the rays from her blinding national fame.

Sandra and Maya hustled over to Lou, who reacted with bewilderment at the sight of Sandra. "Stephen said you weren't going to make it."

"What are you talking about? I wouldn't miss it," Sandra fibbed.

"I'm sure Elisabeth will appreciate you being here," he said, turning his attention back to Stephen, out on stage, who was now whipping up the crowd. He had not seen Maya yet.

He was about to move away from them when Sandra reached out and grabbed some fabric of his tacky blazer. "Oh, by the way, Lou, have you met my partner, Maya Kendrick?"

He stopped and turned around. His face suddenly drained of color at the sight of Maya, who smiled innocently.

"N–no, I-I don't believe I have," he stuttered. "Lou Dooley."

Maya nodded.

He shakily held out a hand, but Maya didn't take it.

"We were hoping we could talk to you," Maya said flatly.

Lou shot a look over toward his wife, who was completely oblivious to her now discombobulated husband, having just finished a quick TV interview and now flipping through some notes she had written down on a small stack of index cards.

Lou backed away. "I'm afraid I can't . . . Elisabeth is about to take the stage and I want to go out in the audience to watch from a good vantage point."

"It's very important, Lou," Sandra said sternly.

"I–I'm s-sorry, maybe later, after the speech. . ." he stammered as he backed into a spotlight, nearly knocking it over. A stagehand raced over to reposition it.

"It's about Cole Perry," Maya said loudly.

Lou nearly collapsed to the floor on the spot at the mention of Perry, but he unconvincingly tried to slap on a befuddled expression. "I–I don't know anybody by that name."

"That's odd. According to his phone records, the two of you spoke on a number of occasions," Sandra said.

"No, t–that's impossible—" Lou squeaked, eyeing his wife, who was just about to go onstage and was a little curious why her husband suddenly looked so alarmed.

From the stage, they could hear Stephen yelling into the microphone above the deafening cheers, "Give it up for your United States Senator, Elisabeth Dooley!"

Senator Dooley tore her eyes away from her addled husband and strutted out onto the stage, excitedly waving to the boisterous crowd. Stephen gave her a big bear hug and then she took his place behind the podium. Stephen stepped back a few feet but did not leave the stage.

Meanwhile, behind the curtain, Lou Dooley was having a meltdown. "I'm sure I–I don't know what you're talking about. If a call was made to this person from my phone, I didn't make it," Lou said emphatically.

He nervously glanced at Maya.

Sandra noticed. "You seem to recognize my friend Maya here. Are you sure you two haven't met?"

"Yes, I'm sure!" Lou barked.

"So you're saying perhaps one of your wife's staffers borrowed your phone and made the six calls to Mr. Perry? Is that your story?" Maya asked, folding her arms.

Lou nodded nervously. "Yes, that's the only plausible explanation—"

"I have another plausible explanation," Maya said, inching closer to him, intimidating him. "Cole Perry is known as a fixer. Someone you call to fix your problems. And you were facing a big one. Your wife, who is in the middle of a big reelection campaign for her senate seat, was about to be exposed in a college admissions kickback scheme involving Coach Josh Kirby."

"I have no clue what you're talking about," Lou said.

He was a terrible liar. The guilt wasn't just written all over his face. It was embroidered.

Maya almost gleefully plowed ahead with her theory. "Coach Kirby was getting cold feet. He was going to blab everything to the authorities. Your wife would have been swept up in it because she paid Kirby to get your daughter, Kendra, into college on a field hockey scholarship, a sport she didn't even play."

"If the truth came out," Sandra said solemnly, "Elisabeth's campaign would have sunk, not to mention the legal exposure she would be facing."

"So you hired a two-bit thug to rough up Kirby as a warning. Keep him from talking. But then you found out there was a detective out there, poking around, who was close to uncovering the whole scandal, so you enlisted Perry's help again to intimidate her too," Maya said. "Unfortunately for you, I don't intimidate easily."

Lou bowed his head.

There was no point in arguing. He knew he had been caught.

"I–I had no idea you two knew each other. . . ." Lou groaned. "I swear, Sandra, Kirby never mentioned you by name. I never would have knowingly done anything to harm you—"

"Just my partner," Sandra spat out.

Lou raised an eyebrow. "*Partner?*"

"Yes, I'm a private detective."

"Not licensed yet," Maya quietly reminded her.

"I will be soon," Sandra said through clenched teeth, shooting her a look. Then she turned back to Lou Dooley. "We're a team. You go after one of us, you go after both of us."

Lou decided to shift gears, try to clean up his monumental mess. "Look, can't we talk about this? I may have made a few rash decisions, but I'm sure we can work something out—"

"You're pathetic, Lou," Sandra scoffed. "Does Elisabeth even know what you were willing to do to protect her?"

Sandra noticed Senator Dooley onstage, addressing the audience, railing against her opponent Hal Dunlap, a Republican state senator, but keeping one eye on the commotion happening in the wings. She stumbled over her words a few times because she was obviously distracted. She could tell that something major was happening, and that it was not good.

Stephen also was now aware of the scene and was in a much better position to investigate because he was just onstage for moral support. He soundlessly exited the stage and joined Sandra and Maya as they surrounded Lou Dooley, who was melting in front of them.

"What's going on?" Stephen asked.

"Ask Lou," Sandra said pointedly.

Suddenly, Lou grabbed Maya and shoved her. She smacked into a wall and Lou made a run for it. He got about twenty feet when he was intercepted by Lieutenant

Beth Hart and Detective Roman Marino. Maya and Sandra had alerted Hart on their way to the State Theatre, so they could be positioned outside to move in and grab Lou in the likely event he tried to escape.

Marino began gruffly reading Dooley his rights as they handcuffed him. That grabbed the attention of the press backstage, all of whom swarmed over to find out what exactly was happening and why the husband of the senator rallying the crowd onstage was suddenly being placed under arrest.

Senator Dooley could not see her husband being led out of the theater in handcuffs, but she instinctively knew something intense and dramatic was continuing to unfold backstage.

After Sandra explained what was happening to Stephen, whose mouth hung open in disbelief, he slowly, sadly made his way to the wings and, after signaling Senator Dooley, gave her the signal to quickly wrap up her speech.

She could tell from Stephen's ashen face that this was probably not just a small fire they would have to put out. This was a full-on, raging California wildfire that would burn through and flatten her campaign.

Chapter Thirty-Seven

After abruptly ending the rally, Senator Dooley's team, along with Stephen and Sandra, immediately retreated to the senator's campaign headquarters in downtown Portland. Maya, who instinctively knew her presence would be neither welcome nor tolerated, decided to hang back and not insinuate herself. These were more Sandra's people.

A somber mood hung over the whole staff as they slowly came to realize that the future of the campaign was now in jeopardy. The only one not accepting this cold, hard fact yet was the senator herself. She remained defiant, obstinate and unrepentant as details of her husband's troubling actions emerged. She even considered painting him as a lone wolf, making his own decisions, none of which she approved of or endorsed in any way. Sandra watched in awe as Elisabeth Dooley was perfectly willing to throw her devoted husband right under the proverbial bus.

It was chaos at first, as staffers argued and panicked over how to handle a situation that was rapidly deteriorating, and Stephen rather forcefully suggested the key players find a quiet office where they could deconstruct events and come up with a plan. Senator Dooley finally agreed, calling the family lawyer and ordering him to go straight to the police station, where Lou was being booked. Sandra tagged along behind Stephen as he escorted Elisabeth, her campaign manager and her communications director to a corner office where they all hustled in, unintentionally leaving the door slightly ajar.

"We can get ahead of this," Senator Dooley said, a hint of desperation in her voice.

Sandra was stunned by her lack of understanding of the position she was in.

So was Stephen, and he wasn't shy about saying so. "Elisabeth, don't delude yourself. This is bad. Your husband's just been arrested for conspiracy to commit murder, and you're knee-deep in this college admissions scandal. This is not going to simply go away."

"I may have been a little overzealous in trying to get Kendra into a good school. All parents do things out of the box if it helps their kids—"

"What you did is *illegal*!" Stephen barked. "You bribed a high school coach to claim your daughter was a star field hockey player when she's never played the sport in her life!"

Senator Dooley grimaced.

She knew it was wrong. But she still wasn't willing to admit it.

Not yet.

"What else?" Stephen asked.

"I–I'm not sure what you mean—" Dooley sputtered.

"What else is out there that we don't know about?" Stephen barked.

"There's nothing . . ."

The campaign manager, a young, good-looking, ambitious millennial, cleared his throat.

Senator Dooley flicked her eyes toward him, then sighed. "Okay, there was one other small thing."

Stephen also let out a heavy sigh. "Tell me."

"I fudged a little detail in order to give Kendra at least a fighting chance for a better SAT score because she's a terrible test taker. She always has been. She panics when she gets too stressed and freezes up, so I wanted to give her a little more time to get the answers right."

"What did you fudge?" Stephen demanded to know.

Senator Dooley hemmed and hawed.

"Elisabeth, this is no time to hold back. Your entire campaign is hanging in the balance," the campaign manager said quietly.

Dooley sighed. "I told the test officials that Kendra has attention deficit hyperactivity disorder. . . ."

"Why?" Stephen asked.

"Because kids with that affliction have brains that are unable to screen out distractions, like someone sneezing or the rustling of papers, so they're allowed to take the test in a secluded room by themselves."

"Oh my God . . ." Stephen muttered.

"Come on, it's not *that* bad," Senator Dooley scoffed.

"Yes, Elisabeth," Stephen said solemnly. "It *is*."

"What was I supposed to do? Kendra needed a boost to get into a decent school, let alone an Ivy League one."

"How do you know?"

All eyes turned to the person asking the question.

It was Sandra.

Dooley gave Sandra an icy stare.

It was obvious the senator blamed her for this entire mess, for poking her nose in where it did not belong. None of this would be happening right now if it had not been for Stephen's meddling, bored wife, who needed a hobby.

"How do I know *what*?" Dooley asked, dripping with disdain.

"How do you know she needed a boost? You could have just let her try on her own," Sandra said in a hushed tone.

"And risk her winding up at a community college? I hardly think so. Kendra is a frustratingly average student. Lou and I came to that sobering conclusion very early on, that our only child, bless her heart, is not exceptionally gifted when it comes to academics."

There was silence in the room.

Sandra heard someone sniff behind her and turned to see Kendra standing just outside the door, which was open slightly, listening to everything her mother was saying about her.

When she saw Sandra staring at her, she bolted.

Sandra hurried out after her. She chased her down before she fled out of the headquarters into the chilly, wet streets from the heavy downpour just a few minutes earlier.

"Kendra, wait—"

"My life is ruined!" Kendra wailed, tears streaming down her apple cheeks.

"No, it's not. . . ."

"I'll forever be known as a liar and a cheat! I know a girl, a really nice girl, who has that attention disorder, and now she'll probably never talk to me again because my parents used it to—"

"I know this doesn't make it right, but your parents did what they did because they love you—"

"They're embarrassed by me! My mother always has been, because I'm not beautiful and perfect and great in school like she was! Do you know I didn't even want to go to college? I wanted to take a year off and backpack around Europe with some friends, figure out what I wanted to do, maybe find a way to help people, join the Peace Corps, but no, my mother insisted I apply to colleges, all the top schools. Can you imagine that, with my grades? And now look what's happened!"

Sandra couldn't argue Kendra's point.

She was right. What her parents had done to her was appalling.

But everyone could find a way to rise above the adversity they faced in life. It was just harder for a young girl, not yet of voting age, trying to find her way, still so vulnerable and impressionable, who up to now had very little say in how she lived her life thanks to her obnoxiously controlling parents.

Kendra broke down, sobbing.

Sandra hugged her tightly and gently patted her back. "You will get through this, and on the other side, things will look sunnier, I promise."

Sandra believed her words. She knew it would get better for Kendra eventually.

But right now, she could see this poor girl overcome with a crippling sense of hopelessness.

After a long few minutes consoling Kendra, Sandra took her to a coffee shop next door and bought her a hot chocolate and a peanut butter cookie. They hung out together, mostly in silence, until Kendra's eyes were dried of tears and she was on her phone texting a few friends she trusted for moral support. Once Sandra was reasonably certain that Kendra was in a better place emotionally, she left her there to wait for a couple of friends who were on their way to meet her.

Sandra returned to the campaign headquarters and the corner office where Stephen was still presiding over the emergency meeting with Dooley and her staffers. The senator was still ignorant of the fact that her daughter had overheard her harsh words about her. Sandra was determined to remedy that with an earful once she got Elisabeth Dooley alone.

Still in a cloud of denial, Senator Dooley slapped down her hand on a desk. "Okay, what are our options?"

There was an uncomfortable silence.

Senator Dooley raised an eyebrow. "Anybody?"

Stephen rubbed his chin, looking down at the floor, then he raised his eyes to meet Dooley's. "Elisabeth, I'm afraid there is only one option. You need to drop out of the race."

"*What?*" Senator Dooley gasped. "No, absolutely not!"

"It's the only chance we have of saving the seat. We can recruit Congressman Harkins to take your place in the primary."

Harkins was the handsome young vet who had just delivered such a rousing speech at the rally.

Senator Dooley, suddenly terrified as it began dawning on her that her privileged life as a powerful US senator was slipping through her fingers, choked out, "No . . ."

She was still in a state of denial.

But the fight was gone. The grim reality finally began to creep in.

Senator Dooley's shoulders sagged, and she sank down into a chair, covering her distraught face with her hands, and cried.

Chapter Thirty-Eight

Sandra's head was down as she rummaged through her bag for her phone to call Maya with the surprising, soon-to-be-top-of-the-news-cycle story of Senator Dooley's impending resignation, and she wasn't watching where she was going. Suddenly, without warning, she smacked into someone, shoulders colliding, and they both stumbled back.

Sandra raised her eyes to see Deborah Crowley rubbing her upper arm with one hand while clutching her own phone in the other.

There was an awkward silence before either of them spoke.

"I'm so sorry . . . I was texting and wasn't paying attention. . . ." Deborah said numbly as the two women stared at each other uncomfortably.

"It's okay . . . I was distracted myself. . . ."

Another excruciating pause.

Finally, realizing she was going to have to take the reins in order to sidestep this agonizingly awkward moment, Sandra took a deep breath, plowed ahead and stuck out her hand. "Deborah, right? Sandra Wallage. We met some months ago at my husband's office in Washington."

"Oh, yes," Deborah said with a nervous giggle. "It's so nice to see you again, Mrs. Wallage."

The two women tentatively shook hands.

"Sandra, please."

Another arduous lull in the conversation.

This time Deborah took charge. "Were you in with Senator Dooley just now? I heard something happened at the rally."

Sandra nodded soberly. "Yes. You should probably talk to Stephen."

"That doesn't sound good," Deborah whispered, concerned.

Sandra shook her head, replying ominously, "It's not."

Deborah's phone buzzed. She glanced down at the screen. "Speak of the—"

She stopped short, catching herself, embarrassed.

"Devil?" Sandra asked, almost enjoying herself as she witnessed the dread on Deborah's face over her obvious faux pas.

There was a quick nod from Deborah. Some of her long, luxurious auburn hair fell in front of her face and she restlessly tucked it behind her right ear.

"You'd better go. I'm sure he's anxious to fill you in," Sandra said.

Deborah cleared her throat. "Stephen and I have been working on some legislation together, and we've been talking to Elisabeth about cosponsoring the bill—"

"Deborah, you don't have to do this."

Deborah tried playing innocent. "Do what?"

"Make excuses."

"Oh . . ." Deborah's whispery voice trailed off.

"I've suspected for some time," Sandra said flatly.

"It's not what you—"

Sandra raised her hand curtly. "Deborah, please. Stephen's a grown man and can make his own decisions."

Deborah looked down at the floor, and her hair fell in front of her face again. She tried securing it behind her ear one more time. She was flustered, and Sandra thought she might break down in tears. The woman must have imagined this moment a hundred times, but now that it was here, she still wasn't ready for it.

The fact was, Sandra almost felt sorry for her.

Almost.

Deborah's phone buzzed again.

Sandra tried not to give her any kind of sharp, inflamed look. No, a mask of calm was what was called for now. She didn't want Deborah to be on the defensive, at least not here at Senator Dooley's busy, bustling campaign headquarters in front of all the staffers, some of whom were pretending to make donor calls but were clearly straining to eavesdrop on their conversation.

"Sounds like he really wants to talk to you," Sandra said.

Deborah nodded again, and her whole body seemed to sag, defeated, as if some personal mission to keep her boyfriend's wife in the dark for a little while longer had failed spectacularly.

Sandra abruptly brushed past her and headed out the door to call Maya. She didn't have to hear anymore from Deborah Crowley. There was no point. She could tell from the wounded, uneasy, shrinking expression on the younger woman's face what she had already known deep down in her gut.

Deborah Crowley was in love with her husband.

Chapter Thirty-Nine

When Sandra entered the foyer of her house she heard intense whispering coming from the living room. Curious, she headed that way. At the sound of her heels clicking on the hardwood floor, the whispering instantly ceased. She rounded the corner to see crackling flames in the fireplace and three boys, two of them her own, seated side by side on the couch with glum looks on their faces. The third boy was Daniel, Henry Yang's son.

"Oh God, who died?" Sandra asked tentatively.

Jack stood up, obviously distressed, eyes pooling with tears. He shook his head. "Nobody."

"Then what happened?" Sandra asked, eyeing Ryan, who stared bleakly at the floor. Daniel had an empty look on his face. But then again, the two times she had met him before, he'd always had that same blank expression and didn't look any different now.

Jack flicked his eyes toward his younger brother, as if unable to speak. Ryan looked up and said gravely, "Jack got a letter today."

Sandra's heart sank.

Boston Tech.

Jack's first choice. He had been rejected.

Sandra went to hug her son. "Oh, Jack, I'm so sorry."

Jack shrugged, trying to remain strong, but then he wrapped his arms around his mother and wept openly. After a moment, he pulled out the letter from his back pocket and handed it to her before spinning around and covering his face with his hands.

"I thought you were a shoo-in. Not even the wait list?" Sandra asked as she unfolded the piece of paper. She began reading.

Dear Mr. Wallage, it is with great pleasure that we inform you that you have been accepted for the class of. . .

For a second, Sandra thought her eyes were playing tricks on her and she was reading what she had hoped the letter would say, but then, after rereading the opening again, it finally dawned on her that she was being punked. She looked up to see Jack exuberant, a giant grin on his face.

"What?" Sandra gasped.

"I got in!" Jack cried.

Sandra glanced over at Ryan, who was doubled over laughing on the couch. As for the resolutely unemotional Daniel, he looked pretty much the same as he had before.

Sandra sighed, relieved, and wagged a finger in Jack's face. "I thought your brother was the actor around here!"

"I have to admit," Ryan guffawed, popping up from the couch and joining them, "he was very believable! But it should be noted I did give him tips on how to work up a few tears to make it look real."

"This is wonderful news. I'm so proud of you, honey," Sandra practically sang because she was so overjoyed.

"Daniel got in too!" Jack exclaimed.

Sandra turned to Daniel, who remained on the couch, hunched over, not exactly in a jubilant mood.

"Congratulations, Daniel," Sandra said.

Daniel shrugged. "Thanks."

"Was Boston Tech your first choice?" Sandra asked.

"Yeah . . ." Daniel replied with all the enthusiasm of being told he needed a root canal.

"Your dad must be thrilled," Sandra said.

Daniel bristled at the mention of his father.

"Does he know yet?" Sandra asked curiously.

Daniel nodded. "I'm sure he does."

Sandra clapped her hands, elated. "Well, this is cause for a celebration. How about I take you all out to dinner?"

"I can't," Ryan said, checking his watch. "I have theater rehearsal tonight. Vanessa's picking me up in a few minutes." He slapped his brother on the back before sauntering out of the room. "Way to go, bro."

"Thanks, man," Jack said.

"But I'm taking over your room the minute you leave for college," Ryan reminded him.

Jack being the oldest got the larger bedroom, and Ryan had made no secret of wanting it the moment his brother finally flew from the nest.

Jack turned to his mother. "That's the only reason he's happy for me. More space to move around in when he's staging his acting monologues."

Sandra folded her arms. "Then I guess it's just the three of us for dinner. How does Mexican sound?"

Daniel glanced at his phone. "That's Bert. He's waiting

for me outside. I have to go. Sorry I can't stick around and go eat with you."

"Next time, then," Sandra called after him as he hurried out the door. She spun back around to Jack. "Who's Bert?"

"His personal driver," Jack said.

Sandra cocked an eyebrow. "Daniel has a personal driver?" She marched over to the living room window and peered out to see Daniel shuffling down the walk and climbing into the back seat of a large black sedan. When he shut the door the sedan peeled away.

"How come I can't have a personal driver?" Jack asked.

"You can, once you come up with an idea like Facebook or Uber, but until then it's carpools and your bike when the weather is warmer," Sandra said.

"I'm officially a college student now, so can I have a margarita tonight to celebrate my acceptance to BT?" Jack asked with a sly smile.

"Absolutely. I hear Guerrero Maya makes a mean virgin margarita."

"Seriously?"

"You're officially a college student who is still officially underage."

Jack feigned exasperation with his mother. "Fine. I'll get my coat."

As Jack ambled out of the living room, Sandra followed him to the closet in the foyer. "Jack, I'm surprised Daniel wasn't more enthusiastic about getting accepted to BT."

Jack seemed to hem and haw a bit as he grabbed his coat and put it on. "That's just Daniel. He's not the type to get too excited about anything."

"But still, it's a pretty big accomplishment," Sandra pressed, suspecting there was a little more to the story. "I would think he would show a little joy."

"Daniel never really wanted to go to college, but he didn't have much of a choice because his father insisted and forced him to apply. I think Daniel would have been happier being a plumber or a carpenter, doing something with his hands, but his dad wouldn't hear of it."

"He must have had good grades, though," Sandra said, fixing her gaze on Jack, who seemed uncomfortable discussing this topic. "Jack . . ."

"Daniel had average grades . . . some would say *below* average. . ."

"Then how did he get in?"

"Soccer scholarship."

"I didn't know Daniel played soccer."

Jack buttoned up his coat and made a beeline for the door.

"Jack . . ."

"What?"

"Was Daniel on the soccer team last year when you played?"

"I don't remember . . ." Jack said, obviously lying.

"Daniel is your friend. I am pretty certain you would remember."

Jack sighed. "No, he wasn't."

"Then how on earth did he get a *soccer* scholarship?"

"I don't know!" Jack snapped. "Maybe you should ask Mr. Yang. Now, are we going to talk about Daniel all night or are we going to celebrate me not having to go to my safety school next year?"

"Let's go," Sandra sighed, waving him out to the car.

Sandra was numb.

She couldn't believe it. A part of her thought she should not be surprised. But she was.

It was becoming apparent that Senator Dooley was not the only parent deeply involved in this scandalous college admissions scheme.

Henry Yang was mixed up in it as well.

Chapter Forty

"You don't seem at all surprised," Sandra remarked as she handed over a coffee she had picked up at Starbucks on her way over to Maya's house. Maya had finally been able to slow down after rushing around all morning and pushing Vanessa out the door in time to catch the school bus, before Sandra had shown up at her door to pick her up so they could ride around together, doing some follow-up investigative work on the case.

Before Maya had even had the opportunity to say, "Good morning," Sandra had urgently updated her on what she now strongly suspected about Henry Yang.

"I guess I'm not surprised," Maya said with a shrug, sipping her coffee and slipping into her favorite brown suede jacket before ushering Sandra out of her house and locking the door behind them.

Sandra seemed frozen in place as Maya brushed past her toward Sandra's Mercedes, parked in the driveway.

"Why not?" Sandra asked, curious.

Maya knew this moment would come. She had kicked it down the road for as long as possible. But now was the time she was going to have to deal with it.

Gripping her coffee, she fixed her gaze on Sandra and said evenly, "I went to see Max and he told me—although he probably shouldn't have—that Henry Yang is under FBI investigation."

Sandra was knocked back on her heels. "What?"

"For illegal practices involving his business. So it doesn't seem like such a shock that he would be caught up in something like this college admissions scandal."

Sandra swallowed hard. "How long have you known this?"

The question was unexpected. Maya at first didn't see the relevance, but after a few moments it dawned on her why Sandra would be asking, and she suddenly dreaded where this conversation seemed to be going.

"A couple of days," Maya said quietly.

"A couple of *days*?" Sandra cried.

"I know, I know, I should have told you sooner—"

"Yes, you *should* have! It might have been helpful if I had known the man I have been seeing was the subject of an FBI criminal probe!"

"I didn't want you to panic until we knew for sure—"

"Panic? What am I to you, a hysterical housewife? I'm your partner! I would have called and told you *right away*!"

Maya was now fully cognizant of the fact that it had been a terrible mistake to sit on the information Max had given her. She took a baby step toward Sandra, who still stood numbly in the driveway. "I'm sorry, you're right."

"I thought we were friends . . ." Sandra mumbled, disappointed.

"We are. I guess I was just trying to protect you."

"From what?"

"From getting hurt. In hindsight, it was a dumb move. I can see that now—"

"I don't need or want you protecting me," Sandra said icily. "I want you to treat me like your equal. I came into this situation with my eyes wide open. I know I'm not as seasoned in this kind of work as you are—"

"This has nothing to do with—"

"Yes, it does," Sandra snapped, cutting her off. "Ever since we started this, you've treated me with kid gloves. I know I'm an amateur, that I don't have any experience, but this is real for me. This is not just some fun hobby for the bored housewife, exhausted from her husband's political career, in search of some amusing outlet, who fancies herself as a private eye between PTA meetings. . . ."

"I know that, Sandra. . . ."

"Then don't patronize me, or sugarcoat anything, or hide things from me that you think I can't handle. I know I'm not a sharpshooter, or a down and dirty street fighter like you, but I'm tough in my own way. . . ."

Maya nodded, chastised.

Sandra raised an admonishing finger and pointed it at Maya. "If we're going to be partners in this, I need to be as hard as nails, like you are."

"You're right," Maya agreed. "I promise to be more direct with you from here on in."

"Thank you," Sandra said in a clipped tone. "Now, let's go."

Sandra clicked her remote, unlocking the door to her Mercedes, then huffily got behind the wheel.

Maya quietly smirked at Sandra's renewed assertiveness as she marched over and opened the passenger side door of the Mercedes and plopped in the seat next to Sandra.

As Sandra put the car in Reverse, turned her head around and slowly backed out of the driveway, Maya could not help but comment, "Although we both know you're too damn sweet to ever really scare people the way I do."

Sandra's hard exterior cracked just a bit. "I know . . ." she moaned.

Maya laughed.

She sipped her coffee, relieved that it looked as if they would get past this.

Chapter Forty-One

Josh Kirby, who had appeared so youthful and energetic when Maya first met him, now seemed to have aged ten years as he wandered around his office in a daze, packing photographs of himself from his college football days and some sports memorabilia and collectibles, most notably a baseball autographed by his favorite players from the Red Sox, into a large cardboard box.

Maya and Sandra stood in the doorway, watching him shuffle around, broken and defeated. When they arrived at the school early that morning, they had no idea the school board had taken swift action, terminating Kirby effective immediately once word of his role in the college admissions scandal had reached the local press and the first story had made its way to the front page of the *Portland Press Herald*.

Josh had assumed Maya and Sandra were there to gloat, humiliate him even further over his illegal wrongdoing. But that simply was not the case. They had shown up at his office to discuss another matter, only to find the beleaguered new coach cleaning out his office, ready to go into hiding.

"You have no idea what it was like for me lifting weights at the gym yesterday, like I do every day, and then seeing this army of FBI agents storm in, surround me in front of all my workout buddies, slap handcuffs on me and drag me out of there as people snapped pictures of me with their phones. . . ." Josh stared wistfully at a framed photo he had taken off the wall, of himself wearing a football uniform in his college days, in happier times. He tossed it into the box. "Then, to see my parents at the arraignment this morning, so heartbroken and ashamed, it was just too much. They're going to have to take out a second mortgage to cover the bail money they posted. I can't see things getting any worse than this."

Maya neglected to mention that things were about to get a whole lot worse given the heap of legal trouble Josh Kirby now found himself in. A hefty prison sentence was certainly not off the table at this point.

Josh finally sighed, glancing around the office to make sure he had not missed any of his personal belongings. "Getting fired is almost a relief. At least I won't have to endure the judgmental, angry looks from my students and fellow teachers."

Maya bit her tongue. This was all his own doing. In her mind, he was 100 percent responsible for the predicament he now found himself in.

Sandra adopted a more sympathetic, it's-always-darkest-before-the-dawn approach. "You're a strong man, Josh. You'll get through this."

Josh seemed to scoff at the notion of being strong. He shook his head silently, then looked up to see the portly, bald, sixtysomething security guard, Ned, a retired cop, hired by the high school, hovering in the doorway behind Maya and Sandra.

"Time to go, Josh," Ned said.

Josh picked up the cardboard box and looked at Maya. "You'll be happy to hear they're bringing Coach Cooper back to fill in until they can find my permanent replacement. He's agreed to put off starting in Chicago until next semester."

He was right. Maya was happy to hear this news.

She missed her old friend. But she didn't allow herself to smile because Josh Kirby was hurting enough as it was.

Josh circled around the desk, and Maya and Sandra parted so he could get by to where Ned was waiting to escort him off school grounds.

As he passed, shoulders slumped, head down, Sandra called after him, "What about Henry Yang?"

The air vibrated with tension.

Josh stopped in his tracks, his back to them. Ned gingerly placed a hammy hand on Josh's arm to keep him moving, but Josh shrugged it off and spun around. "What do you want to know?"

"How involved was he?" Sandra asked.

Josh laughed derisively. "How *involved*? He was the key figure in the whole operation."

Maya glanced at Sandra, who remained steady and calm on the outside, although Maya knew her well enough to realize she had just been gut-punched.

"He was the one who started the whole thing. He was the first parent to pay me off. Big check too. Money was clearly no object. Then he pointed other wealthy parents in my direction to help their own kids, including Senator Dooley. That was all Yang. All of it."

Ned, who was getting nervous about not carrying out his explicit orders to make sure Josh Kirby left the building

ASAP, squeezed his arm again. Josh shot him an irritated, dismissive look but turned back around and kept moving.

Sandra dashed over to the desk in his office, grabbed a pencil and a Post-it note and scribbled something down. She ran past Maya, caught up to Josh and Ned and pressed the note into the palm of Josh's hand.

"What's this?" Josh asked, staring at the note.

"The name of a good lawyer. I know him. He's a decent man and not too expensive. He'll help you."

Josh's eyes pooled with tears. He seemed mad at himself for suddenly getting emotional. That was obviously not the plan. He desperately wanted to keep up his tough exterior, but he had not expected anyone outside his family to help him after the despicable things he had done.

"Thank you," he choked out before allowing Ned to lead him away from the office, across the gymnasium, where a few boys, shooting hoops, stopped to watch their new coach leave the school for the last time.

Maya turned to see Sandra fuming. Her whole body seemed to be trembling, as if she was about to explode.

Maya opened her mouth to say something, but Sandra didn't stick around to give her a chance. She was suddenly marching for the exit.

Maya didn't have to ask where they were going. She already knew.

Sandra was now on a mission. And Maya would just be along for the ride.

Chapter Forty-Two

The attractive, wide-eyed receptionist stared at Sandra, trying her best to act natural, as if she had not instantly recognized her when Sandra breezed out of the elevator and over to the glass-topped desk where the girl sat with an earpiece attached to the side of her head like Lieutenant Uhura from the original *Star Trek* series.

"Sandra Wallage. I'm here to see Henry," Sandra said with a bright smile, acting as if she casually dropped by Henry Yang's high-rise Boston office every day.

"Yes, Mrs. Wallage . . . I mean, Ms. Wallage. I'm aware of who you are, but—"

"You were correct the first time."

The receptionist blinked at Sandra, confused. "I'm sorry—?"

"It's *Mrs.* Wallage. I'm still married to the Senator. Stephen Wallage? At least I am for now. . . ." Sandra chuckled, giving the girl a conspiratorial wink.

"Right," the receptionist said, nodding dumbly.

"Can you let Henry know I'm here?"

"I–I'm sorry, *Mrs*. Wallage," she said, punching the

Mrs. for emphasis. "He's in a meeting with his team and asked not to be disturbed."

"Of course. I understand," Sandra cooed.

The girl had a look of relief on her face.

"Why don't you buzz me in and I'll just wait in his office?"

The look of relief promptly dissipated.

Without waiting, Sandra circled around the desk and tried to open the locked door that led to the offices of Henry Yang's multinational tech firm. It didn't budge. Sandra whipped around and flashed the young woman a puzzled look.

She swallowed hard. "I'm afraid I can't let you in without speaking to Mr. Yang first, and as I told you, he's in a very important meeting. I have strict instructions not to interrupt—"

Sandra stiffened, her friendly demeanor slowly melting.

The young woman noticed her fading smile and it suddenly put her on edge. She appeared to be quickly racking her brain for an acceptable backup plan. "Why don't you have a seat on the couch over there and I would be happy to get you a cup of coffee and maybe a cheese Danish while you wait—?"

Sandra walked slowly back to the reception desk. The girl, literally on the edge of her seat, rolled away, the wheels of her chair grinding against the clear plastic mat underneath. She gripped the glass-topped desk, white-knuckled as she nervously anticipated Sandra's next move.

"What's your name?" Sandra asked coolly.

"Meg," the jittery girl choked out.

"That's a pretty name."

"Thank you," Meg said hesitantly.

Sandra got as close to the desk as she could, so she towered over Meg, who now sat slumped down in her seat like a submissive puppy.

"Like my favorite literary character, Meg March, in *Little Women*."

Meg nodded, pretending to understand, but it was rather apparent she had never read the book nor heard of the character. Still, she managed to nod and squeak out, "Yes."

"Meg, do you have a smartphone or a tablet at your disposal?"

Meg nodded tentatively, still very confused.

"And are you allowed to browse the internet on your desktop computer when you're not answering phone calls or greeting guests out here in reception?"

Meg furrowed her brow. "Um, yes?"

"Good. If that's the case, I'm sure you've seen at least some of the pictures of me and your boss floating around on all the news and gossip sites. Am I right in assuming that, Meg?"

Meg sat frozen, not sure what to do.

"*Meg?*"

"Yes, yes, I have!" Meg yelped, snapping to attention.

"And I'm sure you're aware that Henry does not like the details of his personal life splashed all over the internet. I mean, wouldn't you assume he would see that as a gross invasion of his privacy?"

Meg was ready this time. "I would, yes, I would definitely assume that!"

"Then don't you think it might be a mistake to force me to sit outside in this very public reception area for everyone to see when they get off the elevator, fueling the gossip and innuendo about my relationship with the head of this company?"

Meg's mind was racing as she processed this line of thinking, tentatively nodding, slowly getting it.

"Not to speak for Henry, mind you, but if I were him, I would be rather upset to find out my girlfriend was hanging out on display in reception like some Saks Fifth Avenue window mannequin."

Meg hastily reached underneath the desk to press a button. There was a buzzing sound, and Sandra could hear the lock click open. "Take a right, down the hall, corner office on the left."

Sandra leaned in and smiled at her warmly. "Thank you, Meg." She sashayed through the door, turned right and stopped, waiting for the door to close and lock again. Then, Sandra marched off in the opposite direction. She had no intention of waiting in Henry Yang's office for his meeting to break up.

Passing a long row of cubicles belonging to various assistants and managers, many of whom popped up their heads to see who was zipping past them, a few registering looks of surprise when they recognized the boss's new girlfriend, at least according to press reports.

Sandra ignored them all, rounding a corner and locating the main conference room. Through the walled glass, she could see Henry presiding over a meeting of his top executives. He looked happy, at ease, probably celebrating the latest profit report or recent stock prices.

She was about to ruin all that.

His eyes flicked in her direction, and his jaw dropped at the sight of her. He held up a finger to his people and made a beeline for the door, ready to intercept her. But

Sandra was too quick for him. She was inside the conference room before he had the chance.

"Sandra, this is a surprise," Henry said warily, looking at her, bewildered, totally mystified at what she was doing in Boston, what she was doing in his offices.

"I know. I hope you like surprises," Sandra said, almost giddy.

"I guess it depends . . ."

He was clearly thrown off-balance by her barging into his headquarters, and she could tell he was very worried about what was going to happen next.

Sandra took a place at the head of the conference table and addressed the room full of executives. "I'm sorry for rudely butting into your meeting, everybody, but I'll be brief, and then you can get back to it. As you can probably guess by now, the rumors are true. Why try to hide it anymore? I've been dating the big guy here. So tell me, you know him best, what should I know? Any skeletons in the closet I need to be worried about?"

The executives exchanged furtive looks, totally in the dark as to what was happening here. Was the boss's new girlfriend having a public meltdown? Should they start recording it with their phones and post it to social media?

Henry reached out for Sandra's arm, but she deftly avoided his touch and continued addressing everyone in the conference room. "Nobody? Oh, come on. Someone here must have *something* juicy to tell me."

No one was actually stupid enough to speak up.

Sandra shrugged. "Oh, well. Then maybe I'll start by sharing something with you. Henry should be given a lot of credit for his philanthropy. He's donated huge sums of money to worthy causes, and I applaud him for that."

Henry finally relaxed, falling into a false sense of security.

"But that doesn't excuse what else he's done."

His body tensed. "Sandra, I don't know what you're—"

Sandra spun around. "There have been a lot of hit pieces on Henry about his corrupt business practices, accusations of intellectual property theft; I really don't know anything about any of that. What I *can* tell you, however, is that your boss, Henry Yang, is a *lying cheat*."

Henry Yang stepped in front of Sandra, addressing his employees. "I'm sorry, everyone. I'm not sure what's going on here—"

"Do you want to tell them about how you bribed a high school coach to say your son was a star soccer player to leapfrog over more deserving kids just so he could get into a good college, a college *you* approved of?"

Henry stopped cold.

"Sandra . . ." he whispered.

"It would be bad enough if he stopped there. But no, he started a whole network for his friends, ridiculously wealthy parents eager to *buy* their children's way into the college admissions process, make a mockery of honest-to-goodness, old-fashioned hard work."

There was silence in the conference room. No one knew what to say, how to react.

Henry finally reached out and took Sandra's arm, desperate to get her out of there and regain control of the situation. "Sandra, now is not the time—"

She wrenched her arm free from his grip. "No, I think now is the perfect time to show your devoted team what kind of man they work for."

Henry recoiled, like a cobra ready to strike. "Don't be

so high-and-mighty, Sandra. You're the wife of a powerful US senator. I'm sure you've pulled a few strings once or twice over the years—"

"I'm not a saint. But I can safely say my son got into college without cheating."

The sound station in the middle of the conference room table lit up and Meg's shaky voice could be heard. "Excuse me, Mr. Yang?"

Henry erupted. "Not now, Meg! I told you I didn't want any interruptions!"

"Yes, sir, I know, but there are some people here—"

"What people?" Henry snapped.

"Hi, Meg!" Sandra said cheerily, leaning across the table to speak directly into the sound station. "Are they from the FBI?"

"Um, yes," Meg replied warily.

Henry shot Sandra an enraged look.

"I figured they would be right behind me after I tipped them off. Funny thing is, when I got them on the phone they told me they were already running an investigation on you, so you can't say that it's all my fault you got caught, Henry."

Henry glared at her, mouth agape. He could not believe what was happening.

Then, without warning, he bolted from the conference room and down the hall. Sandra turned to the group and smiled. "I bet he's heading for some secret back elevator; am I right?"

A couple of the shell-shocked executives nodded.

Sandra walked out of the conference room to see Henry Yang pacing back and forth in front of a private elevator next to his office. There was a ding and the elevator door opened, at which Yang was greeted by several

FBI agents and Maya. One of the agents pulled out a pair of handcuffs and snapped them on his wrists. Yang was now sweating, bouncing up and down, panicked. "Please, don't walk me out of the building like this. There's probably press outside. Can't you smuggle me out in a van or something?"

"They're just giving the public what they want," Maya cracked.

The FBI agents frog-marched Yang onto the elevator as Maya stepped out to join Sandra, who waltzed up to watch them whisk Henry Yang away.

As the elevator doors began to close, Sandra announced loudly for everyone in the office to hear, "In case it wasn't clear before, Henry, we are officially *through*."

Before he could respond, the elevator doors shut on him. And Henry Yang was gone.

Chapter Forty-Three

Henry Yang looked exhausted. He blinked his bloodshot eyes and ran a shaky hand through his wavy black hair as he stood outside the Boston high-rise that housed his company as a crush of reporters shoved microphones in front of his weary, drawn face. "I just want to say that this incident has nothing to do with the fine, upstanding people who work for me. Yes, I have failed personally . . . as a man, as a father . . . but I want to assure everyone that this company remains robust and strong. . . ."

Yang was desperately trying to do some necessary damage control. After his arrest, the stock price of his company had plunged nearly 37 percent on the Dow Jones. After word got out that he had pleaded guilty at his arraignment, the price did another nosedive, dropping 22 percent. There was a scramble to stop the bleeding and Yang, who had probably wanted to crawl inside a cave and hide out until all this bad publicity blew over, knew that to save all he had built, he needed to get out ahead of it. With all the evidence mounting against him, Yang instinctively knew a long court fight to preserve his reputation would be futile. The truth would come out eventually. Because he was, without a doubt, guilty as sin.

So the guilty plea was, in the end, the only direction he and his lawyers felt he could go. Coming out early and apologizing, appeasing the prosecutors, was his best hope for a lenient sentence, perhaps even no jail time at all. They had locked Martha Stewart away for five months and she had come back stronger than ever.

A full-throated mea culpa at a hastily arranged press conference had not been his first choice, but he had seen too many CEOs take a dizzying fall from grace after trying to lie their way out of a big mess.

"Will you be stepping down as CEO of your company?" a reporter from CNN yelled.

"I don't know . . ." Henry murmured, scanning the gaggle of reporters, desperate to change the subject.

"Were you the ringleader behind the kickback scheme?" someone from Fox News asked.

Henry Yang pursed his lips and lowered his head in shame.

The Fox reporter tried again. "Was this whole thing your idea?"

Unable to avoid the question any longer, Yang swallowed hard and nodded, choking out, "Yes."

Sandra, sitting on the couch with Jack in her living room, watching Henry Yang trying his best to appear contrite during his press conference on TV, did not feel sorry for him for what he was going through, or proud of him for quickly taking charge and coming clean.

In fact, she didn't feel much for him at all.

The person she most felt for at the moment was Yang's son, Daniel, who through no fault of his own, was now caught up in the eye of this category five storm. She had suspected from his skittish behavior when Jack had told her that Daniel had been accepted to the same college that Henry's son had been aware of what his father was doing. But she in no way blamed him for it. The boy had undoubtedly been under intense pressure to succeed, to ace his SAT tests, maintain a perfect GPA, be able to boast of a long, impressive list of extracurricular activities, including soccer, which he had never played at all. In Sandra's mind, Daniel Yang had only gone along to please his father, who was the actual cheater, the real criminal.

As if reading his mother's thoughts, Jack leaned forward on the couch, eyes fixed on the television mounted on the wall above the fireplace, and mumbled, "I feel so bad for Daniel. I can't imagine what he must be going through right now."

Sandra turned to her son. "You should call to check on him."

"I texted him about an hour ago, but he hasn't responded yet," Jack said solemnly.

"He's going to need you," Sandra said softly.

"I'll keep trying," Jack promised.

A reporter on TV shouted, "Did you have anything to do with Diego Sanchez's death?"

Henry Yang's face dropped. "*What?*"

The reporter jostled to get her microphone closer to Yang, nearly bumping it against his chin. "Some people are saying you poisoned him because he found out what you were doing and was threatening to expose you to the authorities!"

Yang vigorously shook his head. "No! That's vicious, unfounded gossip! Whoever is spreading it doesn't know a damn thing! Let me state for the record, I had nothing, repeat, nothing to do with Mr. Sanchez's murder! And I will sue any of you, and your news organizations, if you even hint otherwise!"

Sandra studied Yang's face intently. He appeared viscerally dismayed by the unexpected accusation. Sandra wanted to believe him. He at least seemed convincing in his denial. But given the recent facts that had come to light about Henry Yang, she certainly had no reason to trust anything that came out of the man's mouth again.

The lights from a car pulling into the driveway caught Sandra's attention. She stood up from the couch and peered out into the night to see who it was.

"That's probably Dad," Jack said.

Sandra cocked an eyebrow. "What's he doing here?"

She could see Stephen getting out of his Lexus, popping open the trunk and grabbing a suitcase.

"He emailed me this morning and said he was going to be coming home and staying in Maine for a while."

"Why?"

Jack shrugged. "It has something to do with Senator Dooley resigning."

"And he's staying *here*?"

Jack bristled slightly. "Where do you expect him to stay, Mom, a hotel? This is his home."

She didn't argue with him.

Jack was happy his dad was coming home if only temporarily. The family would be together again, under one roof. Jack hated his father living full-time in Washington, much more so than Ryan, and on some level, Sandra feared Jack blamed her for the whole separation.

But this was entirely inappropriate.

There were rules that had been put into place when they had sat down to hammer out the details of their separation. Cooking his homemade marinara sauce for the family and crashing in the guest room for one night was one thing. Moving back indefinitely was quite another.

Sandra marched out of the room and intercepted Stephen just as the front door opened and he entered with his suitcase. Stephen quickly raised a hand. "Hold on, don't get mad. This is not what it looks like."

Sandra folded her arms. "What is it, then?"

"Why haven't you been answering your phone? I've left at least five messages."

She knew he had been calling. But she had been so swept up in confronting Henry Yang and witnessing him arrested, she had ignored all his voice-mail messages. She'd figured she would get back to him later, but then, when she arrived home, Yang's press conference had started on TV, and she and Jack had dropped everything to watch it.

"Jack says you're going to be here for a while?"

"Yes. They put me in charge of the search for Elisabeth Dooley's replacement on the ticket."

"They, who?"

"The Democratic Party. We need a strong contender who can come in at the last minute and win, someone with name recognition, solid experience. So I've got to hit the ground running tomorrow. The election is only a few weeks away and we can't afford to have Hal Dunlap winning the seat."

Hal Dunlap was the Republican minority leader in the Maine state senate. Stephen despised him, not so much for his personality, but mostly for his brazen embrace of partisan politics that divided the people of his home state. He would do everything in his power to prevent Dunlap from snatching the election away from them. And Dunlap probably felt the same about them.

Stephen dropped his bag in the foyer. "Look, the reason I've been trying to reach you is because there is some convention in town, so all the hotels are booked. I just need a place to stay through the weekend and then I'll be out of your hair again. I promise. . . ." He picked up on her hesitation. "I won't even take the guest room. I can stay in the office, sleep on the pullout couch, you won't even know I'm here."

Jack had ambled out from the living room. "Can I take your bag upstairs for you, Dad?"

It was as if he was challenging his mother. Daring her to kick his father out of the house.

Sandra glared at Jack. She wanted him to know that she was fully aware of what he was doing and that it wasn't fair. But she had already made up her mind. She turned back to Stephen and gave him a slight nod.

Stephen smiled, relieved, then picked up his bag again and handed it to Jack. "Thanks, college boy. You can take it to the office."

Jack took the bag and headed off.

Stephen then flicked his eyes back to Sandra.

She could tell he knew she was not comfortable with this situation.

"Thank you," he said.

Chapter Forty-Four

Daniel Yang dove into his caramel sundae with a sharp focus that impressed Sandra, attacking it with such gusto she wondered if Henry Yang even allowed his son to consume any sugar at home.

Daniel sat across from Sandra and Jack in the turquoise booth of the popular diner near the Wallage house where they usually grabbed a fast meal at least once every weekend. She had asked Daniel if he would allow her to treat him and Jack to lunch there because she knew her two sons were major fans of the hot spot's extensive menu of greasy comfort food. Daniel had declined at first, but Jack worked hard to convince him to come and hear his mother out.

When they had first arrived and were seated in the corner booth, out of earshot from the buzzing lunch crowd, Daniel had slumped down in the booth opposite mother and son and never made eye contact with Sandra. Only when Jack spoke did Daniel occasionally glance up and nod. He had used the large, plastic menu as some kind of force field to separate himself from Sandra, who was directly opposite him. But when the harried, no-nonsense waitress had scribbled down their order on her pad and then snatched the menu out of Daniel's hands and scurried away, he was suddenly defenseless. He now had no choice but to finally acknowledge Sandra's presence. He clearly now considered her a sworn enemy.

When his double cheeseburger and curly fries arrived, he offered Jack his pickle because he hated them, and Sandra was relieved that at least he was willing to talk about something, even if it was just a kosher pickle. The second time he opened his mouth was to ask the passing waitress for more napkins; he had nervously wadded up the one in front of him into a ball, so when he needed to wipe a dab of ketchup from the side of his mouth, he was forced to use his shirtsleeve.

Sandra allowed him to polish off his burger, making small talk with Jack in the meantime. But once his dessert arrived and he was busy shoveling ice cream into his mouth, she finally reached out across the table and gently touched the boy's arm. "Daniel . . ."

He recoiled at her touch. His eyes narrowed and he was suddenly suspicious.

Sandra continued after quickly withdrawing her hand. "I just want you to know that I understand this is a very difficult time and I am here to help you in any way I can."

Daniel raised an eyebrow as he stared sullenly at her. "*Help?* You want to help me? This is all your fault!"

Jack looked down at his lap, nervously twisting his own napkin around his finger.

Daniel's face betrayed a plethora of emotions: fear, anger, hopelessness. He spat out, "BT has withdrawn my acceptance. They don't want me to be associated with the school in any way. You can imagine how good that feels!"

Jack decided to jump in and help Sandra. "My mom was only doing what she thought was—"

"Your mom was hired to find out who killed Diego Sanchez!" He whipped his head back toward Sandra, incensed. "How is that working out? Did you find the killer yet?"

Sandra slowly shook her head. "No, not yet."

"Maybe it's because you've been too busy ratting out my dad and destroying his life!"

Sandra and Jack exchanged sorrowful looks. They knew how much Daniel was hurting. He needed some way to get out his overwhelming frustration, someone to lash out at, and right now Sandra was the perfect punching bag.

"My life is over too, thanks to you!" he raged. He hurled his big silver spoon down on the table and watched the top of his sundae slowly start to melt.

They sat in silence for a few moments.

Jack sat back and folded his arms. "What your dad made you do isn't my mom's fault."

Daniel's lip quivered slightly. He wiped his nose with the same ketchup-stained shirtsleeve. "I know. . . ."

Sandra leaned forward. "Your life is *not* over, Daniel."

"It sure seems that way," Daniel mumbled. "Everybody's calling me a liar and a cheat. I'm not even eighteen yet and the consensus on social media is that I'm, for sure, like *done*."

"You're a strong, smart young man, Daniel. You will get past this," Sandra assured him.

Daniel stared at his lopsided, half-eaten sundae as vanilla ice cream dripped slowly down the sides of the tulip-shaped glass cup. "If I was so smart, I never would have pretended to be a soccer star and posed for those pictures kicking a ball around in somebody else's uniform."

"It's only because your dad pressured you," Jack argued.

Daniel looked up. "My dad—" He stopped suddenly,

staring at the door of the diner. His eyes widened. "My dad is here."

"What?" Sandra gasped, swiveling around in the booth.

Sure enough, Henry Yang was standing near the host station in the front of the diner. He was rubbing his hands together, blowing on them in an effort to warm them up from the chilly air outside. He spotted the three of them in the back, took a deep breath and then walked deliberately over to their booth. He forced a smile and nodded. "Hello, Sandra, Jack . . ."

They nodded back but said nothing.

Henry then turned his eyes toward Daniel. "Hi, son. . . ."

Daniel gazed up at his father, just in time to see Henry eyeballing the demolished ice cream sundae in front of him. "Please don't judge me like you usually do. I think I deserve it just this once, okay?"

Sandra's initial assumption had been right. Henry Yang rarely allowed his son to indulge in fattening sweets.

"I won't judge you," Henry said quietly.

"How did you find us?" Daniel asked, pressing a finger into a puddle of melted ice cream on the table and licking it off.

"Bert," Henry answered.

Bert may have been Daniel's personal driver, but he was on Henry's payroll, and it was probably part of the job description to keep him informed of his son's whereabouts while Henry was busy at the office.

"After you tried giving him the slip, he managed to follow you here, and then he called me," Henry explained.

Daniel rolled his eyes. "Figures. He knows who signs his checks."

The waitress breezed by and glanced at Henry. "Would you like to see a menu?"

"He's not staying," Daniel snapped.

The waitress shrugged and continued on her way.

Henry glanced at Sandra and Jack. "Would you mind giving us a little privacy?"

Sandra and Jack made a move to get up, but Daniel stopped them and blurted out coldly, "No! Why should they leave? You're the one who showed up here uninvited. Whatever you need to say, you can do it in front of them. I don't care."

Henry took another deep breath and exhaled. "Okay." He smiled apologetically at Sandra before returning his attention back to his son. "I know what I forced you to do was wrong, and I should have known better, but for what it's worth, in my own warped mind, I thought I was just helping give you a fair shot—"

Daniel bristled.

Henry raised his hands. "I know, I know, I made a huge mess of things, but I promise you, son, I will do whatever it takes to make it up to you—"

"How about you let me change my name and start a new life far away from here, without you around to ruin it? How about it, Dad? That sure works for me!"

Daniel slid out of the booth, pushed past his father and bolted out of the diner. Henry didn't run after him. He stood there, choked up, suffering inexpressible grief from the litany of misdeeds that had cost him the love and respect he had thought he enjoyed from his only son.

Jack turned to his mother. "I'm going to go make sure he's okay."

Sandra nodded. "Yes, of course, go."

Jack jumped out of the booth. "Excuse me, Mr. Yang."

Henry stepped aside, allowing Jack to chase after Daniel.

Sandra studied Henry. She could plainly see how uncomfortable it was for him to be so honest, so racked with messy emotions, especially in front of her. Maybe if he had allowed himself to be more human, she would not have kept her distance from him this whole time, at least emotionally.

Henry stared at Sandra vacantly. She wasn't sure if he was about to pick up what was left of the ice cream sundae and dump it on her head. After all, it was because of her that his company was now teetering on the edge and his son had pushed him away. She had upended his whole life. But he didn't lash out at her. In fact, he appeared more wounded than filled with rage.

"Sandra . . ."

He didn't sit down. Nor did she invite him to.

"I'd just like to explain—"

She cut him off. "No."

He appeared confused. "I'm sorry?"

"I don't need to hear you explain anything. What I need is for you to forget about me and get to work repairing your relationship with your son."

She opened her purse and slapped some money down on the table to pay the bill. Then she zipped it shut and stood up. "Good luck with your sentencing."

And with that, she marched out the door, praying he would take her advice, leaving Henry Yang behind her.

Forever.

Chapter Forty-Five

When Sandra and Jack arrived home, they could hear Stephen in the office, talking loudly on the phone. Sandra shed her jacket, hung it on the rack and followed the sound of her estranged husband's voice as Jack padded off into the kitchen to grab himself something to drink.

As Sandra entered the large office, she found Stephen pacing back and forth, shirtsleeves rolled up, his cell phone pressed to his ear. There were paper cups and left-over coffee cake crumbs on the desk from a Starbucks run, while on the opposite side of the room, Ryan sat behind the large oak desk. He was on the house phone, listening, while absentmindedly doodling a nonsensical picture on a notepad with a ballpoint pen.

"Mitch, I don't need an answer right now, but don't take too long. We wait too long, we risk the whole election . . ." Stephen bellowed. "I understand. . . ." He noticed Sandra standing in the doorway to the office and cupped a hand over his phone. "Too loud?"

Sandra shook her head, glancing over at Ryan, who looked bored listening to whoever was on the other end of his own call. He gave his mother a half-hearted wave.

"I know you're happy in the state congress, but this is your chance to be a United States *senator*. Opportunities like this don't come around very often. . . . Well, speak to Lydia and try to convince her this would be good for the whole family. Would you like me to call her?" Stephen listened and then rolled his eyes, irritated. "Where is she? A safari in South Africa? I'm sure she can take time out for a three-minute call between selfies with elephants!"

Sandra stepped forward and whispered, "Too aggressive."

Stephen nodded, then lowered his voice and spoke calmly. "No one deserves a vacation as much as Lydia. She works very hard. It's just that we're on the clock here, and if you don't make up your mind, I'm going to have to continue going down the list. And just so you know, it's a very short list." Stephen listened some more, then said abruptly, "Okay, call me back as soon as you talk to her."

He ended the call. "You would think Mitch Green would jump at the chance to take Elisabeth's place in the senate run. He's always been so nakedly ambitious. When did he start caring about spending too much time away from the family?"

Sandra smirked at the irony of Stephen's statement.

He caught himself. "That came out wrong."

Sandra decided to let it go. "What about Harkins?"

"A hard pass. He wants to run on his own timetable." She flicked her eyes toward Ryan, who was still doodling and holding the phone to his ear. "Who's he talking to?"

"I assigned him a list of skittish donors to call and gave him a few talking points to calm their fears about losing the election now that Elisabeth is out. Mostly he's just letting them rant, and then he reassures them that everything is going to be fine."

"*Is* everything going to be fine?"

"Who knows?" Stephen shrugged, rubbing his eyes. "But he's doing great. I wouldn't be able to handle all this without his help. I miss working from home here in the situation room."

The family office had served as a de facto campaign office ever since Stephen's early days as a congressman, when the boys were mere toddlers.

Ryan finally slammed down the phone, crossing off a name on the list. "Man, these people sure like to hear themselves talk."

"How many more to go?" Stephen asked.

"That was the last one," Ryan responded, relieved, as he stretched out his arms and let out a big yawn. He noticed the tentative look on his father's face. "That *was* the last one, right, Dad?"

Stephen nodded. "Yes, that was the last name . . . on that list. If you check your email, I just sent you a new one with about forty names."

"Dad, you're killing me here . . ." Ryan groaned.

"Take a break. You've been working hard the last few hours," Stephen said. "I want to talk to your mother."

Sandra suddenly became alert. What could this be about?

Ryan stood up from the desk and circled around the desk. "Anything good in the fridge?"

"I'm sure you'll find something if Jack hasn't found it already," Sandra said as he ambled past her and out of the room.

Stephen smiled, then walked over and closed the door, allowing them some privacy.

Sandra turned to him expectantly, waiting to hear what he had to say.

Stephen seemed to stare into space, gathering his thoughts, figuring out how to present whatever case he was about to make.

Sandra stood patiently in front of him.

"Sandra . . ." He stopped there.

She waited.

He was back inside his head.

She decided to help him out by giving him a little nudge. "Yes, Stephen?"

He exhaled, rubbed his eyes again, his mind obviously racing, apparently torn on how to proceed.

"Stephen, if you have something to say to me, just—"

"I want to get back together," he spat out quickly, interrupting her.

"*What?*"

"I love you, you still love me, at least I think you do, and these past nine, ten months without you have been excruciating. They've only made me realize how much I miss you. We belong together, Sandra, and—"

It was her turn to interrupt him. "I'm not prepared to have three people in my marriage."

Stephen stiffened, suddenly blindsided. "What are you talking about?"

"Deborah Crowley," Sandra said curtly.

"I . . . I told you . . . I'm *not* with Deborah. . . ."

"The woman is obviously in love with you."

Stephen gaped at Sandra, confused, then pressed forward. "Okay, yes, Deborah and I got together and dated for a while, but it never felt right, so I ended it a while ago—"

"You lied to me. You told me your relationship with her was platonic."

"It is. Now." He winced, fully aware of how he was coming across.

"You're playing word games, Stephen."

"No, I'm not. I told you we're not together, and I promise you we're not."

"Did you bother to tell Deborah that, because when I spoke to her at Elisabeth's campaign office, she seemed to be under a somewhat different impression."

"I don't know why she would think that. I was very clear that continuing our relationship wasn't fair to her because I was still in love with my wife."

Sandra worked hard to keep up her mask of calm, although she was reeling inside. Why was Stephen springing this on her now? So soon after the Henry Yang debacle. Or perhaps the timing was intentional. The first time she had even considered another man in her life, the result had been an unmitigated disaster. Perhaps Stephen instinctively knew that if he had a chance to win her back, it had to be now, and fast, before she was off the market again.

Stephen rubbed his chin and said softly, "On some level, I think Deborah always knew that."

"Tell me something, Stephen: When did you start seeing Deborah Crowley?" Sandra asked pointedly.

"What does it matter?"

"Was it before we separated or after?"

"After," he said forcefully, almost too swiftly.

Sandra studied his face carefully.

Was this a lie? It wouldn't be the first.

He could tell she didn't believe him. "*After*," he said more emphatically.

She let the word hang out there a little while longer, to the point where it was making him visibly uncomfortable.

"It was after we separated, Sandra. I promise you."

"When I came to your office that day in Washington to tell you that I wanted to spend some time apart, and she was there for a meeting, you two seemed to be very chummy."

"Yes, there was a chemistry between us, but we were simply work colleagues at that time. Nothing more. She didn't ask me out until after she learned we had separated."

She wanted to trust him.

He was a good man. A good father. She just wasn't sure if he was still a good husband.

She was wavering, and he could sense it.

Stephen was also a good debater and an even better politician. "We shouldn't throw away almost twenty years of marriage. I am absolutely convinced we belong together. We make an unbeatable team, and we *can* make this work."

"You're making me sound like your running mate for the presidency," she said flatly.

"That's not a bad ticket actually," he joked.

She gave him a thin smile.

They stared silently at each other for a few more moments before Stephen sighed and said, "Would you at least think about it?"

"Yes, Stephen, I will think about it."

He clasped his hands together. "Thank you."

Another moment of silence.

"Too soon for a kiss?" he asked sheepishly, taking a brave step toward her.

"A bit," Sandra said. "Jack and I just ate, so let me know what you and Ryan want for dinner."

She instantly regretted the offer because it now appeared

as if they were already back to normal, or their idea of normal, before the separation.

Sandra felt overwhelmed by all there was to consider.

It would be so easy to fall back into old patterns. As if nothing had happened. Pick up where they left off.

She would probably have to scale back her involvement in Maya's detective agency, if not pull out altogether, given the number of official duties she would be required to resume as a US senator's wife.

Maybe that wouldn't be a bad thing, given that she had made so little progress on the Diego Sanchez case.

Perhaps she wasn't cut out for this line of work after all.

But she loved working with Maya. She loved her new-found freedom.

Indeed, there was a lot to think about.

Chapter Forty-Six

Melanie Tate was harried and distracted when Maya bumped into her in the middle of the hallway of SoPo High. A few straggling students were making their way to class before the next bell. Melanie had been hauling a large, blank canvas and had not been watching where she was going when she suddenly collided with Maya, who had been on her phone, texting with Vanessa. The canvas dropped to the floor and Melanie sighed loudly, at first assuming a student had run into her. When she raised her eyes to see Maya, the look of disdain quickly dissipated, replaced by a benign, apologetic smile.

"Oh, I'm so sorry, Mrs. Kendrick," Melanie said. "I was in a hurry and wasn't paying attention. . . ."

"The fault was all mine," Maya said, bending over to pick up the cumbersome canvas. "My daughter was supposed to meet me outside twenty minutes ago, but she's MIA," she added before glancing down at the text she had just received from Vanessa. "But now she says she was excused early to study for a chemistry test and got a ride home with some friends and forgot to tell me. Typical."

Melanie gratefully retrieved the oversize canvas from

Maya, who looked at it curiously. "We're doing a group watercolor today, but the school is desperately low on art supplies, so I had to stop by to buy some myself with my own money," Melanie explained.

"That's very generous of you," Maya said. "I thought you taught creative writing."

"I do. But since Emma Forsythe was fired, they asked me to cover her classes until they can find a suitable replacement. I'm happy to do it, of course, but I've also been covering for Diego Sanchez's Spanish classes ever since . . . well, ever since you know . . ." Melanie said, her voice cracking, trying desperately to maintain control and not break down.

"I understand," Maya said. "Sounds like you've got a lot on your plate."

Tears pooled in Melanie's eyes as she nodded. "It's been hard around here lately. . . . I . . . *we* all miss him very much."

Maya could tell that Melanie was working hard not to highlight her own personal feelings for the late Spanish teacher, their history, but it was proving to be almost too much of a challenge.

"They've been looking for someone to take over for him permanently as well, but so far no luck. I'm happy to do it, though," she said, stuffing the bulky canvas under her arm. "Well, I'd better get going. If I'm not in the art room on time, you can bet those kids will be painting God knows what on the walls!"

Maya stepped aside. "Of course."

Before Melanie had a chance to hustle off, Cammie and Daisy appeared behind her.

"Excuse me, Miss Tate . . ." Cammie said sweetly.

Melanie turned in their direction, slightly irked to be detained yet again. "Yes, Cammie?"

"Daisy and I wanted to know . . ." Cammie hesitated, uneasy about speaking in front of Maya.

"What is it, Cammie? I have to get to class, and so should you two," Melanie snapped.

"We just wanted to know about the Spain trip," Daisy interjected.

"What about it?" Melanie asked impatiently.

Cammie and Daisy exchanged apprehensive looks.

"We just wanted to make sure we were on the list," Cammie said with a sense of urgency. "We know it's due today."

Melanie appeared confused at first, but then something must have clicked in her brain, and she nodded. "Yes, yes, you're both back on the list. Don't worry about it. Now go on and get to your next class."

"Thank you, thank you so much, Miss Tate!" Daisy cooed.

"You're the best teacher ever!" Cammie gushed.

"I just told you, you're both on the list, so there's no need to brown nose me!"

"Have a nice day, Miss Tate; you too, Mrs. Kendrick," Cammie said, smiling sweetly as she and Daisy locked arms and scurried off down the hall.

"Bye, girls," Maya called after them, watching them skip away.

Melanie had already scooted off in the opposite direction, toward the art room.

Maya could not help but note that Cammie and Daisy had been convinced Melanie Tate was guilty of poisoning Mr. Sanchez when she was questioned by the police, and now she was their favorite teacher. She was curious to know why.

Maya raced to catch up with Melanie down the hall.

"Excuse me, Melanie, wait up a sec. Can I ask what all that was about?" Maya asked.

Melanie had reached the door to the art room. Inside, she could see some boys rabble-rousing, one getting his friend in a headlock, as a few other boys cheered him on. Melanie popped her head in. "Get in your seats now or you're all getting three weeks' detention!"

The boys laughed, barely taking the threat seriously, but then they mercifully sauntered over to their desks and sat down.

Melanie, who had already forgotten Maya's question, gave her a puzzled look. "I'm sorry, what did you ask me?"

"The list Cammie and Daisy just asked you about. What kind of list is it?"

A light bulb went off in Melanie's head. "Oh, that. I've been trying to save Diego's class trip to Spain in the spring. After he died, Principal Williams wanted to cancel it. But I stepped in and said I'd spearhead completing the fundraising and organizing the details."

"That's so kind of you, especially given everything else they've thrown your way."

"Well . . ." Melanie started getting emotional again. "The trip was so important to him—he was so looking forward to sharing his heritage with his students—and I just couldn't let all of that fall by the wayside."

"It's a lovely tribute to him, Melanie," Maya said softly.

"Today is the deadline for me to submit the final list of students who will be going. I almost forgot. I'm glad Cammie and Daisy reminded me."

"You told the girls they were *back* on the list," Maya said. "What did you mean by that?"

Melanie shrugged. "There had been some disagreement between the girls and Diego."

"About what?"

"I have no clue. I just heard he had banned them from the trip. When the administration office gave me the preliminary list of students, Cammie and Daisy were not on it. I don't know what they did to get themselves barred from going, but they've always been in the top percentile of their class and never personally caused me any problems, so I decided to give them a reprieve and let them go on the trip."

Maya was knocked back on her heels. What had Cammie and Daisy possibly done to anger Mr. Sanchez enough that he banned them from going to Barcelona?

She knew she had to find out.

Chapter Forty-Seven

When Maya knocked on the door of her daughter's bedroom before swinging it open and popping her head in, she had expected to find Vanessa dutifully sitting at her small corner desk, adorned with photos of Ariana Grande and Harry Styles and her other favorite pop stars, studying for the chemistry test scheduled for the next day. But alas, there she was sprawled out on her bed, close to being swallowed up by a stack of oversize comfy pillows, on her phone, briskly typing a text with her thumbs. Next to her on the bed was her closed laptop.

"I thought you were supposed to be studying for a chemistry test," Maya admonished.

"I am. Ryan and I are quizzing each other now," Vanessa exclaimed as she quickly covered her phone with her hand. She glanced up to see her mother's suspicious stare. "Should I say that again and try to sound more convincing?"

Maya chuckled. "No, you can just tell me what you're really doing."

"We've been chatting about what everyone's saying on Instagram and Twitter about Daniel Yang's dad."

"What are they saying?" Maya asked, curious.

"That he was the one who murdered Mr. Sanchez because he found out that Mr. Yang was cheating to get Daniel into a good school and threatened to call the FBI."

"They're just speculating. There is no evidence that Henry Yang did anything to harm Mr. Sanchez."

"But he could have, right? I mean, there's no proof he *didn't* kill Mr. Sanchez."

"I think everyone is looking for someone to blame right now. There shouldn't be a rush to judgment before all the facts are in."

Vanessa flicked her eyes to her phone. "People are going crazy. Jack told Ryan that Daniel has been getting death threats from angry kids who applied to the same college but were rejected or wait-listed. They're saying it's all Daniel's fault."

Maya felt sorry for Daniel Yang. She didn't know him well, but she had the feeling he was an innocent kid caught up in a giant mess of his father's making.

"Practically everyone in my Spanish class has been leaving me and Ryan messages asking if the case is closed and you're done investigating."

"Not quite yet," Maya said, sitting down on the edge of Vanessa's bed. "I want to ask you something."

"Is it about Ryan?" Vanessa blurted out, eyes wide.

This caught Maya by surprise. "No. Should it be?"

"No!" Vanessa snapped.

Maya studied her daughter's face. There were a number of thoughts swirling around in her head. She folded her arms and stared at her daughter. "That was a *really* fast no. Too fast."

Vanessa sighed. "Mom, we haven't gone all the way yet, but if we do, we'll use protection, okay?"

"Wow, that was a three-hundred-and-sixty-degree turn from where I thought this conversation was going to go, but nevertheless, that's good to know."

"Obviously I'm way off base with what we're talking about here," Vanessa said, frustrated. "What were you going to ask me?"

"Were you aware of a conflict between Mr. Sanchez and a couple of your classmates, Cammie Lipton and Daisy Wynn?"

Vanessa sat up straight in her bed. "No, not really. . . ." She thought about it some more. "Wait . . ."

"What?" Maya asked, leaning forward.

"Well, I remember a few days before the bake sale, Ryan and I got to Spanish class a few minutes early, and we were alone and we were—" Vanessa stopped herself, searching for the right words to present to her mother about what they were doing. "Hanging out."

Maya was reasonably sure "hanging out" was another way to describe "making out" or "pawing each other" or some other activity she did not care to think about.

"Anyway, we heard Mr. Sanchez arguing with a couple of students, two girls, but we couldn't see them and we couldn't be sure who they were, but it could have been Cammie and Daisy, I guess."

"Did you know Mr. Sanchez had banned them from going on the trip to Spain next spring?"

Vanessa's mouth dropped open. "*What?* No!"

"Do you have any clue why he would do that?"

Vanessa shook her head. "No, but that would explain why I saw Cammie crying by her locker and Daisy comforting her later that day. I asked what was wrong, but they wouldn't tell me. I just assumed some bullies had been picking on Cammie. Those two can be kind of odd ducks, and sometimes kids are mean to them. I certainly didn't think it had anything to do with Mr. Sanchez. They worshipped him."

"How do you mean, worshipped?"

Vanessa rolled her eyes. "Come on, Mom, you almost went out on a date with the guy. Isn't it obvious? He was *gorgeous*. Cammie and Daisy were like, obsessed with him; they followed him around, hanging on his every word, like cult members." Vanessa jumped off the bed excitedly. "Do you think maybe Cammie professed her love to Mr. Sanchez, and he broke her heart by rejecting her, so she decided to exact her revenge by getting Daisy to help her *kill* him?"

It wasn't the most preposterous theory. In fact, it was almost plausible.

"I don't know . . . maybe . . ." Maya said, rolling the possibility over in her mind before standing back up from the bed. "I'd better get dinner started. You keep studying."

"This topic is *way* more interesting than the chemical structures and mechanisms of toxicity in plants." Vanessa moaned, grabbing her laptop and flipping it open while cradling it in her lap.

Maya stopped cold in the doorway and turned back around. "What are you studying?"

"Never mind. It's *so* boring."

Maya swiftly marched back over to the bed and snatched the laptop from her daughter's lap. She studied what was on the glowing screen. There was a list of seven of the world's deadliest plants. Water hemlock. Deadly nightshade. White snake root. And right there at number four, the one she had suspected, the castor bean plant.

"Mom, what is it?" Vanessa gasped, dying of curiosity.

"Keep studying. I expect you to ace that test tomorrow!"

Maya barked before scurrying out of her daughter's room and down the hallway to her own room, where she entered and closed the door behind her. She wrenched her cell phone from the pocket of her brown suede jacket and speed-dialed Sandra, who answered on the first ring.

"Hi."

"Hey. We need to meet."

"Now? Stephen and the boys and I are just sitting down to dinner."

Stephen?

That surprising news tidbit would have to wait. She had a far more pressing story to discuss.

"I'm pretty sure I know who killed Diego Sanchez."

Chapter Forty-Eight

Dr. Anna D'Agostino blinked her big, dewy eyes at Maya and Sandra, confused, as if she had failed to comprehend their simple question. She was a short, rotund woman with wide hips, a bulbous nose that served as a resting spot for her giant, Coke bottle glasses. She had a rather severe, chopped haircut, and she wore a bright-red wool sweater with a green print in the shape of a tree and white dots all around it that appeared to be snowflakes. With her round shape, she looked like a Christmas ornament come to life. Her mouth hung open, but no words came out.

Maya tried again. "Dr. D'Agostino?"

She suddenly snapped out of her trance. "I'm sorry, I didn't hear you. What did you ask me?"

It was as if she was stalling for time, trying to come up with some kind of answer, which Maya found strange.

Sandra said gently, clearly taking note of the chemistry teacher's disturbed demeanor, "She asked you if any of your students have access to the storage room where you keep all your supplies and exhibits."

Dr. D'Agostino began wringing her chubby hands.

"N-no, they don't. I'm very careful not to allow my students to come in contact with anything remotely harmful."

"So, no one could have gotten their hands on any poisonous substance you might have shown the kids in your lesson on the world's deadliest plants?" Maya asked.

"Of course not! I keep those plants under lock and key!" Dr. D'Agostino snarled. "Why would you ask me something like that? I'm very responsible!" She was on the verge of a meltdown, which indicated to Maya that the woman was lying through her teeth and obviously hiding something.

"Can we take a look? It's very important," Sandra pressed.

"No, I do not think that would be appropriate," Dr. D'Agostino barked.

Sandra folded her arms, challenging her. "Would it be more appropriate if we went to Principal Williams and put in a formal request?"

Dr. D'Agostino stumbled back, a slight gasp escaping her lips. "I don't see any reason why you should do that—"

"Neither do we," Sandra said sweetly. "So why don't you just show us what you've got stored in your room?"

"It's not a room; it's more of a closet. They don't give us much space for supplies," Dr. D'Agostino complained, sighing. She shuffled over to her desk, unlocked the top drawer with a key from her pocket and grabbed a bulky set of keys from inside. Then she escorted them to a door located in the back of the classroom. She fumbled nervously with the keys before finding the right one and unlocking the door.

She led them into the small space that had five gray metal shelves on the back wall that were crammed with boxes of beakers and test tubes and Bunsen burners, all labeled with black felt-tip marker. On the second shelf were six of the aforementioned plants.

"How do they survive with no light?" Maya asked.

"They don't," Dr. D'Agostino answered. "I just keep them here out of reach from the kids during school hours. I take them home with me and store them in my own greenhouse most of the time."

Maya studied the plants. "So, you put these out on display and have your students identify them for the quiz testing their knowledge of the poisonous plants?"

Dr. D'Agostino dipped her head. "Yes."

"Why are there only six?" Maya asked.

"I beg your pardon?" Dr. D'Agostino choked out.

She was buying time again, trying to figure out what to say.

"My daughter, Vanessa, said you were teaching them about the world's seven deadliest plants? There are only six here," Maya said sharply.

"I-I couldn't get ahold of the seventh one. . . ." Dr. D'Agostino sputtered.

"The castor bean plant," Maya said.

Dr. D'Agostino's eyes widened again. "Yes. How did you—?"

"If you lost it, or someone stole it, you'd better tell us now, Doctor, because this is very serious."

Dr. D'Agostino seemed to be running through her list of options, but suddenly, feeling cornered by Maya and Sandra in the tiny closet, she decided she had no choice but to confess. "Yes, the castor bean plant is missing. I don't know what happened to it. It was right there on the shelf a few weeks ago with the other plants when I first introduced them to my classes, and then it was gone."

"Why didn't you report it?" Sandra asked, incredulous.

"Because if word got out that I misplaced a plant with a potentially deadly toxin on school grounds, I would have been fired on the spot for reckless and careless behavior, and I need this job! They've been firing teachers left and right at this place lately, if you hadn't noticed!"

"Do you always keep the key to get in here in the top drawer of your desk?" Maya asked.

"Yes, always," Dr. D'Agostino said.

"So pretty much all your students know where you keep the key to this room," Maya said.

"I suppose so, but you saw that I keep that drawer locked at all times, and the key is always on my person. I never let it out of my sight, so it could not have been one of my students who swiped that plant."

"Think, Doctor; is there anyone else who had access to this room? A fellow teacher, the janitor, a lab assistant, anyone?"

"No, no one," Dr. D'Agostino insisted. "Just me and . . ." She stopped.

Maya and Sandra exchanged brief looks.

"What is it?" Sandra asked.

"Never mind. It couldn't be her—"

Maya eagerly stepped forward. "Who?"

"Well, I don't have a lab assistant per se, but I do sometimes enlist a student helper who sticks around after class to help me clean up, and I have given her the key to the storage closet on occasion. . . ." Dr. D'Agostino was lost in thought, but quickly found her way back, convinced she was wrong. "But she's my best student. Why would she—?"

"*Who?*" Maya asked again, more urgently.

"Cammie Lipton."

Maya clapped her hands.

That was it.

Her suspicion had just been confirmed.

"You're not saying that *Cammie* stole the plant, are you?" Dr. D'Agostino gasped in disbelief.

"Would Cammie have any idea how to remove the poison from the plant?" Maya asked.

"What? This is absurd! Why on earth would Cammie—?"

"Just answer the question, Doctor!" Sandra cried.

Dr. D'Agostino's whole body slumped as the realization slowly began to dawn on her. "Of course. It was on the test. The toxin, ricin, can be extracted from the pulp left over after the oil has been squeezed out."

Maya bolted out of the classroom with Sandra on her heels. They raced down the hall to the administration office, where they broke in on Principal Williams in the middle of her morning staff meeting. After a brief rundown of what they had just discovered, a rattled principal picked up the phone and called the janitor to have him meet them at Cammie Lipton's locker with a bolt cutter. They were already waiting in the hallway in front of the locker when Mr. Smith, the sixty-seven-year-old, seen-it-all, veteran janitor ambled up and cracked open the locker within five seconds.

Principal Williams took the lead, emptying out the contents of the locker: a laptop, some textbooks, a backpack, which she handed to Maya, who began thoroughly rummaging through it.

Maya didn't expect to find a castor bean in a Ziploc bag. Cammie seemed too smart for that, and had probably done away with the evidence. But she did come across a folded-up letter, which she opened and read.

There it was. The motive. In full detail.

She handed it to Sandra, who skimmed the letter, her mouth agape.

"What is it?" Principal Williams asked curiously.

"Where is Cammie now?" Maya asked.

"I don't know what she has first period. We'll need to go back to the office to look it up on the computer."

"Lead the way," Maya said forcefully.

They returned to the office, and Principal Williams had her secretary look up Cammie's schedule.

"She has PE now. She should be in the gym," the secretary announced.

"Thank you, Vera, now call the police and let them know we have a situation," Principal Williams said as her secretary reached for her phone.

They all hustled out of the office and down to the gymnasium, which was located at the far end of the school. When they entered, Maya and Sandra were both surprised to see their own kids, Vanessa and Ryan, among the students playing basketball while the young assistant coach, not much older than the students himself, who was filling in for the recently sacked Josh Kirby, refereed the game.

Maya scanned the gaggle of students, quickly spotting Cammie and Daisy in gym shorts and T-shirts, looking bored, barely participating, letting the other kids play defense while they pretended to go through the motions.

Principal Williams, followed by Maya and Sandra, circled around the basketball court and spoke to the assistant coach standing on the sidelines.

He blew his whistle.

The kids stopped running.

Ryan, who was dribbling the ball, took a long shot from halfway down the court, but the ball bounced off the rim of the basket. His brother was the superior athlete. Ryan's talents blossomed on the stage.

"Cammie! Daisy! The principal would like to talk to you!"

Cammie and Daisy glanced at each other apprehensively, not sure what this was about, certainly not happy about being singled out in front of their fellow students. They huffily shuffled over to Principal Williams, who was flanked by Maya and Sandra.

"Your gym class is dismissed for today," Principal Williams told the students. "You can all hit the showers before next period."

Principal Williams didn't want them hanging around and witnessing a confrontation, but although the kids looked like they were going to leave, they hung back, all supercurious to find out what was about to go down.

Daisy spoke first. "Yes?"

"We just have a couple of questions," Principal Williams said gravely.

"Okay . . ." Cammie whispered, unnerved.

Before Principal Williams had a chance to continue, Maya stepped in. "Why did Mr. Sanchez ban you girls from the spring trip to Spain?"

Cammie and Daisy eyed each other nervously, but then Cammie, the better actress, reacted, indignant. "What are you talking about? He did not! That's a total lie!"

"Is it?" Sandra asked, a skeptical look on her face.

"Mr. Sanchez *loved* us! We were his favorite students!" Cammie protested.

"Maybe you were," Maya said calmly. "But then you both got caught cheating."

Daisy, like her namesake flower, suffering from lack of water, slowly began to wilt.

Cammie continued keeping up appearances, embracing her role as the unfairly maligned student. "I *don't* cheat!"

"No?" Maya asked, eyebrow cocked. She produced the folded letter she had found in Cammie's locker. "According to this letter, Mr. Sanchez wrote to your parents, you and Daisy teamed up for an assignment and plagiarized a report on the Spanish monarchy by copying it from a travel blog and using an online tool to translate it from English into Spanish before passing it off as your own."

"Where did you get that letter? It's a fake!" Cammie tried to snatch the letter away from her, but Maya held it out of her reach.

Principal Williams said angrily, "It sure looks like Mr. Sanchez's signature. Did you intercept it before your parents saw it, Cammie?"

She refused to answer, pursing her lips defiantly.

Daisy was far less resilient as tears began pooling in her eyes that she wiped away with the towel she was holding.

Maya's eyes narrowed as she took a step forward, trying to intimidate Cammie into making a confession. "Mr. Sanchez gave you a failing grade, didn't he?"

Cammie vigorously shook her head.

"We have his online grade book on file, Cammie. Everything is backed up. We can easily check," Principal Williams threatened.

But Cammie still stood her ground, refusing to crack.

"I remember that essay assignment," Sandra said. "Ryan told me it counted for thirty percent of your final grade. That's a lot."

"I bet an F didn't sit well with you, two highly regarded honor students with sky-high GPAs, a couple of teacher's pets," Maya spat out. "Just the idea of failing must have sent you right over the edge."

"We begged him to let us do a makeup assignment, but

he refused. He said we needed to learn a lesson," Daisy squeaked.

"Shut up, Daisy!" Cammie barked, shoving Daisy in the rib cage with a sharp elbow.

Daisy winced but refused to obey the direct order of her BFF. "We kept following him around, trying to reason with him, calling him at home. We couldn't let it go; a failing grade was going to sink our chances of getting into an Ivy League school together!"

"So you harassed him, enough for him to finally snap and ban you both from going on the Barcelona trip," Sandra said. "You felt betrayed by him, your favorite teacher, the one you both had huge crushes on. And that's when you decided you had to do something drastic; your futures depended on it. So you plotted to get rid of him before he ruined your lives."

Daisy nodded, jittery, tears now streaming down her cheeks.

Cammie remained clammed up, defiant, her eyes blazing.

"We know you stole the castor bean plant from the chem lab, Cammie, and Dr. D'Agostino told us you knew how to extract the ricin from it," Maya said.

"So did every other student, if they were listening in class!" Cammie whined.

Maya ignored her desperate argument. "You injected a fatal dose in a cookie and slipped it into the box Mr. Sanchez purchased at the bake sale from Miss Tate, his ex-girlfriend, when he wasn't looking."

"If his death was ever traced back to the cookie, it would look like Miss Tate was the culprit because she was vengeful after he broke her heart," Sandra said.

More remorseful nodding from Daisy.

More contempt and bravado from Cammie.

"And then, poor, unsuspecting Mr. Sanchez ate the poisoned cookie at his home while he was getting ready . . ." Maya's voice cracked as her grief started to get the better of her. ". . . for his date with me."

There was silence in the gymnasium as everyone, including the slack-jawed students, who had stopped pretending they weren't listening, took all this in.

Daisy sniffled, then she began to swoon, her eyes rolling up in the back of her head. She toppled over, fainting dead away. Both Maya and Sandra rushed to catch her before she hit the floor.

Cammie seized the opportunity to make a run for it.

She bolted across the basketball court past the cluster of sweaty students, heading straight for the doors that led to the school parking lot. Halfway across, the assistant coach sprang forward, surprising Cammie, and grabbed her by the arm. Cammie lashed out like a wild animal, clawing at his face, drawing blood, shocking him enough to loosen his grip, allowing her to wrench her arm free and continue running.

She was almost to the door when Vanessa grabbed the basketball up from the floor and hurled it at Cammie. The ball slammed into the back of her head, tripping her up, sending her smacking, face-first, to the hardwood floor, body splayed, her left ankle twisted.

Cammie slowly raised her head and grabbed her bloodied nose, which she had banged hard upon impact. Cammie screamed with an unbridled rage neither Maya nor Sandra had ever witnessed before from either a child or an adult.

This girl was seriously disturbed.

"My nose! I think it's broken!" Cammie howled as blood poured down on her lips and teeth.

"I think you'll survive," Maya said.

Ryan and a couple of other boys surrounded Cammie in a circle to make sure she didn't try another getaway attempt.

"Keep an eye on them. I'm going to see if the police have arrived," Principal Williams announced solemnly to Maya and Sandra, who were on either side of a moaning, distraught Daisy, propping her up.

The principal marched out of the gym.

Cammie pulled herself up, pinching her bloody nose with two fingers, and nearly spat at Maya and Sandra. "You dumb grown-ups think you're so smart! Well, I'm smarter! I will figure a way out of this! Just you watch! They will never send me away! I'll make sure of it! And then I'm going to sue you!"

"Good luck with that," Maya said, shaking her head.

Sandra tried reviving Daisy by shaking her arm, to no avail. The girl's head just drooped and she moaned some more. Sandra looked at Maya and said, "I think we'd better get this one to the nurse's office."

Chapter Forty-Nine

Sandra took absolutely no joy in watching two young girls arrested at the high school for the murder of their Spanish teacher. It was a tragedy all around, especially for the shell-shocked students, her own boys included, who would have to deal with the fact that Diego Sanchez was taken away by two of their own.

She had remained behind with Maya until the police arrived to spirit Cammie Lipton and Daisy Wynn away for booking at the precinct. Word had quickly spread through a flurry of texting about what had gone down in the gym. After debating on whether to dismiss the student body for the day, Principal Williams ultimately opted to carry on with classes, then made a brief announcement over the public address system that she was scheduling an assembly for the following morning, where students, teachers, and administrators could all gather and talk about the startling and unsettling revelation that was now reverberating through the entire school.

After the hoopla had died down and the police had left with Cammie and Daisy, both handcuffed, as teachers and students gawked in disbelief through the classroom windows, Sandra had told Maya she needed some time to decompress. Maya agreed, and they both wandered to their cars in a daze and drove home.

When Sandra arrived at her house, there was a car she didn't recognize in the driveway, a blue Volvo S60 in pristine condition. She knew it didn't belong to Stephen. She parked next to it and headed into the house, entering the foyer to hear muffled voices coming from the office. She figured Stephen had a meeting with someone and almost walked up the stairs without seeing who it was, but something in her gut told her to pop her head in to say hello.

She shed her coat and hung it on the rack and then walked slowly to the downstairs office off the living room. As she got closer, she could hear the voice belonged to a woman. It was then she knew exactly who it was. The door was open a crack and she could see a pair of shapely legs crossed. She pushed open the door with one hand and it creaked open, alerting Stephen, who was sitting next to the woman on the office couch, Deborah Crowley.

Deborah uncrossed her legs and shot to her feet.

Stephen quickly slapped a bright smile on his face. "Hi, honey. I didn't expect you home this early."

That was always an easy go-to line for a husband who was caught off guard and feeling guilty, even if he didn't have anything to feel guilty about.

"There was an incident at the school," Sandra said. "I'll explain everything when you're not so busy. How are you, Deborah?"

"I-I'm fine, thank you," Deborah sputtered nervously. "Stephen and I were just meeting to discuss . . ." Her mind went blank.

"Boring health policy issues," Stephen said, helping her out.

"I didn't know you spent so much time all the way up here in Maine," Sandra said coolly. "I've been seeing you around a lot lately."

"I'm heading back to DC tomorrow," she said, deftly avoiding having to address the issue of her presence and if it had anything to do with Stephen.

"I'll leave you two alone," Sandra said, turning to leave.

"We were just wrapping up," Stephen said.

Deborah gathered up her papers and folders and stuffed them inside her bag. She glanced at Stephen. "Yes, I really should be going. I'll get those performance and cost reports to you in a couple of days."

"Sounds good," Stephen said, still smiling.

"Always nice to see you, Sandra," Deborah said, brushing past her.

"Likewise," Sandra responded with a nod.

She waited until she heard the front door open and close before she locked eyes with her husband. "Stephen . . ."

"I know what you're going to say. It's *over*, Sandra. Like I told you, I ended it. There is *nothing* going on between us. We were just having a professional meeting. Otherwise I would never have brought her into our house."

Sandra watched her husband tap-dancing.

He had always been good in a crisis. Always able to stay calm and measured. Impressively unflappable. Charmingly diplomatic. That was his greatest talent as a politician. Not that this moment constituted a crisis. Maybe in his mind it was a small one. Having his wife walk in to see him sitting on the couch with a lover, or a former lover, depending on what she was willing to believe. If that wasn't a crisis, it was at the very least a diplomatic kerfuffle that needed to be dealt with decisively.

Sandra had momentarily zoned out, but he was still talking. "I do not want this to in any way confuse the issue at hand."

Sandra snapped back into the conversation. "I'm sorry, what issue is that?"

Stephen seemed surprised to suddenly learn she hadn't really been listening to him. "That I love you, and that I am wholly committed to making this marriage work. It's unfortunate, but I do have to maintain a professional relationship with Deborah for the sake of certain policies I want to get done. I know it's awkward, but it's necessary. I hope you're okay with that."

Sandra waited for Stephen to say more—he always had more to say—but he had finished his speech. She knew it was finally her turn to respond. "Yes."

Stephen looked at her, confused. "Yes, what?"

"Yes, I'm okay with it."

He breathed a sigh of relief. "Good. I was hoping you would say that."

"I like Deborah. She seems like a very nice person whose heart is in the right place. She does good things at the Commonwealth Fund."

Stephen nodded, a little taken aback by her unexpected effusiveness.

"But Deborah Crowley was not what I needed to talk to you about," Sandra said.

"Oh, okay," Stephen said tentatively. "What is it, then?"

"I want a divorce."

Stephen's face fell. "*What?*"

"I've been thinking about this for a long time—"

"Sandra, I told you, Deborah and I—"

"Yes, and I believe you. But this has nothing to do with you and Deborah. You can see her professionally or romantically; that's up to you. It's none of my business because what I have finally come to realize is that we are over. Our marriage is done."

"Sandra, please, no—"

"I know it. And I think you know it, Stephen."

He stared at her, crushed, mouth open in shock. Perhaps for the first time since before he took the debate stage in high school and became a state-wide champ, he had no argument prepared.

"But I love you, Sandra."

"And I love you. Which will make this process far less messy than it might have been. We have had a marvelous life together. I have the utmost respect for you and what you've done with your life. And that's good. This shouldn't be messy at all. For the sake of our greatest accomplishment together, our boys."

Boys.

They were young men now. But she would always see them as her little boys.

Stephen simply nodded again, still shell-shocked.

He knew there was no talking her out of this decision.

And she could see in his face that he was impressed with how strong she had become. That had been no accident. The past year, on her own, working with Maya, she had felt she had finally come into her own. It was time to start fresh. And although she knew this process would be painful and emotional, and undoubtedly there would be bumps along the way, she was excited to come out on the other end more independent, and perhaps even stronger than ever.

Chapter Fifty

Maya watched as a guard led Max into the hot, stuffy room. There were handcuffs around his wrists in front of him and he twiddled his thumbs nervously, confused about what was happening. This was not a scheduled visiting day, and that appeared to make him anxious. If he was being dragged out of his cell, there had to be a good reason. And if history was any indication, the reason was rarely good.

When Max's eyes fell upon Maya sitting at a small Formica table in the far corner of the room, he broke into a wide smile. But as he approached her, the smile slowly faded, replaced by a furrowed brow as he contemplated the possibility that Maya was bringing him some kind of bad news.

Maya waved at her husband as the fit, muscular yet baby-faced guard led him over to the table. Max sat down opposite her. The guard uncuffed him, checked his watch, and said gruffly, "Five minutes."

"It won't take that long," Maya assured him.

The guard sauntered away to the other side of the room and took up his post near the door.

Max gazed at Maya. "How in hell did you pull this off? Coming here on a weekday when there are no visitors allowed?"

"I still have a few friends in high places who owe me a favor or two," Maya said with a wink.

Max leaned forward, his face full of apprehension. "Is everything all right? Where's Vanessa—?"

"Vanessa is just fine. She should be taking a chemistry test at school right about now. You'll see her next Saturday at our regularly scheduled visit."

Max twiddled his thumbs some more. "Okay, good. All good on the home front?"

"Yes, Max, everything's good," Maya said. "There is nothing to be concerned about."

"Well, that's a relief," Max said tentatively. "Then what brings you here?"

"I have something to say to you, and I didn't want to say it in front of Vanessa, at least not yet."

Max studied her intently. "Okay."

"I didn't plan on doing this now, but I wrapped up a case this morning, and I was driving home, ready to take the rest of the day off, and I was thinking about you, and the next thing I knew, I was driving here and on the phone with the assistant warden, who I used to work with, and asking if he could arrange a quick face-to-face so I could tell you . . ."

"What is it?" Max shifted restlessly.

Maya took a deep breath, held it, then exhaled and whispered, almost imperceptibly, "I still do."

Max, befuddled, leaned in toward her again. "Still what?"

"I still love you."

Max stared at her, then glanced at the guard, who was

fighting the urge to crack a smile but finally managed to remain stone-faced.

"You came all the way here to tell me *that*?" Max asked.

Maya nodded. "Yes."

Max beamed. He couldn't quite believe it.

"I always have and I always will," Maya continued softly.

"I love you too, Maya," Max said, reaching out and touching her hand. "You're my whole world. You and Vanessa."

"I don't know how any of this is going to work, but I just wanted you to know, I will wait for you, for however long you are in here, and when you finally get out—and I pray it's soon—I want us to try to be a family again."

Max choked up, again glancing at the guard, not wanting to blubber like a baby in front of him, but he was overwhelmed with emotion and couldn't fight it back. A tear streamed slowly down his cheek. He squeezed her hand tighter.

"That's it. That's all I wanted to say," Maya said, standing up. "Vanessa and I will see you next Saturday."

They both resisted the urge to fall into each other's arms and kiss. There were rules to these visits, and even with her inside contacts, they were expected to be obeyed.

Max rose as well, finally letting go of her hand.

The guard marched over and snapped the handcuffs back on Max's wrists. Max blew Maya a kiss as he was led back out of the room.

Maya watched him go. When Max had first been arrested and then subsequently convicted of corruption, she had assumed their marriage was doomed. How could they possibly go on with him serving years, perhaps even a whole decade behind bars? But once he was sent away, something unexpected happened. She had managed to forgive him, especially when he was so remorseful and vowed to make amends to those he had harmed. And then, something miraculous happened. She did not stop loving him. And although she had tried to move on, raise Vanessa as a single mother, even considered dating again, something she had not done since college, she just could not do it.

Max was never going to leave her heart. And she had finally come to accept that.

Maya knew she had just made the right decision.

And for the first time in a long while, she had hope for a brighter future.

Connect with Us

Visit us online at
KensingtonBooks.com
to read more from your favorite authors, see books
by series, view reading group guides, and more.

Join us on social media

for sneak peeks, chances to win books and prize packs,
and to share your thoughts with other readers.

facebook.com/kensingtonpublishing
twitter.com/kensingtonbooks

Tell us what you think!
To share your thoughts, submit a review,
or sign up for our eNewsletters, please visit:
KensingtonBooks.com/TellUs.

Catering and Capers with
Isis Crawford!

A Catered Murder	978-1-57566-725-6	$5.99US/$7.99CAN
A Catered Wedding	978-0-7582-0686-2	$6.50US/$8.99CAN
A Catered Christmas	978-0-7582-0688-6	$6.99US/$9.99CAN
A Catered Valentine's Day	978-0-7582-0690-9	$6.99US/$9.99CAN
A Catered Halloween	978-0-7582-2193-3	$6.99US/$8.49CAN
A Catered Birthday Party	978-0-7582-2195-7	$6.99US/$8.99CAN
A Catered Thanksgiving	978-0-7582-4739-1	$7.99US/$8.99CAN
A Catered St. Patrick's Day	978-0-7582-4741-4	$7.99US/$8.99CAN
A Catered Christmas Cookie Exchange	978-0-7582-7490-8	$7.99US/$8.99CAN

Available Wherever Books Are Sold!

All available as e-books, too!

Visit our website at **www.kensingtonbooks.com**